GUY HATER

by
J. STERLING

Guy Hater
Copyright © 2017 J. Sterling
All Rights Reserved

Editing and Formatting:
Pam Berehulke
Bulletproof Editing

Cover Design:
Michelle Preast
Indie Book Covers

Cover Model:
Vince Azzopardi

Cover Photography:
R + M Photography

Print Edition

ISBN-10: 1-945042-09-5
ISBN-13: 978-1-945042-09-6

Please visit the author's website
www.j-sterling.com
to find out where additional versions may be purchased.

Thank you for purchasing this book.

Please join my mailing list to get updates on new and upcoming releases, deals, bonus content, personal appearances, and other fun news!
http://tinyurl.com/pf6al6u

DEDICATION

Who we fall in love with isn't always a choice. Hell, most of the time it isn't a choice. It's more like an indescribable pull, a connection, an invisible thread that binds our heart to another person's whether we want it to or not. I've learned this year, more than any other in my lifetime, that love is *the* most powerful force on earth.

Don't worry; I can hear you saying it. *Duh, Jenn, I know.*

Love can challenge every single one of your beliefs. It has the potential to turn you into someone you don't recognize. And it can save you.

Love can save you.

It can help you find your way out of the darkness and into the light. It can guide you safely to shore when you thought you'd drown at sea. It can change *everything*.

I hope you find the kind of love that changes it all. And I hope you're happy. I really, really hope you're happy, because if you're not, then what's the point?

Find your joy.

Chase it. Live in it. Drown in it.

And then share it with the whole damn world! You deserve it.

PROLOGUE

Frank

WHEN I OPENED my eyes, harsh hospital lights temporarily blinded me, causing me to forget where I was. Without thinking, I tried to prop myself up on the bed and groaned as my right arm and shoulder exploded with pain. *Fuck.*

It was a real shit thing, remembering that your dream had been obliterated to dust. Yes, I could choose to rehab my shoulder after surgery, but I was out for the rest of this season and most likely part of the next.

When you played college baseball, there wasn't that kind of time. You didn't have the luxury of recuperating on the bench for almost two seasons. New players would join the team and pass you by, replacing you on the field, and just like that, you'd be forgotten.

It wasn't bad enough that the collision at third base had dislocated my shoulder on impact. No, my doctors discovered that I had a torn labrum—cartilage in my shoulder socket—when they assessed the damage. No one knew how long the labrum had been breaking down because I'd kept playing through the discomfort this season, even when my arm felt more than a little sore. I knew better than to do that, but hated admitting that I was hurt.

In all honesty, I'd been lucky they'd even found the tear. It wasn't something that fixed itself on its own or got better with rest and time. No, a torn labrum required surgery in order to heal, and the prognosis wasn't good. Most players never recovered from a torn labrum, and I knew it.

In the time it took to throw a baseball or swing a bat, everything I'd worked so hard for as long as I could remember was gone. If I could have snapped my fingers to reiterate the point to myself, I would have.

But I couldn't.

Because my fucking shoulder was destroyed, and I couldn't move my arm.

"Hey, Frank."

My girlfriend's voice cut through my pity party, and I turned my head to meet her eyes. My relationship with Shelby was brand new, we'd only recently started dating, and I was certain it was about to end as quickly as it had begun.

I expected to find her looking either as sad or as devastated as I was, but she wasn't. She seemed calm, a small smile tugging at her lips. She was a sweet girl, someone I could fall in love with someday. Well, as much as I could fall in love with anything other than baseball.

But there was no baseball for me anymore.

What the hell was I going to do with my life? I had no backup plan because there was never a reason to. Getting hurt had never crossed my mind . . . all I'd been able to think about was going pro.

Until now.

"How long have you been here?" I tried not to sound like a dick, but my thoughts were focused on life-changing questions like, *What am I going to do now? Who am I going to be?*

Shelby shrugged, and her long brown hair fell over her shoulder.

"You don't have to stay," I grumbled. "I know you have classes."

She pulled her chair closer to my bed. "I've already talked to my professors. I'm going to stay, if that's okay."

"Are you sure? You realize my career's over, right?" I practically barked at her. "You sure you want to hang out with a has-been?" It was irrational and mean, but I was mad and she was the only one in the room with me, so I directed my frustration at her.

She stiffened a little before relaxing, reaching out to rest a hand on my left arm. "I'm sure. I won't pretend to know how you're feeling right now, Frank. I can only imagine how hard this is for you and how sad you must be, but I never liked you because you were a baseball player."

"No? That had nothing to do with it?" Too late, I realized that now I totally sounded like a complete dick.

Shelby narrowed her eyes for a second before letting out a soft sigh. "I like your dedication and work ethic. But that's a part of your character and it has nothing to do with baseball. I love the person you are, not the person you thought you were going to become. I don't care if you're a baseball player or a plumber as long as you're happy."

I reached for her hand and squeezed it with my good one because I knew she meant the things she was telling me. Even though I was pissed off about everything I'd just lost, I still had one very important thing. And she was sitting right next to me, refusing to give up on me. I never knew how much I needed that kind of acceptance until Shelby sat there patiently, giving it to me willingly, no matter how frustrated I was.

Over the next few weeks, even my former teammates disappeared. They still had the game, their dreams within reach, and seeing me only reminded them of how easily it could all be stolen away. They stopped asking if I was okay, how I was feeling, and finally, they stopped coming around altogether. That was another blow to my ego, watching them drift away one by one. Guys I'd thought were like brothers just walked away as if I'd never mattered.

But not Shelby. She never left my side.

When I finally declared a new major and switched my focus to business management and finance, hanging up my cleats for good, she encouraged me and told me I'd be great at it. All the days when I didn't believe in myself, she believed in me enough for the two of us. I don't think I would have gotten through that time in my life without her.

Funny how things can change.

WINGWOMAN
Claudia

"**P**LEASE COME WITH me, Claudia," my roommate pleaded as she batted her eyelashes at me. "You know I can't be trusted on my own. I shouldn't be left unsupervised. I'll get into trouble. Probably end up in jail, and you'll have to come bail me out."

When I didn't answer right away, she propped her hands on her hips and glared at me. "You know I can't go to jail. I'm the wimpiest person around. I'll be someone's bitch in like two seconds, and I don't want to be someone's bitch. Someone should be my bitch, but I don't want that either. I don't want a bitch. I don't like girls in that way. Claudiaaaa!"

I let out a dramatic groan, my mind already made up that I would go. I could use a night out after the day I'd had. It was just far more fun to torment Britney.

"Why are we going there again?" I asked. "And why can't you be trusted on your own?"

A small scowl transformed her freckle-dusted face. "I really think tonight is the night. He's been flirting so much more than usual lately. I need you, and I don't want to miss my opportunity. There's no way a guy like Ryan stays single for long. He's probably already taken. I mean, he is breathing."

Britney was talking about one of the hot bartenders at her new favorite bar, Sam's. She recently started going there, and claimed that the drinks were, hands down, the best cocktails she'd ever had in all of Santa Monica. I hadn't been able to go with her yet, so this would be my first time. But since she'd started going, she hadn't shut up about the three hot brothers who owned the place.

The only downside to her new favorite bar was that it was quickly becoming *everyone's* favorite bar. Apparently, the youngest brother, Nick, (yes, I knew all their names—thank you very much, Britney) was responsible for making sure Sam's was prominent on every social media site, online blog, and regional magazine, not to mention appearing in locally filmed reality shows, which we had plenty of.

To be fair, that's the only reason Britney found out about the bar in the first place, one of those trashy reality-TV shows. She'd caught a glimpse of Ryan, or maybe it was Frank, and had to go see the place for herself. I had been out of town visiting my parents when she went the first time, but that didn't stop her from filling me in on every single detail she'd learned and talking about the place nonstop until I finally agreed to go with her.

Hiding my grin, I pretended to still be unconvinced. "It's Wednesday night, Brit. Who the hell goes out on a Wednesday?"

Britney narrowed her eyes and tossed back her brown ponytail. "We do. We go out on Wednesdays. You're just messing with me, right?"

It was true; we did go out pretty often when we weren't exhausted from work. But, to be fair, we were twenty-six-year-old single women with no kids. Of course we wanted to socialize and blow off steam. Plus, it was really hard to meet guys in this town if you never left your apartment. Our only other option was at work, but our male coworkers were either married or too old for us.

Britney and I had met at the bank three years ago, when we were both tellers working our way up the corporate ladder. I now handled all our bank branch's small-business loans. Nothing gave me more satisfaction than helping people make their dreams a reality. Starting a small business meant taking a giant leap of faith and required a lot of belief in the power of your dreams. I was inspired by my clients at least once a day.

I was also depressed at least once a day. I hated when I couldn't approve a loan, or the bank turned someone down. Extinguishing their glimmer of hope by telling them their loan wasn't approved was like a knife in my heart every single time. Part of me believed everyone deserved the chance to make their dreams come true. Some needed more help than others, but did that make them less deserving? I never thought so, but the bank was a business and it didn't like risky endeavors.

Sometimes America didn't build your dreams with you; it took them from you and stomped on them and told you that you weren't worthy of having them.

My mom and I emigrated from Colombia to the United States when I was seven. We came here legally but outstayed our visa, which was illegal. I had never seen my mom so worried as she was between the time our visa expired and when she met my stepdad, Bradley. She was constantly afraid that we would be found out and deported. I didn't know what that word meant at the time, but I sensed it wouldn't have been a good thing. She was more worried in America than she had been before we left Colombia, and that was saying a lot.

Mom and Bradley got married, and three years later, she and I became official citizens of the United States of America. Again, I wasn't sure what that meant, but the end result was that my mom didn't worry anymore. She was happy, and so I was happy too.

We were lucky to have found Bradley, or that Bradley found us. I'd never really gotten to know my real father, and Bradley treated me like I was his own. As I grew older, I became more and more grateful for him, realizing that he chose to be in our lives. He didn't have to stick around for an immigrant wife and stepdaughter, a child that wasn't technically his, but I'd never felt unloved or unwanted in his home, two things that were important in any young girl's upbringing.

At Britney's frustrated glare, I burst out laughing. "Of course I'm coming. What kind of wingwoman would I be if I didn't accompany you on your mission to bag this Ryan character?"

"Thank you, thank you, thank you. I owe you." She jumped up and down before pulling me into her arms for a quick hug.

"You say that a lot. I think you owe me a Mercedes by now," I teased. "Or a house in Malibu."

"If I land Ryan freaking Fisher, I'll buy you whatever the hell you want," she said with a huge grin. "I mean, you might not get it until we're eighty, but still, I'll come through in the end."

I had liked Britney from the moment I first met her at work, charmed by the smile that brightened her face. She always laughed instead of complaining, which made her fun to be with.

Our bond was solidified during lunch one day when we discussed the cost of living at the beach versus the suburbs. I confessed that I wanted to move closer to the water, but I couldn't afford it on my own. She suggested moving in together, and I only balked at the idea of having a roommate again for about two seconds. Living alone had been isolating and lonely, and I wanted to love where I lived. And I didn't love living in Burbank, surrounded by couples with growing families while I was still very annoyingly single.

It was the best decision I'd made in years. Britney and I moved into our apartment in Venice three months later.

Shaking my head, I told her to go get dressed and headed to my room to do the same. No matter how many times I'd tried to convince Britney that Ryan's flirting was simply his way of being good at his job, she refused to believe me. She insisted there was something more between them and accused me of being cynical.

She wasn't entirely wrong. I was a little jaded when it came to love and guys in this town, but that had nothing to do with my opinion about bartenders. Being charming and flirtatious was part of their job description. How nice and fun they were affected their livelihood. I equated it to the way female strippers flirted with their male clientele for better tips and repeat business. The majority of male bartenders did the same. I didn't blame or begrudge them that in any way. I simply didn't want my roommate falling head over heels for some guy who just flirted with her for better tips.

Hell, maybe I was overly cynical.

It wasn't like the guy couldn't prove me wrong. If he really liked Britney, I was certain I'd be able to tell just by looking at him.

WEDNESDAY NIGHTS

Frank

NICK AND RYAN took care of the bar patrons while I went over our books in the back office. As I tallied this week's take so far, I was pleased to see how much the numbers had improved since Nick had joined us. It was nice having our youngest brother officially a part of Sam's now.

After graduating from State, Nick had gone to work for our father, not that Dad had given him much of a choice in the matter. The father that Nick had grown up with was totally different from the dad who'd raised Ryan and me, and we had a hard time reconciling that fact until it was thrown in our faces. Dad had changed after becoming successful, turning into someone Ryan and I didn't recognize . . . or like.

As a result, Nick was forced to live through some over-the-top drama that should never happen to anyone. I wouldn't have believed any of it if I hadn't witnessed it firsthand. Thankfully, our dad eventually pulled his head out of his ass, let Nick out of his contract, and became a normal human being again. He and our mom even hung out here on the weekends sometimes, which was a huge shock at first, but was sort of cool now. I loved having all my family together.

As soon as he was free, Nick had immediately bought into

the bar as an equal partner with Ryan and me. I never realized just how much I loved those two knuckleheads until we were all together, working side by side every day. I hadn't really grown up with Nick since he was ten years younger than me, only eight years old when I'd left for Arizona to play baseball. Ryan and I were closer, but that's because we were only a few years apart.

I couldn't imagine running a business with anyone else, couldn't imagine being related to anyone else. They were both insane, mostly Ryan, but I loved them anyway.

A knock at the door made me pause in the middle of the note I was scribbling in the corner of my handwritten ledger. I still did some things the old-fashioned way, writing ideas and taking notes by hand instead of putting them into the computer. Something about doing it this way made it feel more authentic.

Or maybe it was simply more my style. That was probably more like it.

"Come in," I called out without looking up.

"Sorry to bother you, brother, but do we have any more Grey Goose?"

Nick stood in the doorway as I pointed toward the stacks of boxes containing vodka to my left. His jet-black hair was like mine, but his blue eyes were the exact same shade as Ryan's. It tripped me out sometimes when I looked at them.

"Ah, I see it. Thanks." The glass bottles clanked as he freed what he was looking for and closed the office door behind him.

My brothers knew that when I was in the office, I was handling a part of the business neither one of them wanted to tackle—the finances. They left me alone, for the most part, and I was grateful for it.

I never stayed in the office for long during the evenings when the bar was busy. Our bar was popular, and contrary to popular belief, I liked being a part of it. Most people assumed that I would rather stay in the back and not speak to anyone, but that wasn't true. I enjoyed tending bar when the guys needed my help, and was fascinated by watching the way people interacted with one another. I was an observer, always watching, but that didn't mean I never wanted to come out and play.

Stepping through the office door and into the bar, I scanned the area. Ryan was grinning like an idiot at some girl who was grinning back at him just as big, and Nick was busy ringing up a tab.

Of the three of us, Ryan was the only unattached one. Nick had met his girlfriend, Jess, during his last year at State. Their relationship had weathered some nasty storms, but we were all thankful they'd made it through and stayed together. Nick and Jess were solid, and anytime she showed up at the bar, he would make some ridiculous announcement to the entire place before very publicly molesting her. It always caused half the girls in the bar to swoon out loud and the other half to groan.

"Look who made it out of the office," Nick shouted, and a handful of our regulars yelled, "Hi, Frank!"

I nodded at them and glanced at Ryan, who gave me a shit-eating grin. I was starting to think it was the only grin he had anymore.

Maybe if we had been smarter, we would have pretended

we were all single to keep up the sexy, available bartender illusion, but none of us wanted to lie. Besides, women continued to come back week after week, so it didn't seem to hurt our business any.

Plus, Nick would have never gone for it. He would have told me to fuck off faster than I could have caught my next breath. The boy had come a long way from being controlled and manipulated by our father. It was like once he found his voice, he couldn't stop using it.

Me, on the other hand, I was in a relationship I didn't know how to get out of.

Shit. I hated saying that, hated even thinking it, but it didn't make it less true. My girlfriend, Shelby, had been there for me when no one else was. She'd nursed me back to health after I got hurt in college, and she believed in my new dreams. No one was more excited than she had been when Ryan and I had first talked about possibly opening a bar.

She'd assumed, and rightfully so, that when I decided to move back home to give it a shot with Ryan, that she was a part of the plan. I hadn't been happy for a really long time, but I could never find it in my heart to tell her that. I didn't know how. I felt like I owed her. She didn't deserve to be left behind when she'd never left my side.

Shelby had done nothing wrong. Hell, she was fucking perfect. But somewhere along the line, I'd stopped wanting her.

What kind of asshole did that make me?

"Hey, buddy, can I get a Guy Hater?" a guy with spiked blue hair and a lip piercing called out in my direction. "I really hate that name," he added with a smirk.

I grinned back. "Me too, but don't let Ryan hear you say that. He's sensitive." I nodded in my brother's direction, and Blue Hair laughed.

"Girls like it, though," he said. "The name. They think it's funny."

"Why do you think we keep it on the menu?" I said with a grin before I turned to grab the ingredients for the cocktail.

Honestly, I hated most of our drink names, but Nick and Ryan had been right—the sillier the name, the more conversation it inspired. Everyone ended up ordering one, if only to try it, even if they made fun of the name at first.

All I had wanted was for our drinks to be different (and better) than the ones you could get at any other restaurant or bar. It didn't make sense to have a menu filled with alcoholic beverages that could be bought down the street at a TGI Friday's or some shit. People needed to come here for a reason, and we wanted to give them more than one. We had built the business plan around the concept that people needed good atmosphere, good company, and great drinks.

I handed off the whiskey-based drink to Blue Hair and took his credit card to open his tab. When he shouted at my back, "This is really good," I turned around to give him a thumbs-up before feeling stupid. Since when did I give anyone a thumbs-up?

"You okay?" Ryan asked as he stepped next to me, drying a glass.

"Fine, why? Are you okay?"

"I'm always okay. Just checking in. You have that look on your face." He punched me in the arm before walking away.

Confused, I held my hands out wide. "What look?"

Nick answered for him. "That one." He pointed at me before sharing a laugh with Ryan.

Shit. There was no look on my face; they were just busting my balls.

"Why do I even leave the office?"

"'Cause you love us," Ryan shouted, then leaned over to try to hug a pretty brunette from behind the bar. The adoring look in her eyes was no different from any other woman's who came in here and fell for Ryan's charms.

She liked him and wanted him to like her back.

She hoped his flirting meant that he did.

But it didn't.

I was shaking my head when I noticed the woman standing behind the brunette. Her jet-black hair swung as she tossed her head back and laughed, her olive complexion practically glowing under the soft lights of the bar.

Something inside me stirred. This woman was beautiful, her dark eyes expressive, and the smile she wore as she shook my brother's hand stirred something to life inside me that felt like jealousy. Or maybe it was envy? I had no idea what the hell I was feeling, but no emotion had ever gripped my chest like that before.

I couldn't stop staring at her. Couldn't have looked away if I tried. And I clearly wasn't trying very hard because she caught me staring, her eyes locking onto mine with such intensity that I could almost feel it hanging in the air between us. Her lips pressed into a shy smile before she looked down, breaking our eye contact but not the connection between us.

"Hey, brother, who are these beautiful ladies?" I called out as I made my way over to Ryan.

He shot me a surprised look before it morphed into a grin. I had never asked Ryan who he was talking to before, had never attempted to be charming at the bar. I wasn't sure what qualities I might have gotten from our parents, but charm certainly wasn't among them. No, all the charming genes were divvied up between Nick and Ryan.

"This is Britney and her roommate, Claudia . . . like *cloud-ee-ah*. Not like *clawed-ee-ah*."

I watched as she smiled again, pissed off that it wasn't me who was making her do it. "It's nice to meet you both. Thanks for coming in. Is it your first time?"

I tried to make eye contact with Britney to include her in the conversation, but I couldn't stop looking at Claudia. It wasn't so much the rich coffee-bean color of her eyes as the way she was looking at me with them. Maybe she was thinking I was a psychopath, while I was hoping she liked what she saw.

"I've been here before, but it is Claudia's first visit," Britney said, but Claudia and I were still looking at each other without a word, not acknowledging that anyone else was in the room.

I blinked and gave Claudia a brief smile before looking away, confused about what was happening to my body and running through my head. I wasn't available and had no right to act like I was, but this woman had me twisted up with just a look. That kind of thing didn't happen to me. I wasn't Ryan, the hopeless romantic looking to find his Cinderella.

"I hope you ladies have a nice time. Next round's on me," I said before walking away.

I had to get away, had to get some distance from this girl. My heart needed to stop pounding like a wild gorilla inside my chest.

Ryan chased me down as I hurried back toward the office. "What the hell was that?"

"I have no fucking idea," I said before slamming the door in his face, willing him to keep his ass outside.

I dropped into my desk chair and sat there stewing, trying to figure out what had just happened out there. What did it all mean? Why did this woman set me on fire when I wasn't available to burn?

Ten minutes later, I was no closer to any answers. Logic was shouting at me to stay put, but my ego begged me to go back out there. What if some other guy was hitting on her? A woman like that got hit on all day long, every single day. I was certain of it.

Feeling guilty for my thoughts, I shot Shelby a quick text to say hi, something I rarely did anymore. And then I instantly regretted it, worried she might take it as an invitation to head to the bar.

I hoped she wouldn't. I needed her to stay home tonight and not come here.

All thoughts of Shelby were pushed away, replaced by thoughts of Claudia. Claudia, like *cloud-ee-ah*, was right outside the door, somewhere in my bar.

And I had to see her again.

I THINK I HAVE A FAVORITE BROTHER

Claudia

I FINALLY UNDERSTOOD Britney's obsession with this bar. One step inside its warm interior and I loved the vibe already. Soft music played in the background, but was drowned out by the conversations happening everywhere. A whole section of wall was dedicated to Instagram pictures only, with Sam's bar prominently advertised in the corner. It was brilliant marketing and I respected it. Nick's handiwork, I knew from Britney.

"It's amazing, right?" she asked as we navigated through the crowd, and I smiled and nodded in response.

We found Ryan and Nick tending bar—smiling, taking orders, and mixing drinks. They were definitely good-looking, both with gorgeous blue eyes that looked almost identical in the dim light. I absolutely understood the appeal and why women kept coming back for more.

When Britney introduced me to Ryan, I smiled, realizing within seconds why she crushed on him. He was charming, but not in a cheesy kind of way, with sandy-brown hair and a sprinkling of sun-kissed freckles that reminded me of Britney's. His charm seemed easy and genuine, like it was part of who he was, not like he was giving you his best sales pitch. It would be way too easy to think he was into you when he talked to you.

While I observed Britney and Ryan flirting with each other, my skin prickled for no apparent reason. I looked around the room, my eyes latching onto a pair of green ones that I couldn't look away from.

It had to be Frank, the oldest Fisher brother. His jet-black hair matched Nick's, and their features were similar.

I struggled to look away. He was devilishly handsome, his jawline so strong and rugged, it caused my breath to catch in my throat. We stared at each other for what felt like minutes, but was probably only a few fleeting seconds, until I tore my gaze away.

Someone had to.

Even though I was no longer looking his way, I could still feel him, sense he was near. Unnerved, I hesitated before looking up at the sound of what had to be his voice. Everything about this man caused my body to physically react, and I had no idea why.

When Ryan introduced Britney and me to Frank, I was once again ensnared by those green eyes. I couldn't look away this time, refusing to stop the buzz that charged inside my head just from looking at him. Everything else went quiet as I lost myself in a sea of green.

This time it was Frank who broke our eye contact. He hustled away so quickly, I almost thought that I had done something wrong or had offended him in some way. When Ryan chased after him, I shot Britney a questioning look.

"That was . . . weird." She gave me a wicked grin. "And hot."

"I just thought it was weird," I lied, willing the heat that had flared through my body to die down.

"I've never seen Frank look at anyone like that before," Britney said as Ryan made his way back to us. "Not that I ever pay him that much attention, because he usually stays in the background."

"Sorry about that, ladies," Ryan said with a smile. "What can I get for you?"

As I scanned the menu, I couldn't help but laugh at some of the cocktail names. "Guy Hater? No Bad Days? Adios Pantalones? Friendship Bracelet? These are ridiculous," I said, still grinning.

Ryan faked a pout. "You're hurting my feelings, Claudia."

"I'm sure you'll recover. I'll take an Adios Pantalones." I cast a sideways glance at Britney, who ordered a No Bad Days.

We watched as Ryan meticulously made each drink, taking his time before he presented us each with our works of art.

Tapping the bar, he said, "Next one's on my socially awkward brother."

I sat up straighter. "He's not socially awkward," I said, defending Frank as Britney shot me a surprised look.

"He's not?" Ryan hiked one eyebrow. "What would you call it?"

I laughed. "I don't know. But I don't think that any of you Fishers have an awkward bone in your body." I grinned, unable to stop myself from flirting back with him. "Except maybe you, Ryan."

"I'm wounded." His mock pout came back as he placed a hand over his heart.

"I'm sure you'll survive. Britney here's a great nurse," I said, then we turned around to fight our way through the small crowd gathered at the bar.

"I didn't know you were a nurse," Ryan called after Britney, and I swallowed the laughter that threatened to bubble up.

"Oh yeah, I can heal you right up," Britney called over her shoulder as she followed me.

Once we were clear of the crush at the bar, I scanned for somewhere to sit, or at least stand comfortably. Spotting enough space on one of the couches, I made a beeline for it and sat down before anyone else got the same idea.

Britney chastised me as soon as we sat. "A nurse? He believed you, dummy!"

"I was joking. You forgot to tell me that he was so gullible."

She sipped her drink. "If thinking I'm a nurse gets me a date with Ryan, I don't care. I'll be anything he wants me to be."

I shook my head. "You're insane, you know that?"

"I know, but my God." She craned her neck to look toward the bar. "Look at him. I mean, just look at him."

I followed her gaze toward where Ryan would be, but froze as the office door swung open and Frank stepped out. Tattoos I hadn't noticed before snaked down his arms, tribal designs that were sexy as hell.

"Yeah, he's something, all right," I mumbled, drinking in the sight of him.

"Want to talk about insane, let's talk about you and Frank Fisher. What the hell was that between you two? And don't say *nothing*, because everyone saw it."

"Saw what, exactly?" I asked, playing stupid but curious

about her take on what happened.

"That eye contact. The two of you staring at each other like you were the last drops of water on the whole entire dried-up planet." Britney narrowed her eyes at me before she took another sip of her drink.

"He's really good-looking," I said, not meeting her eyes as I sipped at my drink.

"That's it? He's really good-looking? No shit, Sherlock. Everyone within a fifty-mile radius knows the Fisher brothers are good-looking."

I shrugged. "What do you want me to say? That I was so lost in those green eyes that I wouldn't have noticed if the building had caught fire? That having him look at me the way he did made me forget where we were? That just looking at him made my heart race like I was running a marathon?"

She reached out and squeezed my shoulder. "True or false?" It was something we did when we were being serious and wanted an honest answer. Lying wasn't permitted.

I sucked in a quick breath. "True."

"At least it wasn't Ryan. I might have had to plot your murder if he made you feel all those things."

I was startled as Frank suddenly appeared in front of us, his large frame towering over ours as we sat on the squishy couch.

"Ladies, how are you doing on drinks?"

Britney downed the rest of her No Bad Days before thrusting her glass toward Frank with a pout. "Mine's all gone."

Flustered, I tried to fight off the heat that spread throughout my body simply from being near him. I rarely reacted to anyone this way, and I was having a hard time keeping myself in check.

Sure, I was attracted to a handsome face and a hot body as much as the next girl, but this . . . this was something entirely different. Looking at Frank sent shock waves through me. And when he looked at me, it was like he really took his time and *saw* me. Men in Los Angeles rarely took the time to pay attention to anyone or anything, unless it was their own reflection in a mirror.

"Would you like another, Claudia?"

He spoke slowly, pronouncing my name correctly, and I decided then and there that my name had never sounded as sexy as it did coming out of Frank's perfect mouth.

I glanced at my glass, which was half full. "I still have some," I said, swirling the remnants of my Adios Pantalones around inside the glass.

"I could still get you another." His lips tilted into a slight smile as his gaze burned into mine.

"Okay. Sure." I smiled back. Or, at least, I hoped I did. My body was numb with all the crazy feelings that Frank triggered in me.

As he walked away, I couldn't help but watch him go. His ass looked incredible in his jeans, the way they fit him snug and hugged every muscled curve on him. His biceps flexed as he walked, stretching the sleeves of his T-shirt.

"Here." Britney handed me a cocktail napkin and I took it cautiously, narrowing my eyes in question. "It's for the drool."

I tossed the napkin back into her lap. "Asshole."

"The two of you should get a room. I mean it. I've only been here a few times, but I have never, and I mean never, seen Frank mingle with the commoners."

"And?" I tried to sound like I didn't care, but I liked what she was hinting at.

"And . . . I think he likes you."

"He doesn't even know me."

"What do you think he's trying to do? It's a hell of a lot more than Ryan's ever done, and I was convinced he liked me. Now I'm not so sure." Britney tilted her head toward the bar, and I looked to see Ryan smiling and reaching out to touch a woman's cheek.

He was flirting, but like I'd always thought, it was part of his job. Maybe that's what Frank was doing too, just being good at his job. I couldn't let myself pretend something was there that wasn't. Chastising myself, I tried to reel my heart back to reality.

When a voice called out, "I see the love of my life!" Britney clapped her hands.

I spotted Nick Fisher looking toward the door as a pretty young blonde walked through it, her face flushing red at his words. A petite Latina trailed behind her, smiling and waving at everyone as if they were staring at her. The sight of it made me laugh.

"God, you're gorgeous. Isn't she gorgeous, everyone? I love this woman!" Nick shouted, making his way toward the blonde before planting a kiss on her lips and giving the other girl a hug.

"That was the cutest thing I've ever seen." I smiled, envious of the very public display of adoration.

"I know, right?" Britney let out a heartfelt sigh. "I want someone to love me like that."

"Don't we all?"

I might not be a hopeless romantic like Britney, but I appreciated romance as much as the next girl. I wanted passion in all aspects of my life, especially when it came to love. Finding love in Southern California had been difficult, and meeting a guy who was as passionate about me as he was his career seemed even harder.

Frank reappeared, three drinks in hand, and nudged a small footstool over with his shoe. He sat facing us before handing us each a fresh drink.

"What should we toast to?" Britney asked playfully.

"Your call," Frank said with a shrug.

"We should toast to finding guys to love us the way Nick loves his girlfriend," Britney said with a little too much enthusiasm, causing her drink to slosh.

Frank scoffed. "I don't want a guy to love me like that."

I burst out laughing. He was so serious, his demeanor kind but reserved. He seemed like he was holding back, but I liked that about him. There was an air of mystery that surrounded Frank. He seemed like the kind of guy who only let a few people get close to him, and that quality only intrigued me more.

"Well, I do," I said firmly. "I totally do."

That got Frank's attention. His eyes bored into mine again. "You do?"

"Definitely."

He studied me, his head cocked a little to one side. "You're into over-the-top public displays of affection?"

I thought for a moment, gathering my feelings before wording them properly. "I'm into someone loving me passionately and not caring who knows. When I love, I love hard. I love deep. My love is all consuming. I want to be loved back in the same way. I want to be consumed."

I took a deep breath after my declaration. The words felt good spilling from my lips, pouring from my heart. I rarely confessed such private feelings to a stranger, but he had asked.

Frank's lips pursed together with my answer, drawing my attention. "What nationality are you?"

"Colombian," I said proudly, happy that he asked, that he seemed to care.

"Hence the need for passion."

I nodded in agreement and offered him a tight-lipped smile. "Hence the difficulty in finding any American guys who have it."

"Maybe you're looking at all the wrong guys."

Was he flirting? I really, really wanted him to be flirting.

"Maybe you're right. Know anyone I should be looking at instead?" I was definitely flirting.

"I might."

When he pushed to his feet, I stifled my disappointment. I hadn't wanted my question to make him leave.

"I have to get back to work," he said. "If I leave Ryan alone for too long, he'll burn the place down."

I had completely forgotten that Frank was working. It was easy to forget when you sat in a place like this, drinking delicious cocktails and having good conversations. Or what was the start of a good conversation.

Britney lit up at the mention of Ryan's name. "Frank, wait!" she called out, and he stopped to turn back to her. "What's his deal, anyway?"

"Ryan's?" His dark eyebrows drew together.

"Yeah. Does he have a girlfriend? Does he date? He's super flirty with me all the time, and I'm just trying to get a good read on him, because I can't really. At all. I don't know what any of it means coming from him."

Frank shifted his weight, like the question made him slightly uncomfortable. Or maybe it was that he'd been asked it a million times before. "Ryan's extremely flirty. He always has been. He does date, but he hasn't in quite a while. Do you want me to tell you the truth or keep you hopeful?"

"Truth," I said at the same time that Britney answered with, "Hopeful."

We both laughed, and Frank smiled.

"The truth is that he's not looking for a relationship right now. He's most likely just flirting with you because that's the way Ryan is. He can't help it; it's in his nature. He's really friendly, and he wants everyone to love him."

"Unlike you?" I asked, and Frank shot me a look.

"I don't need *everyone* to love me. Just the right ones." With that, he turned and headed back toward the bar, which had finally started to clear out.

Britney seemed to deflate, her enthusiasm draining out of her in a long, dramatic sigh. "I guess it was all in my head."

I tossed my arm around her shoulder. "The flirting was real. It just didn't mean what you wanted it to. I'm sorry, Brit."

"It's okay. I'll still crush on him because I can't even help it." She took another sip of her drink. "And you'll still crush on Frank because you can't help it either."

I choked on my drink before pulling away from her.

Pounding on my chest, I shot her a crazed look. I wanted to argue with her, but the denial died in my throat.

She was right, and it was pointless to try to say otherwise.

WHAT WAS THAT

Frank

I SAT IN the office, willing time to pass faster.

Actually, I was hiding. Hiding from Claudia, hiding from whatever these feelings were, hiding from my brothers.

Hiding from the truth.

Since we'd opened the bar, I'd never spent time hanging with any of the customers. Unlike Nick, who lost all control of his balls whenever Jess walked through the doors, I didn't want to mix my personal and professional life. I'd convinced myself that they shouldn't cross over, and told Shelby that as well.

Thank God she listened and stayed away most of the time. She was a middle-school teacher and was always busy planning lessons or grading papers, and went to sleep at a decent hour like regular people. On the rare occasion that she had stopped in the bar, I tended to hole up in the office, wishing she'd leave.

Fuck, that made me sound like a real asshole. And you know what? Maybe I was. I didn't know anymore.

I wasn't sure of anything after tonight, and I hadn't even technically done anything wrong. But I had acted out of character, and Ryan and Nick both knew it.

I could tell they couldn't wait to give me shit about it by

the way they were both casting glances at me. Ryan especially. I wasn't sure exactly what I'd say when they started questioning me, but I knew I needed to deny, deny, deny.

Whatever the hell the truth was, I wasn't ready to admit it to my brothers, let alone to myself. I was the responsible one, the oldest, the one who didn't fly by the seat of his pants. Somehow in all of my making the right decisions and choices, I'd ended up in a relationship that no longer brought me happiness. And to be honest, I hadn't been happy in years.

Yet Shelby still stayed and never complained. God, that woman was a saint. What kind of man falls out of love with a saint?

Glancing at the clock, I noted the time and headed out of the office and into the nearly empty bar. Almost everyone had left, including Jess and her friend.

Claudia and Britney, however, were right where I'd left them.

I wasn't sure if I was relieved that Claudia hadn't left without saying good-bye, or nervous that she was still here. I stared at her profile, memorizing the way her hair moved as she did, wondering what it would feel like in my hands. Was it as soft as it looked? What did it smell like?

"Last call!" Nick shouted as he rang the bell that hung in the corner of the bar, making my thoughts crash-land back into reality.

Ryan and Nick both turned to me, waiting for me to deliver my regular line. With a smile, I addressed the small crowd.

"You don't have to go home," I yelled.

And they responded, "But you can't stay here!"

"That's right!" Man, I loved this bar. I threw my fist in the air and glanced toward Claudia, who was staring right at me. I gave her a small smile, and that strange pull I'd felt before came roaring back to life as she smiled back.

"Hey, Ryan?" a woman shouted, and I rolled my eyes.

"Yeah, sweetheart?" Ryan answered with a fake Southern drawl and tipped his nonexistent cowboy hat.

Shaking my head, I looked at Nick, who watched with an amused grin.

"Can I get an Adios . . ." the woman called out, pausing.

A handful of women shouted "Pantalones!" in unison, finishing her order.

I groaned as my idiot brother removed his shirt and tossed it on the register behind him, then proceeded to make the drink.

Every.

Damn.

Night.

We really needed to stop this stupid tradition. I wasn't even sure how it started in the first place, but I couldn't remember a night it hadn't happened. Maybe once Ryan got an actual girlfriend, he'd keep his damn clothes on. Or maybe I could convince him to only take his clothes off on the weekends instead of every single night?

After most of the customers had left, I was closing out the registers when I heard the sound of Claudia's voice.

"It was nice to meet you, Frank." She leaned against the wood railing and gave me a smile.

That smile, just for me, was fucking beautiful. *She* was beautiful. I wanted to hop across the bar that separated us and give her a hug good night, and I didn't hug women I didn't know.

Screw that. I wanted to pull her body against mine so I could feel every curve, every bit of her softness pressed against me.

Suddenly, I was torn between not wanting her to leave and needing her to get the hell out of my bar as soon as possible. It was a damn challenge keeping my body away from hers.

Jesus, Fisher, pull it together.

"It was nice to meet you too." I smiled back at her and kept my distance. But as she and her friend neared the front door, I found myself shouting, "See you soon?"

Claudia stopped and turned around, her gaze locking on mine. "Couldn't stay away if I tried." Her lips curved into a mischievous grin, and I watched her ass as she disappeared from view.

"What the hell was that?" Ryan raised his brows at me as he locked the front doors behind the girls. They had been the last ones to leave, no doubt waiting for something.

I hid any reaction from him, remaining stoic. "I don't know what you're talking about."

"Bullshit," Nick said with a laugh, and I shot him a murderous glare that shut him up.

I continued going through the night's receipts as I tried to ignore them, but my brothers were nothing if not persistent. And annoying. They were fucking annoying.

"What was that? Seriously, I've never seen you act like that before." Ryan tossed a wet rag at my back, and I picked it up and fisted it before turning around to face him.

Twirling the rag quickly with one hand, I asked, "Like what, exactly?" before whipping it against his thigh with a loud snap.

"Fuck! That hurt!" Ryan hopped around on one foot like I'd shot him as he attempted to rub out the welt that was probably forming underneath his jeans.

I smiled, happy with my rag-swatting abilities as Nick chimed in.

"I haven't worked here long, but even I've never seen you get all dopey around a chick before."

My smile fell instantly. "I do not get dopey."

"You were a little dopey," Ryan bit out, still hopping around. When I pretended to ready the rag for action again, Ryan's hands flew up in the air. "Fine, you were smitten. Or grumpy. Or whatever other dwarf names there are. Definitely not dopey."

"There's no dwarf named Smitten. What's wrong with you?" Nick scowled at him as he unloaded a tray of dirty glasses.

"It's not like we don't get the appeal," Ryan said before turning to Nick. "Right, Nick? Claudia was insanely hot."

Nick simply shrugged. He didn't talk about other girls now that he and Jess were back together.

Obviously frustrated, Ryan continued to push. "Just admit that you were attracted to the girl. Can you do that?"

"Why do you even care?" I demanded, doing my best to deflect. "Oh, I get it. You like Claudia, and you're pissed she likes me."

Ryan and Nick both started laughing, and Nick said, "Oh yeah, Frank. That's exactly it."

Tamping down the urge to throw something heavy at each of their heads, I tried desperately to think of a way to shut them up.

I wasn't the kind of man who flirted with women, didn't want to do dirty things to women who weren't my girlfriend. But, apparently, I did. And I needed my brothers to stop reminding me about what an asshole I had apparently become in the course of one evening. The guilt stampeding through me made me irritable.

"Can you two just shut up for one second?" I snapped as I pulled the final paperwork from the registers and credit card machines.

"We're not trying to upset you, bro. It's just that we've never seen you go out of your way to talk to anyone before. You looked happy." Nick shrugged one shoulder. "That's all I want to say."

"You did look happy," Ryan said. "It's okay to be interested in someone, or find a girl attractive. It's normal."

I bristled because it wasn't okay. "Not when you have a girlfriend, it's not."

Nick nodded. "Can't argue with that."

For once I was thankful for his over-the-top love for Jess. I only wished that my feelings were for the same reasons, but I knew they were more out of obligation and doing the right thing than my actual love for Shelby.

"I'm gonna go update the books," I said, ending the conversation and heading into the office.

The sound of them talking quietly filtered into the office, and I did my best to tune them out. I left the door open, but hoped they would leave the subject—and me—alone.

*

THANKFULLY, BOTH RYAN and Nick took the hint and laid off me for the rest of the night. They even walked with me out to our cars without saying another word about Claudia, which was both a surprise and a relief.

I'd have another twenty-four hours' reprieve from them since Thursdays were my days off. We each took one day off during the week, but sometimes even that turned into a workday. It was hard to stay away from the bar when you loved it as much as we all did.

After walking through the door to the condo I shared in Marina del Rey with Shelby, I slipped off my shoes and padded softly down the hallway. She'd be sleeping, and I hated waking her up on a school night. Not that she would have minded.

I flipped on the light in the bathroom, then turned on the shower and peeled off my clothes. I stepped in, closing my eyes and allowing myself to get lost momentarily in the steam, enjoying the hot water pounding on my head and shoulders.

Claudia's image appeared in my mind, and I shook my head in vain to get rid of it. She smiled, and my dick sprang to attention. It was too late. There would be no getting rid of her now.

It was wrong, but I couldn't stop. Squeezing some body wash into my hand, I gently lathered it up before rubbing it on the length of my dick. I moved my hand up and down as Claudia's dark brown eyes appeared in my imagination. My hand worked my flesh harder and faster as I pictured her full lips sucking the head of my cock. I closed my eyes, mentally fisting her jet-black hair in one hand as she took me deep into her mouth, as far as she could take me.

My hand worked faster, my dick nearly ready to explode with Claudia's name on my lips. Faster. Harder. *Claudia*.

I came, panting as I slowed to a near stop, draining my dick of every last Claudia-inspired drop. My heart pounding, I watched as the water swept away the evidence of what I'd just done.

And just as quickly, guilt set in.

Fantasizing about Jessica Biel and her lips around my dick was one thing. Celebrities were unattainable and therefore totally acceptable spank-bank material. But thinking about the woman I'd met at the bar tonight, while my girlfriend lay sleeping in our bed in the other room, was not.

What the hell was wrong with me? I stood under the hot spray a little longer, trying to get my head on straight, hoping the water would wash away my unease.

I ran some of Shelby's girly shampoo through my hair. I liked the way it smelled. And then I used her conditioner because that shit made my hair crazy soft, and the stuff I had for men didn't do that. What could I say? I liked having soft hair.

After rinsing off, I stepped out of the shower, relieved from my release but still feeling guilty about the cause of it. Wrapping the towel around my waist, I tiptoed out of the bathroom and headed toward our dresser.

Shelby stirred, and I looked at her as she sat up slightly. "Hi." Her voice was sleepy as she rubbed at her eyes.

"Hey, go back to sleep. I'll be there in a minute," I said softly, and she smiled at me as she lay back down.

Before stepping into my boxer briefs, I dropped the wet towel to the floor. I glanced at it for a second, hearing Shelby in my head asking me why it was so hard to hang things up.

Reaching for it, I tossed it on the hook behind the bathroom door and brushed my teeth, then headed for bed, Claudia still on my mind.

I fluffed the pillow and briefly considered spooning Shelby purely out of guilt. Deciding against it, I turned my back to her and closed my eyes.

Shelby's warm arms wrapped around my midsection as she snuggled her front against my back. "I'm glad you're home. Did you have a good night?"

I found her hand with mine and squeezed it. "It was busy, but good. How was yours?"

"I watched a movie while I graded papers. Ate dinner alone. You know, the usual."

At her words, more guilt surged. Shelby was on her own most nights. I used to tell myself it was because the bar wouldn't survive an hour without me, but the truth was something I wasn't ready to confront yet. It seemed like I'd never be ready to confront it.

"I'm sorry," I said, not really meaning it as I brought her hand to my lips and pressed a quick kiss there.

"I keep thinking that eventually you'll be able to spend more time away from the bar. You guys have employees now, and you don't have to be there 24/7. But you're still there all the time."

This subject was nothing new. Shelby wanted my time, and I wanted to spend all of it at work.

"It's hard to give up control over something you own," I said for what felt like the thousandth time.

"I know," she said, her voice soft. "I understand."

Shelby was always understanding, never really fighting with me. Even when she wasn't happy about something, she swept that shit under the rug and pretended everything was fine, like she could continue hiding her pain from me. I supposed I pretty much did the same thing, avoiding topics that really mattered to maintain the peace.

Or maybe I was simply denying the truth.

My brothers and I were finally in the position to hire employees, which meant the three of us didn't have to be at the bar every night, but that didn't matter. We all still showed up, for the most part. It wasn't that I didn't trust the people working for us. It's just the bar was our baby, our pride and joy, and it was hard for me to sit at home at night doing nothing when I could be at my business either working or supervising. Doing something.

It seemed easier for Nick when it came to his day off. He rarely showed up unless Jess was in tow. I didn't know if it was because he hadn't been around when the bar first opened like Ryan and I had, so maybe he didn't feel the attachment to it that we did, or if it was because he was so truly in love that he had found a way to balance his life.

This was too much thinking, too many deep thoughts for almost four in the morning. I needed sleep.

I should have said something reassuring to Shelby, should have told her that I'd try harder or that I'd figure it out, but I didn't. No, I kept my mouth shut, choosing to close my eyes in the hope that sleep would come quickly. I didn't want to lie to her and say a bunch of things I didn't mean but thought I should say out of obligation.

It was getting harder to keep living like this. And the fact that I had been attracted to Claudia tonight certainly didn't help matters.

NIGHT OFF
Frank

THE NEXT EVENING, I found myself standing in the kitchen, doing my best to make Shelby a home-cooked meal. I'd called my mother earlier and asked for her enchilada recipe. Mom offered to come over and help, but I needed to do this on my own. I was a grown-ass man; I could cook dinner for my girlfriend without my mom's help.

I think.

I'd woken up this morning, guilt still torturing me as I flung my arm across Shelby's empty pillow. Claudia's image had filled my mind on more than one occasion throughout the day, and no matter how much I tried to keep her out of my head, it hadn't worked.

Irritated because I didn't even know the woman, I'd headed to the store to buy the ingredients needed to make dinner for the woman I should be thinking of at all times. Shelby deserved my effort, so I decided I'd try to do something nice for her since it was my night off.

When she walked through our front door at the end of the day, file folders in her arms, she sniffed the air. Her gaze roamed the condo before landing on me in front of the stove.

A curious smile spread across her face. "What's all this?"

she asked as she laid the folders and her purse on the counter.

"Dinner." I tried to sound confident. "If I don't fuck it up."

We both laughed. It seemed like ages since we'd done that.

"It smells amazing. Is that your mom's recipe?"

I nodded as she made her way to me and placed a kiss on my lips. "Why don't you go shower and I'll finish this up?"

She looked so damn surprised, and it only made me feel worse. "You sure?"

"I got this," I reassured her, and she headed down the hallway toward our bedroom.

As she walked away, I knew exactly why I'd fallen in love with Shelby all those years ago. After my baseball career ended, I hadn't been easy to deal with, but she never wavered. She loved me when I was unlovable. She hadn't quit on me, and I felt like it was my obligation to not walk away from her in return.

When my feelings started to change, I'd been too chicken-enshit to admit it to her—or to myself, for that matter. I was too wracked with guilt over all she'd done for me, all she'd lost in her life. There was always something keeping me put . . . if it wasn't one thing, it was another. And for as unhappy as I was, it seemed easier to stay with her. That was a shit reality to accept, but it was the truth. It was easier to stay than to upend our lives. The last thing I wanted was to hurt her feelings, to break her heart and force her—and me—to start over.

I'd almost worked up the courage to end things between us once before, but then her dad got sick. Her mother wasn't in the picture, so it had only been Shelby and her father for her whole life. Within five months of getting sick, he was gone too, and only I was left. I carried the weight of that squarely on my shoulders, and mourned the loss of my own happiness for the sake of hers.

"Take care of my little girl," her dad had begged me on his deathbed.

How the fuck did you disappoint a dead man and look at yourself in the mirror each day?

I should have stopped things before I moved back to California to open Sam's, but I hadn't. It was the perfect opportunity to ask for space to see where we stood, to see if we had a future. But Shelby had assumed that she would be moving with me, and once again, I didn't have the balls to do the right thing and tell her she wasn't invited. Instead of speaking up—or breaking up—I sucked it up and watched unhappily as she packed her bags, eager for this new phase in our life, assuming it was what I wanted as well.

But I hadn't wanted it.

And she hadn't even asked if I did.

Somewhere along the line, I'd begun to feel like a passenger in my own damn life, making decisions based on a sense of obligation instead of what I truly wanted. And now I didn't know how to stop it. I was in too deep. Or, at least, it seemed that way.

"Wine?" Shelby asked from behind me, and I turned to face her, her brown hair still damp from the shower.

"Already on the table."

I pointed to the bottle, and as she opened it, the oven timer buzzed. Praying the enchiladas were okay, I pulled them from the oven and looked them over. *Huh, I might have actually pulled it off.* They looked edible.

"This was really nice of you." Shelby came back with two wineglasses and handed me one.

I leaned over to place a kiss on her cheek. "I know things with us haven't been the way you hoped—"

Interrupting me, she waved me off. "I know how much the bar needs you. It's just that I need you too." The last part was almost a whisper.

I swallowed hard, wondering what to say and how to say it without hurting her. "I just haven't figured out how to balance it all yet." It wasn't entirely a lie. Pulling her into my arms, I held her close.

"I miss you. We never see each other anymore," she said into my chest, her breath warm against my beating heart.

Pulling back, I placed a kiss on her forehead but didn't say anything more about it. "Let's eat." She moved toward the table, and I grabbed the casserole dish and carried it over.

I asked her about work, and she filled me in on all the latest news with her students. It was only when she talked throughout the entire meal that I realized just how little conversation we actually had anymore. Everything she told me about her classes was news to me.

"Megan got engaged," she said as she finished off her glass of wine. Megan was her best friend from Arizona.

"Really?" Surprised, I held my breath, hoping to avoid this topic of discussion.

"Well, she and Christian have been together for four years." Shelby cocked an eyebrow at me, and I ignored her not-so-subtle hint. She and I had been together much longer. "Are we ever getting engaged, Frank?"

Shit.

Any hopes of her not going there were suddenly dashed,

along with my appetite. I didn't know what the hell to say. I refused to lie about it and pretend I was ready to get married when I wasn't sure that I'd ever be.

"My friends all think if it hasn't happened by now," she said, "it's never going to happen. Are they right?"

Great. She'd talked about this with her friends. If I knew anything about women, and I did, this couldn't be good. Women fed off each other, each thinking they knew more about a man's psyche than the other. They were usually wrong.

"I don't know," was all I managed to say in response. It was a chickenshit non-answer, an asshole move.

"Don't you think that after ten years together, you should know?" Her eyes filled with tears, making me feel even lower than I already did.

"Shelby, I said I don't know," I snapped, hoping my tone signaled the end of this non-conversation.

For as unhappy as I was in the relationship, I hated hurting Shelby in any way. I cared about her and probably always would, but it wasn't enough. A part of me knew that I wasn't being fair to her by staying together. I wasn't doing either of us any favors, but I wasn't strong enough to end things. I couldn't bear the thought of disappointing her dead father or letting her down. And I sure as hell didn't want to admit that I wasn't the good person I'd always thought I was.

So I stayed, the weak side of me hoping that maybe one day Shelby would be the one who got fed up and left. That way I wouldn't be the bad guy.

When had I cared more about perception than right or wrong?

LET'S GO BACK

Claudia

I SHOULDN'T HAVE been so fixated on Frank, but I was.

It had been two days since Britney and I had been to Sam's, and I hadn't been able to stop thinking about Frank. I daydreamed about his deep green eyes and the way they had delved into me, truly seeing me. The tattoos that snaked up his arms had been the subject of more than one fantasy. I'd imagined those arms lifting me as my legs wrapped around his middle, all the hard parts of him pressing against the softer parts of me.

Yes, Frank Fisher was what fantasies were made of. At least, they were what mine were made of, apparently.

An odd sound interrupted my thoughts, and I blinked at the sight of Britney standing in front of my desk, snapping her fingers at me.

Oh God, I'd been daydreaming of Frank at work.

"What the hell's wrong with you?" Britney demanded. "I've been standing here forever, and your client has been waiting in the reception area for ten minutes."

"Shit." I rushed to my feet and straightened my skirt. "Sorry."

"Ah, crap. I know that look." She waggled her eyebrows at

me. "You've got a fish wish."

"A what?"

"A fish wish. You want to be smothered by a Fisher brother. Spanked by Frank."

"What the hell are you talking about?" I sputtered.

She laughed. "Look it up online. It's a real thing. Hashtag Fish Wish, all one word."

"You're joking." *I hope.*

"I'm really not. Next time we're at Sam's, look around at the women. They all have a crush, and they're all hoping they'll be crushed on back. Hence, Fish Wish. You'll see half the bar with the same look on their faces that you have right now. Hell, I probably had it too before Frank talked some sense into me," she said with a sad smile. "Go get your client, you fish-wishing floozy."

I quickly typed the hashtag FishWish into my computer and watched as numerous other Fisher Brother hashtags emerged.

#Dyin4Ryan

#WannaBeLickedByNick

#SpankMeFrank

Laughing, I closed the browser. Maybe I did have a fish wish, but I couldn't think about that now. I had to help someone make their business dreams a reality.

I looked down at my clipboard as I entered the customer lounge. "Mr. Frankson."

As I read the name out loud, I stumbled a little on the Frank part of his name. *You've got to be kidding me. Like I need more reasons to have Frank Fisher on my mind.*

An older man stood up from the chair and extended his

hand.

"It's nice to meet you," I said. "I'm Claudia, and I'll be going over your paperwork today. Right this way."

I led him into my office, hoping like hell we'd be able to make his dreams come true.

*

"CAN WE GO to Sam's tonight?" I asked with a little too much enthusiasm when we got home that evening, and watched as Britney shot me a knowing glance.

"I don't know, Claudia, the place is a madhouse on Friday nights." She tried to sound serious, but she couldn't stop giggling. "Hell yes, we can go. Of course."

"Just for the record, I know I'm completely transparent, okay?" I said before she could say another word.

She knew damn well that I wanted to go there so I could see Frank. I had a crush, but I couldn't be blamed for it. He was delicious and mysterious, and I was drawn to him like a moth to a flame. Stupid, stupid analogy, but I'd never fully understood it until now.

"I didn't say a word." She threw her hands in the air. When she walked toward her bedroom, I swore I heard her mumble "FishWish" under her breath as I shook my head.

"This is all your fault, by the way," I called out and waited for her to shout back.

Instead, she peered around her doorframe. "How's that?"

"You're the one who made me go there in the first place. I was perfectly fine before you forced me to see those brothers in person." I faked a glare and she scoffed.

"First of all," she said, putting one finger in the air, "it's not my fault that you and Frank Fisher have some weird sort of connection going on. And second," she added another finger, "this is the most exciting thing that's happened since we moved in together."

I laughed in agreement, but focused on the part where she mentioned that Frank and I had a connection. Was that what it had been?

"You really think we had a connection?"

"Have. Not had. And we'll see when we go tonight if it was a one-time thing," she said before disappearing again.

Yes, I had been drawn to Frank, but he was extremely attractive. And attraction didn't necessarily equal a connection. Chemistry was one thing, but a real connection was something else entirely. I had no idea what we had between us, but I was more than willing to attempt to find out.

Britney had been right about Friday nights at Sam's. It was packed, and I worried for a second that we might not be able to get in. Thankfully, there was no issue with security at the door as we were ushered straight through.

"Good God. We'll never get a drink," I practically yelled into Britney's ear so she could hear me over the noise of the crowd. I immediately scanned behind the bar, looking for my favorite Fisher brother. When I realized he wasn't there, my heart sank an inch or two.

"Come on." Britney waved before reaching for my hand and pulling me toward the other end of the bar. As we weaved through the throng, a couple of guys tried to stop us, but we kept moving.

I hated when guys manhandled me in public places. Did I

give you permission to grab my arm, pinch my ass, or *accidentally* graze my boob as you reached for something you didn't need in front of me? I never understood why men behaved this way, but it always pissed me off. I didn't get angry often, but my Colombian temper showed up the second any of that kind of stuff happened. Britney always said that my face turned an unnatural color whenever I was angry, so she knew when to keep her distance.

Once we were at the other end of the bar, a door swung open and my Fisher god stepped through it. Frank was frowning, like he'd been working on a difficult problem behind those doors that no one else was aware of.

Breathless, I watched as he scanned the length of the bar before his gaze fell on me. It didn't take long for him to find me, but once he did, all seemed right in the world.

I smiled, felt my mouth curving upward without my control, and the tension in his face melted away and a smile appeared. My heart rose back into its proper place, demanding kudos for being the one responsible for that smile.

"Claudia," he said as he stepped around the bar and made his way to us.

"Hi, Frank. It's a madhouse in here."

I sucked in a breath as his arms slipped around my waist and he pulled me against him in a tight hug. I had no idea if Frank Fisher was a hugger, but I was currently on the receiving end of a really good hug and wasn't about to complain.

Thrilled, I squeezed his muscles, my fingertips digging into his biceps as I pulled him close, refusing to let go. His nose dipped toward my neck, and when I felt him inhale, goose bumps prickled my skin.

"You smell good," he whispered into my ear, and for a second, his arms were the only things holding me upright.

"Thank you."

He pulled away slowly, like he didn't want to break the connection any more than I did. "Hi, Britney." He gave her a quick friendly hug, and her eyes met mine as it happened.

"Hey, Frank. Your bar is stupid successful," she said, and he laughed.

"How unfortunate. What can I get you ladies? Same as last time?"

He remembered our drink orders? I tried not to read into that as I crinkled my brow, wondering if I should try something new this time.

Frank caught my eye. "What's the dilemma, Claudia?"

How he could read me so easily? Was he in tune with my thoughts already? That couldn't be possible.

Trying to play it cool, I shrugged. "I was wondering if I should get the same thing or try something new. What do you think?"

"Ryan is trying to create a new tequila-based drink. I'll have him make it for you, and you can tell him if it sucks or not." He looked at Britney. "Still want a No Bad Days, or want to try a rum-based drink instead?"

"Rum!" Britney shouted like a schoolgirl, and I smiled.

"Don't go anywhere," Frank said as he walked away.

Like I'd even dare.

"Well, I guess we know the connection is still there." Britney raised an eyebrow at me. "My hug was pathetic in comparison to yours."

"I noticed," I said, not even pretending to play games. I called them like I saw them, and was happy that Frank hadn't touched Britney the same way he'd touched me.

"He's definitely into you."

I nodded in agreement. I got the same impression from Frank, and the feeling was so very mutual on my end. But now what?

"What's wrong? What are you thinking about?" Britney asked, but Frank reappeared carrying two drinks before I could respond.

"Okay. Claudia, don't hold back on this. If it isn't good, you have to tell Ryan what you don't like about it. And, Britney, you're going to love this. Even I think it's delicious, and I don't like sweet drinks." Frank's green gaze touched on me when he said the word *sweet*.

"Just sweet girls?" Britney said with a laugh.

He bristled for a millisecond, but I noticed. Frank regained his composure, his gaze bouncing between us. "Eh, not too sweet."

"That's good, because Claudia's mostly sour."

I choked out, "Shut up. Frank, please don't listen to her. She's an idiot."

"Like my brother." He tipped his head toward Ryan, and I burst out laughing.

"Hey! Ryan's not an idiot." Britney defended him, her gaze finding Ryan at the bar. "Why does he have to be so hot? Ugh," she said before taking a sip of her drink. "Shit. This is good."

"I knew you'd like it." Frank smirked before looking at me. "Your turn."

I felt pressured, like I was under the microscope as they both watched me sip on Ryan's latest creation. I really hoped it was good as I eyed the orange wedge perched on the rim of the glass before taking a sip. The tequila hit my taste buds, followed by bitters, and then a hint of something else.

"Is there banana in this?"

Frank smiled. "There is. Do you like it?"

"It's unbelievable. It's so good," I said before taking a gulp instead of a sip.

"Ryan!" Frank shouted.

Ryan's head shot up. He pointed a finger in the air to signal one second, and headed our way once he finished the drink he was working on.

"What's up? Hi, girls. I wondered what the hell Frank was doing out here." Ryan's blue eyes met mine, and I felt myself blush.

"Claudia loves your new drink," Frank said proudly as Ryan's face lit up.

"Really? You like it?"

I smiled. "It's so good. I don't know how you make these flavors blend so well together, but it's amazing."

"Yes!" Ryan pumped a fist in the air.

"Do you already have a name for it?" Britney asked, and I was practically on pins and needles, waiting to hear the answer.

He smirked. "Nick came up with this one." He paused before looking at Frank. "Awkward Moment."

Britney cried out, "Yes! That's awesome!"

"It's perfect," I said with a laugh. "And fun." I took another big sip, almost finishing it off.

Ryan leaned toward Britney, and I swore I heard her breath catch. "Do you like yours?"

"It's delicious. Does it have a name?"

"Of course it does." He looked over at Frank, who rolled his green eyes. "It's called Jazz Hands," Ryan said with a laugh as he wiggled his fingers in the air.

Frank just shook his head.

"You don't like the names?" I asked him.

"They're so stupid half the time, but people seem to love them."

"He doesn't understand because he's not creative," Ryan said. "He's all finance and smarty-pants up here." He tapped on Frank's head and Frank jerked away, glaring at his younger brother. In response, Ryan threw his jazz hands in the air, taunting him.

"Don't you have drinks to make?" Frank shoved him, and Ryan snickered.

"Yeah, yeah. You're just trying to keep the pretty ladies all to yourself," he said before walking away to take more orders.

"I should go help." Frank nodded toward the bar, which was still packed. "But I'll get you both another first." He smiled again, and I swear I melted at the sight.

"You're in trouble," Britney whispered.

I swallowed hard because I was, and I knew it. I had never been so sure of anything.

SHE'S BACK

Frank

SEEING CLAUDIA'S FACE when I walked out of the office lifted my entire mood. One look into her eyes, and I knew it was going to be a good night just because she was there.

Somehow, she changed things for me. I had no fucking idea why or how, but it didn't make it any less true. Seeing her made me happy, making me realize just how foreign that feeling had become for me. I didn't know how dead I'd been inside until the sight of her brought me back to life.

Nothing about this made any sense, and I tried to fight it but failed. My brain told me to walk away, to give her a curt smile and stay behind the bar making drinks. But my legs refused, taking me to her instead. My mind said one thing, but my body did whatever the hell it wanted.

I cared for all of two seconds until I had her in my arms. Then I couldn't have cared less if the bar burned down around us. That's how much this woman affected me.

"Hey, I need your Moleskin," I shouted, and Ryan and Nick both turned toward me.

Most bartenders in the business had their own Moleskin notebooks that they carried around with them everywhere, making notes as they tried to blend new cocktails or came across a recipe they really liked. I carried one too, but it was filled with the cost of inventory items and where I could try to negotiate a better deal. Mine probably didn't a single drink recipe in it, and Ryan would probably freak out if he knew.

"For what drinks?" Ryan asked with a smirk.

He was going to make me say the names out loud . . . in front of everyone. Sometimes I really hated my brother. I frowned, but Ryan wasn't deterred.

"I need to know which pages to show you. Just tell me which drinks?"

"Jazz Hands and Awkward Moment," I all but growled out under my breath, and he cracked up.

Ryan grabbed the small black book from his back pocket and flipped through it. "Here and here," he said as he dog-eared two pages for me.

Focusing on the list of ingredients that was barely legible, my mind found itself on a temporary Claudia reprieve. Her presence consumed me, and I wasn't the type of man to be consumed by any woman. For a moment, I was thankful that trying to read Ryan's handwriting was a feat in itself. That didn't last long, because I made the mistake of glancing back toward the girls and found Claudia watching me.

I was going to royally fuck up these drinks.

"Want a little help?"

Nick appeared at my side, and I breathed out in relief.

"I can't read half of this," I complained, and he took over.

"I was here when Ryan first made them. I know how he did it," Nick said.

I wasn't sure if he meant it or if he was only trying to make me feel better. Either way, I didn't care. Nick was making the drinks, which meant they'd be drinkable.

I busied myself with a few beer orders, a whiskey sour, and a vodka cranberry. Those were the kinds of drinks I could handle. No frills.

"Here you go," Nick said as he slid the finished concoctions toward me.

"Thank you." I shot him a smile, then grabbed the drinks and headed toward the other end of the bar. The girls hadn't moved.

"Sorry that took so long," I said before handing them each a fresh drink.

"Don't apologize," Claudia said as she sipped it. "Thank you for this."

"Yeah, Frank, thank you," Britney added.

"It's no problem. Have fun, okay? Don't leave without saying good-bye." I directed the last part to Claudia. I wasn't even sure where that had come from, but it slipped out before I could stop it.

"Never," she said back, her tone confident, flirty even.

I needed to get away.

Berating myself, I went back behind the bar and handled more orders. The place was packed, which was great for business, but seemed to wreak some kind of havoc on my mind. I found myself needing to know where Claudia was at all times. I scanned the bar several times throughout the evening, looking for her in all the chaos. And each time I found her, just like that, I felt centered again.

Nick sidled up next to me and tilted his head in Claudia's direction. "Just go talk to her."

"I've already talked to her," I said, trying to sound cool.

"You watch her," he said, and I turned my head quick to shut him up, my jaw flexing. "I just meant that you watch her the same way I watch Jess when she's here, making sure she's safe. Just an observation, bro."

He made a face at me before his gaze shifted and his entire expression changed, brightening in an instant. I knew that look.

"Speaking of," he said, his focus not wavering, "my reason for existing has now entered the bar!"

People cheered and laughed, but everyone—and I mean everyone, guys included—watched as Nick romanced Jess.

Ryan stepped next to me. "Think he'll ever stop doing that?"

"Think you'll ever stop taking your damn shirt off?" I snarled at him a little, but he just grinned.

"Touché."

I had my answer. Ryan would be taking his shirt off every night until we were old and gray. *Great.*

"You're just jealous," I added, rubbing salt into the wound that was my younger brother's heart.

You wouldn't know it by watching Nick in this moment, but Ryan was definitely the most romantic of us three. I wasn't sure if he'd watched Disney movies on the sly growing up, but he was dying to find his one true love. It killed him that he hadn't found the love of his life yet.

I never understood his overwhelming need for it, but then again, I wasn't really one to talk. Maybe I didn't understand romance at all? Apparently, I wasn't very good at it, as I was learning.

"Damn straight I'm jealous," he said with a smirk.

"This girl right here is my entire world," Nick said.

He wrapped an arm around Jess and kissed her like no one else was in the room, making her cheeks redden the way they always did whenever he made his public declarations of affection for her. I think Nick secretly loved embarrassing her.

"I love her more than anything, my brothers excluded. I hope you all get as lucky as me someday." He planted a kiss on Jess's cheek. "But not with her, because she's taken and I'll kill you."

Jess tossed back her head and laughed, then looked for a place to sit as Nick made his way back behind the bar.

Ryan caught my eye. "I want that. Don't you want that?"

I cleared my throat, casting a glance at Claudia, who happened to be looking right at me. No, I didn't want that. It wasn't my style.

"Or maybe you have that?" he added. "Nah, you and Shelby are like a miserable old married couple."

"Shelby and I aren't cheesy and twelve years old," I said with a scowl.

"No, you both act like you're eighty. And you can't stand each other, yet you stay together. It kills me for you, especially when I see the way you look at Claudia. I've never seen you even look at another girl before."

"Can we do this later?" I growled, not wanting to have this kind of discussion ever, but especially not while the bar was open and packed with people I didn't want knowing my personal business.

"Count on it," Ryan said before disappearing.

A couple cleared their seats at the bar for Jess and her crazy best friend, Rachel. I made my way over and greeted them both with a quick hug. If I ever tried anything less, Rachel would do something insane like hop on my back the second I turned around and claim that I was her horse as she waved a hand in the air. I always pretended to be annoyed by her, but the truth was that she was a lot of fun, and I loved it when she was around.

"Frank, ready to date me yet?" Rachel asked. She was always flirting with me, but it was all in good fun. She had a mad crush on Ryan that she knew was never going anywhere, so I got the brunt of her playfulness.

"I'll take you out tonight if you'll let me," I said, flirting back. Hell, it was easy to play with someone when you didn't really mean it.

"You sweet-talker." She winked before shouting at Ryan, "Why is your shirt still on, Fisher? Don't you know I come here for the free show?"

"Please don't encourage him," I begged.

Rachel leaned toward me. "I can't help it, Frank. If you took your shirt off, I'd encourage you too. But you're all," she frowned and waved a hand up and down the length of my body, "covered up all the time."

Jess laughed. "Oh my God, please ignore her." She ducked her head and covered her face with her hands.

"He couldn't ignore me if he tried. Frank loves me." Rachel batted her eyelashes, and I couldn't help but laugh.

My gaze left the girls momentarily in search of Claudia, and I noticed that she and Britney were talking with a group of guys. I ground my teeth, not liking the idea of someone else getting Claudia's attention, or that she might like it. I must have looked for a minute too long because both Rachel and Jess turned around, curious.

"Who are you looking at?" Rachel asked, and Jess pursed her lips.

I stayed silent, refusing to answer the question. I shouldn't have been surprised, but I realized in that moment that Nick had told her everything. Jess knew all about Claudia, but mercifully kept the information to herself.

Rachel kept glancing around, clearly taking stock of the women in the room. "Please tell me, Frank. I'm dying." She coughed into her fist. "See? Literally dying to see what your type is."

"My type?" I asked, somewhat baffled.

"Yeah. What kind of girls do you find attractive? I want to know my chances, duh," she said as if it were the most obvious thing on earth.

"Frank, I'm sorry. She should never be allowed to leave the house," Jess said in a rush, but Rachel refused to be deterred.

"Ay, *dios mio*, please tell me it's not that stick-figure bleached blonde in the corner?" She pretended to gag in mock disgust.

I turned to search out who was referring to, and it wasn't long before I spotted the typical Southern California blonde. I had no idea who she was and had never seen her before.

"No. Definitely not her." She couldn't have been more different from Claudia in every way.

"Aha! So you were looking at someone!" Rachel clapped her hands with delight. "But really, thank God it wasn't her. I would hate it if you were that cliché."

When Jess cleared her throat, Rachel's eyes widened. "No

offense, *amiga*. You're not cliché just because you're blond and have blue eyes. You're smart and don't look like you're searching for a sugar daddy."

"Admit it. You would totally hate me if you didn't know me," Jess said, pretending to be offended.

Rachel growled and narrowed her eyes. "Probably."

"I knew it. How are we even friends?"

"Your life would be so boring without me," Rachel said as she threw out her hands. "Plus, you'd have no culture!"

As Jess covered her mouth with her hand, I laughed. "I wasn't looking at anyone. You know I have a girlfriend."

"Who isn't blond, right?" Rachel asked jokingly.

I shook my head. "Nope. Not blond."

"Why isn't she ever here? I've never seen her before. Do you have a picture?" Rachel bounced in her chair, getting a little too animated. She was like a Latin cocker spaniel, if there were such a thing, hopping around, tail wagging, peeing on the floor in excitement.

"Leave him alone, Rach," Jess said, and I shot her a thankful look.

"On that note, I'm going to make the rounds. You two try to stay out of trouble. Mostly you." I pointed at Rachel. "Don't start a bar fire with Ryan or anything."

"I'd do anything that boy asked. Fires included," she shouted at me, but I was already walking away from them and straight toward Claudia. Who was anything but blond or typical.

No, Claudia was exotic. She was cultured and classy, and downright beautiful in every way. The shape of her body, the curve of her hips, and her ample breasts were what guys dreamed of. But for me, that wasn't it. It was more the way she carried herself, so self-assured and confident. And her eyes. I saw those eyes in my head more times than I cared to admit.

As I neared, I could hear the men flirting with them, doing their best to run some sort of game, but Claudia wasn't buying into it. I knew it by the tone of her voice, which sounded bored. For some reason, that made me ridiculously happy, and I had no business being that happy.

"Frank!" Claudia jumped up as soon as she saw me and moved through the throng of guys effortlessly. They all turned to see who had her attention.

Yeah, it's me, motherfuckers.

She practically leaped into my arms, and I held her all too willingly. Nothing felt better in this moment than that woman in my grasp, no matter how wrong it should have felt. Her body fit mine like it was made for it, each curve melting against mine. I inhaled the scent of her hair as it spilled around me. I had no idea what it smelled like, exactly; I just knew that it smelled good.

"Hey there." I smiled as I released her. "These guys bothering you?"

She cast them a quick look before focusing those beautiful brown eyes on me. "Nah, they're harmless. Just typical, is all."

I leaned toward her, my body feeling like it was way too far away from hers, when the reality was it was probably way too fucking close. "Typical how?"

"Oh, you know. All talk about their expensive cars and their fancy jobs. Apparently, they have more money than God."

I laughed at how she mimicked their voices, and tried to read her into reaction to them. "You're not into cocky rich boys?"

"Not really." She smiled at me. "I do like men who work hard and value what they do, but not because they want to show it all off. Don't get me wrong, Frank." She placed her hand on my chest, and the heat from her skin instantly warmed me. "I like nice things, but not at the expense of what truly matters."

"And what's that?"

She dropped her hand and cocked her head. "Your eyes are so pretty."

Shit. Was she drunk?

She shook her head. "Sorry, I . . ." She frowned, stumbling over her words. "What did you ask me? I swear I'm not drunk. You're just distracting, is all."

In that second, I felt like a million bucks. "I'm distracting?" I started to compliment her further, but stopped myself by clearing my throat. "I asked what you think truly matters."

"Oh, right!" She pointed a finger in the air. "Not money. Sure, it's nice to have, and it does make things a lot easier. But I'd rather be happy. I require honesty and trust in my relationships. And I want the man in my life to have passion not just for his work, but for me too. I need passion. I can't be an afterthought."

Her voice changed when she said the last part. She sounded vulnerable, yet confident. It was an odd mixture but was as sexy as hell. I wanted to take her into the back office and show her just how much passion I had flowing through my veins in that moment.

"I can't imagine anyone seeing you as an afterthought, Claudia."

She dropped her gaze to her feet for a second before meeting my eyes again. "You'd be surprised."

I had the sudden urge to deck every guy in her life who had ever treated her badly. It didn't make any fucking sense, especially since she told me how she valued honesty, and I wasn't being entirely truthful with her. Not that I had lied, but she obviously didn't know I had a girlfriend, and I clearly wasn't filling her in on that fact. Maybe I needed to deck myself first before I decked anyone else. Nothing made any sense when it came to her and my reactions.

"Sounds like you're dating all the wrong guys."

She sucked in her bottom lip, pulling it between her teeth, and I lowered my gaze, entranced by the way that lush lip moved gently in and out of her teeth's grasp. And when her tongue darted out to lick it, I thought I might lose my load in the middle of my own damn bar.

"It's hard to find any good ones," she said. "Have any recommendations?" She smirked, her cheeks blushing the tiniest bit, but I noticed.

"I might. I'll get back to you." I winked and turned to leave.

"Wait!" she called out with a melodic-sounding laugh. "Where are you going?"

"I have to get back to work."

I walked away knowing that I was leaving her wanting more, and hoped like hell I could convince myself to want her less.

GO BE BOLD
Claudia

"**Y**OU CAN THANK me later," Britney said as she reached for my hand and pulled me back onto the couch next to her.

"Thank you for what?" I shot her a look.

"For getting those assholes to leave." She tipped her head in the direction of the guys who had been hitting on us earlier. They had already moved on to other women, thank God.

"What'd you do?" When her lips formed a mischievous grin, I got a little nervous. "Britney, what'd you say to them?"

She laughed. "I told them you were Frank's girlfriend and that he wasn't really friendly. I might have equated him to a rabid dog who bit if provoked."

"A rabid dog? Seriously?"

"They're gone, aren't they?" She shrugged. "If I had to listen to one more story about who they knew in Hollywood or all the parties they get invited to, I would have rolled my eyes so hard into the back of my head, they would've stayed there."

"So you'd rather go blind than listen to them talk anymore?"

"Yes."

"Kind of dramatic, don't you think?"

"I'm nothing if not a little dramatic." She flipped her hair with one hand. Dramatically.

"Clearly."

She rested her head on my shoulder. "Now, tell me what Fuckable Frank said to you."

I coughed and choked out, "Please. For the love of our friendship, don't ever call him that again."

"Fine. What did Freaky Frank say?" She glanced up at me and waggled her eyebrows seductively.

I shoved her head from my shoulder and turned toward her. "Please stop with the weird names. Freaky Frank is not sexy. It sounds creepy."

"You're no fun. What did No-Fun-Frank say to No-Fun-Claudia, then?"

"Nothing, really. He was flirting, I think."

"You think? Of course he's flirting. He's been flirting with you since the first time he laid his stupid gorgeous green eyes on you."

"It's hard to tell with him," I admitted.

Did I want Frank to be flirting with me? Hell yes, I did. But I couldn't always tell if he was. I didn't know him well enough, and I found him hard to read.

"He's so hot and cold. One second, I think he's into me, and the next, he's running away like I have chicken pox or something."

"Chicken pox? Are we five?"

"You definitely are," I teased.

"Don't care. I'll be five." She shook her head. "But for the record," she turned and glanced behind us, "he's watching you.

He's always watching you."

I looked in Frank's direction and our eyes held for a moment longer than should be considered comfortable. My cheeks warmed and I looked away, feeling silly. I didn't know what him watching me was all about. I knew what I hoped it meant, but had no clue if there was any significance at all.

"Now what?"

"You have to leave him your number tonight before we leave," she stated, like it was the most obvious next step.

My eyes widened as I pulled back. "Leave my number? But he hasn't even asked for it."

"And he probably never will," she said in almost a whisper.

"Then what the hell are you talking about?" I snapped out, sharper than I had intended.

Britney wanted me to leave my phone number for Frank, but she didn't think he'd ever ask me for it? Why the heck would I give my number to a guy who didn't want it, or wouldn't ask for it?

She huffed out an annoyed breath. "I'm saying that if you wait for Frank to ask for your phone number, you might die first. And it's not because he doesn't want it."

She wasn't making any sense, but I played along anyway. "So I should just leave my number for him? Write it on a piece of paper like some . . ." I paused, annoyed at the stereotype I felt like I was so quickly becoming. "Like some—"

"Like some bar floozy?" Britney laughed.

I didn't want to be a typical bar floozy. I was fairly certain that Frank got hit on all the time, and the last thing I wanted was to be like all the other women who came into his bar.

Not to mention that if I were the aggressor, it meant that

Frank didn't have to be. Just the idea of that turned me off. I wasn't attracted to weak men, no matter how good-looking they might be. My heart required strength and confidence. A passive man would never do. I'd eventually eat him alive.

"He's a grown man, Britney. If he wants my number, then he should ask me for it. Do I really want to be interested in someone who doesn't even have the nerve to ask for my number?"

Britney belted out a loud laugh. "Do you really think Frank lacks nerve? Look at him. Honestly, I think he's just the quiet type. He isn't like Nick and Ryan, you know? He's not overly in your face like they are, all charming smiles and flirtatious words. He keeps to himself, and I wonder if he's trying not to cross a line with you for some reason."

"Like because he's not interested, maybe?" My heart stung a little just saying those words.

"No! God, you're so annoying." She groaned. "That man knows where you are in this bar at all times. If that's not interested, then it's just plain stalkery behavior. Not that I'd mind being stalked by him."

She bit her lip suggestively, and I found myself feeling territorial. If Frank was going to stalk either of us, it was going to be me.

Wait, what the hell am I even thinking?

"So, will you do it?" she asked.

I shrugged. "I'll think about it."

"Just be bold. What do you have to lose?"

"My pride. My confidence. The ability to look at myself in the mirror each morning without cringing."

"All over a stupid phone number? Now who's being dramatic?" She finished the last of her drink and slammed the empty glass down.

I sighed, weighing Britney's words against my heart's desire. What did I want when it came to Frank?

Everything?

Nothing?

"What are you thinking about? You have that stupid look on your face," Britney said, interrupting my thoughts, which weren't forming all that well anyway.

"I'm just trying to figure out what the hell I want when it comes to him," I admitted a little too honestly.

"You don't have to have it all figured out right this second."

"I know that."

"Are you sure?"

Her tone was a little too judgmental for my taste, and I stiffened. "Yeah, I'm sure. I think I know myself better than anyone else," I said with attitude.

She slouched back into the couch. "I'm not trying to upset you. I'm just saying that it's okay if you want to get to know him and see where it goes. Maybe you'll hate him after talking to him more. He might be stupid. Who knows? But you won't know unless you try."

Dammit. I hated that she was right. Because I was pretty sure that she was drunk, and it annoyed me that even inebriated, Britney could make this much sense.

I growled, "Fine. I'll leave him my damn number. Happy now?"

"Yes!" she shouted, pumping her fist into the air.

I reached for my clutch, opened it, and looked inside. "Just one problem."

"What's that, my little Colombian friend?" she said in an

accent that I was sure was meant to mimic my own. It was a horrible mix between Al Pacino in the *Godfather* and a drunk white girl from the Valley.

I shook my head. "No paper. No pen."

She hopped up from the couch like it was on fire. "I got you!" she said before sprinting off toward the bar.

I refused to turn around and watch her, my body already humming with slight humiliation at what might come out of her mouth while she was unattended.

When one of the annoying guys from earlier saw me sitting alone, he headed toward me. With one shake of my head, I made him stop in mid-step and turn back around. In that moment, I was thankful he and his friends thought I belonged to Frank.

Britney reappeared and plopped back onto the couch, bouncing me a little as she landed.

"Here you go! One pen and some paper," she said, handing them over as if she was the cleverest person in the entire bar.

"Please tell me you didn't ask Frank for them," I pleaded, willing my potential embarrassment to back down.

"Hell no! I asked Ryan." She giggled, her eyes a little glassy, and I wasn't sure if it was from the alcohol or the lust. "I'll take any excuse to talk to that man."

"You're incorrigible."

"Ooh, big word," she teased.

I wrote my name and number on the paper, thinking about how I was going to slip it to Frank without an audience.

"Are you ready to go soon?" I asked, more than a little nervous. I had always considered myself a confident woman, but when it came to that particular Fisher brother, I found myself questioning everything.

"Whenever you are." She allowed her head to fall back onto the couch, as comfortable as if we were in our living room.

"I'm ready." I didn't want to close the bar down like we had the other night. If I was leaving Frank my phone number, I wanted to do it and then get the hell out. Why was my mind making this into such an ordeal?

Britney leaned forward, a little off-balance as she scooped the piece of paper from the top of the table and peered at it. "Just making sure you didn't give him the wrong number."

A laugh bubbled up. "Why on earth would I give him the wrong number?"

"I don't know." She waved my question off. "I'm drunk. I ask stupid questions when I'm drunk."

"Can we go now?" I practically begged.

"Yeah. Go be bold!" she said way too loudly, and I covered her mouth with my hand.

"Seriously," I hissed at her. "Be quiet or I won't do it."

I looked around at the small scene her shouting had created. Too many heads were turned toward us, watching us with curiosity. I was already nervous enough, wondering how to give Frank my phone number on the sly. The last thing I needed was all eyes in the bar on us.

"Sorry," she whispered.

I reached for her arm to steady her. "How many drinks did you have?"

How the heck could she be so much more inebriated than I was? In our hours at the bar, I'd only had three drinks, but

Britney must have had more than that when I wasn't paying attention. And normally, I always paid attention.

"It was those douchey guys. They kept giving me shots."

Shit. I hadn't seen that happen at all. "I didn't realize. Are you okay?"

"I'm good enough to be your wingwoman!" She threw her arms out to her sides and pretended to fly as we walked.

I stopped short, pushing her in front of me before grabbing her arms and forcing them down to her sides. "Behave, or I'll tell Ryan you're pregnant with his love child."

She spun around to face me. "Wouldn't that be a dream? I wish I was pregnant with Ryan's love child!"

Everything she said was too loud. The bar was loud on its own, but Britney was louder. I heard Ryan's voice before I turned my head to meet his gaze.

"Who's pregnant with my love child?" He laughed, and the people lined up the bar for drinks all turned around and stared at us.

When Britney waved both hands in the air, I wanted to die. *I'm going to kill her.*

Thankfully, Frank appeared at my side. "You ladies heading out?"

I looked up at him, appreciating the way his tall frame towered over my five feet five inches, thinking of all the ways he could use his height to his advantage. As my mind wandered, I almost forgot he'd asked a question.

"Gotta take the drunk one home." I nodded toward Britney, whose arm was still in my grasp.

"I am not," Britney said. "Okay, fine. I'm drunk. So what? I hope it doesn't hurt the love baby."

"On that note . . ." I tightened my grip and reached into my pocket with my free hand, pulling out the paper. "We better go. But I wanted to leave this for you." I shoved the paper at him.

Frank looked down, his fingers folding as he palmed the small note.

"No pressure or anything. I mean, you don't have to use it. It's just . . ."

Oh my God. I couldn't stop stumbling over my words, and Britney started laughing hard.

"Frank makes you stupid, Claudia. I swear, she never acts like this."

"Gotta go," I said, then yanked on Britney's arm, leaving Frank and everyone else in the bar behind.

I was officially mortified.

CONFESSIONS

Frank

I WATCHED AS Claudia pulled Britney out the front doors, half tempted to chase her outside. If I thought for one second that it wouldn't embarrass Claudia further, I would have done it.

Unfurling my fingers from the paper I clenched, I instinctively knew what would be there. Just like I thought, Claudia had given me her name and number, taunting me, daring me to dial it.

Pulling out my cell phone, I almost sent her a text message, but I hesitated. It was in that millisecond of hesitation that guilt pushed its way in. That was all it took to make me to refocus. Shoving my phone and the note into my pocket, I headed back behind the bar to finish the evening with my brothers.

Once the bar was cleared out and locked up for the night and the rest of the staff sent home, Ryan started in on me. The little shit had been waiting hours to have this discussion.

"Can we please have a serious conversation?" He washed a glass as he spoke, but his eyes met mine, and they looked almost sad.

When Nick stopped what he was doing and inched closer

to where Ryan and I stood, I played dumb. "What are we getting serious about?"

"You know what," Nick said, but Ryan waved him off.

"Let me handle this," he whispered to Nick.

"Um, I can hear you, you know?"

"Of course I know," Ryan snapped. "Now, listen. There's something I can't figure out, okay? And I don't want you getting all pissed off and closing up on us when I ask you."

I groaned, wishing that Ryan would cut to the chase already and stop beating around the bush like a fucking girl. "Spit it out. I can handle whatever it is you're too chickenshit to ask."

He dropped the glass into the soapy water and it splashed all over his shirt. Thank God he'd put it back on after last call. "What's the deal with you and Shelby?"

That was it? *That* was his big dramatic question?

"What kind of question is that? How am I supposed to answer that?"

Nick said slowly, "I think what Ryan's trying to say is, we can see that you're not happy. We don't understand why you stay."

I wasn't sure how to answer that question, or if I wanted to. I'd kept everything to myself for so long, not wanting to burden anyone with my mess, but maybe it was time to unload. I wasn't good at asking for help, but maybe that's what these two were here for. God knew I'd do anything for either of them, and I knew they'd do the same for me. I just hated the very idea of needing anyone.

Without a word, I grabbed a bottle of whiskey and snagged three shot glasses. We'd done the same thing for Nick when we needed him to talk to us about all the crazy shit that was going on in his life. He'd tried to keep the things our father was doing to him a secret from us, but we'd plied him with enough alcohol that he started talking. It was our thing, I supposed.

Nick picked up the shot I pushed toward him. "I'm sensing a theme here."

"That we're alcoholics?" Ryan picked his up too.

"No. That we confess our truths over shots of hard liquor," Nick said. "It's how we bond."

"I need it if you want me to have this discussion with you," I said, my tone somber.

"Drink up." Nick grinned and tipped back his first shot. "Start talking, Frank."

"Don't push me," I growled.

Ryan shoved my shoulder. "Just start talking. Hell, start from the beginning. Give us the CliffsNotes, but tell us something." He tossed back his shot before filling his glass again.

Starting at the beginning wasn't something I was interested in. Plus, most of that no longer applied. Too much time had passed between who we were then and where we were now. After downing my shot, I refilled my glass and knocked it back too.

Ryan narrowed his eyes. "Did Claudia give you her number tonight?"

"She did."

"We'll get to her in a minute," Nick said, waving a hand. "Shelby first."

I rounded the bar, pulled out a stool, and sat facing them.

"I don't know where to start."

Both Nick and Ryan jumped in, shooting out questions, talking over each other like a couple of little kids. I raised a hand to shut them up.

"I don't know how to end things with Shelby." There. That was as good a place to start as any.

"But why? What keeps you so firmly rooted?" Nick asked. "You're not being blackmailed, right?" He swallowed hard, no doubt remembering the hell he'd gone through before being reunited with Jess.

"No, it's nothing like what you went through," I reassured him, thinking back at the absolute insanity my baby brother was forced to shoulder on his own before he let us in.

Ryan's face paled slightly. "She's not pregnant, is she?"

I recoiled, realizing how much more trapped I'd feel if she were. "No. Stop guessing."

"Then tell us, already."

"I think about ending things a lot, but then I feel so guilty that I can't get past it," I admitted, embarrassed at how weak I sounded.

"Why the guilt? Because she was there for you after baseball ended?" Ryan asked. He was so sincere, I could tell that he really wanted to understand the position I was in, and he didn't know any of the details.

"For one, yeah. She was there when no one else was. She literally picked me up from the floor when I didn't want to stand anymore." I sighed, recalling the dark time when I realized I'd lost everything I'd worked my whole life for.

"I can understand that," Ryan said, and Nick nodded in agreement.

"But there's more. You guys know she was raised by a single dad, right?" I furrowed my brow, wondering if I'd ever filled them in on that.

"I didn't know," Nick said. "I probably know the least since I was so young when this all happened."

Nick and I were ten years apart, so he was just a little kid when I had moved out. And when everything went downhill for me in college, the last person I was going to talk to about it was a ten-year-old.

"Shelby's dad was all she had. It was just the two of them her whole life. He was a great guy, really supportive and loving. I swear to God, I was actually working up the nerve to end things with Shelby," I said, shaking my head as I recalled the memory. "I wasn't happy in the relationship anymore. Not for any particular reason, though."

Sighing, I admitted, "I just realized that I stopped looking forward to coming home and having her there. I started doing everything I could to put off going home. I'd run errands and get shit we didn't need, all because I felt trapped and hated walking through that front door. One night, I'd given myself a pep talk the whole drive home, but when I walked in, Shelby was on the kitchen floor in tears, her cell phone at her side. It was her dad. He was really sick. We'd just had dinner with him a few nights before, you know? And we didn't have any idea because he kept it from us. He thought he would eventually get better and not have to ever tell us, but he didn't."

I stopped and took a deep breath. Losing Shelby's dad had been one of the hardest things I'd ever witnessed. It wasn't easy watching a strong man you admired fade away to nothing, right before our eyes. It was beyond heartbreaking, and it happened so quickly.

"I'd never felt more powerless than in those months before he passed. But on his deathbed . . ." I tried to compose myself as I remembered how tired his eyes had been, but also how much hope they still held out for his only daughter and me. "As he lay there dying, he made me promise that I'd always look after Shelby. He begged me to take care of her, told me he was leaving her in my hands, and that he couldn't imagine her with a better guy. He said he trusted me to always do the right thing by her."

My head dropped, the obligation I felt toward Shelby and her father weighing on me like a Mack truck. Telling my brothers about it had relieved the pressure a little, but it could never remove it from me completely.

"I never told Shelby what he said to me. I couldn't."

"Jesus, Frank," Nick said softly. "That's some really heavy shit. And you're walking around all day every day carrying all that on your shoulders?"

I looked up to see both my brothers watching me, their eyes filled with a mixture of sympathy and pain. I hated seeing it. I didn't want them feeling sorry for me. Every decision I had made about Shelby was of my own doing. No matter the reasoning behind it, I was still responsible for my situation.

"Everything makes so much sense," Ryan finally said.

"Yeah?" I asked.

He nodded. "But, Frank, I don't think Shelby's dad would want you two to stay together if you weren't happy."

"But she is happy," I said quickly. "I mean, I think she is. Hell, I don't know anymore."

"You gotta talk to her," Nick said, "really have a conversation with her about it. What if she's just as miserable as you are, and you're both punishing each other by staying together because you're each too scared to leave?"

I shrugged, not knowing what else to say.

"I'm really sorry you've been dealing with that alone all this time." Ryan reached out and gripped my forearm. "Don't forget you have us." He glanced at Nick before meeting my eyes again, his voice wobbling a little as he said, "We're always going to be here for you, no matter what. Don't keep shit like that to yourself anymore. We're your fucking brothers. That's why we're here."

"It wasn't your burden to bear," I said.

"It's really not yours either," Nick said, his voice stronger than Ryan's. "You can't live your life because of a promise you made to someone on his deathbed. I mean, I get it, that's a lot of pressure, and you've always been a stand-up guy who wants to do the right thing, but this—" He swallowed. "This is too much to ask of anyone."

It was almost humorous hearing that kind of advice come out of Nick's mouth, of all people. Until recently, he'd let other people dictate his entire life and every decision in it. He'd almost married a girl he hated because of it, and here he was now, doling out life-altering advice to me like it was the most natural thing ever.

And it wasn't. It was fucking weird.

But that didn't make him any less right.

I just wished that I believed letting down Shelby's dad was something I could live with. I wasn't sure that it was. Obligation and guilt had kept me rooted for this long, what was the rest of my life?

"I agree with Nick." Ryan rounded the bar and pulled up a stool next to mine. "You can't do this to yourself. It's no way to live."

"I know." And I did know. I just didn't know how to get out of it. "But how do you end things after that long when nothing's really wrong? She's going to want to know what happened, and I won't have an answer for her."

My mind spun, imagining scenarios that hadn't happened but probably would if I tried to break up with Shelby. "She'll want to fix it, but there's nothing to fix. How the hell do you explain that to a woman like Shelby? I've wasted so much of her time when she's been nothing but perfect. Seriously, the woman is a saint."

Nick tilted his head to the side, studying me. "Just because she's a good person doesn't make you a bad one for not wanting to be with her."

"You can't force yourself to have feelings for someone if you don't," Ryan added with a slight frown. "Sometimes feelings fade or change over time. That doesn't make you a bad guy either. At least you haven't married the girl while you've been so unsure."

I bristled at the thought. "I've been dodging that bullet for quite a while now, but she's getting impatient."

"Of course she is. She's a chick and she wants to get married. Even if it's for the wrong reasons," Ryan said matter-of-factly. I had forgotten for a second that he was a fairy-tale romance specialist.

"What wrong reasons?"

"She thinks it's the next natural step in your relationship.

Whether she's truly happy or not isn't the issue. She thinks that by now you two should be engaged, buying a house, getting ready for marriage, and planning how many kids you're going to have."

Ryan was right. Shelby was absolutely on that page when it came to us, but I kept doing my damnedest to steer her off it.

"How do you get her to back off? When she brings it up, what do you say?" Nick asked.

"I keep telling her that I don't know if I want to get married. That I'm not sure I believe in it." I looked down at my empty glass, avoiding their eyes.

"And she buys that?" Ryan asked incredulously.

"It's not like I give her much room. I close off and go silent if she pushes too hard. I never know what the hell to say without hurting her, and I don't want to lie."

"But staying with her is a lie," Nick said in a quiet voice.

"I know I should have the strength to walk away, but the thought of hurting her after all she's been through in her life fucking kills me. I may not be in love with Shelby, but I care about her feelings. The last thing I want to do is hurt her." It was fucked-up logic, if it was even logical at all, but it was the truth.

"I feel for you, brother." Ryan clapped his hand on my shoulder. "I really do. But I want better for you. You deserve to be happy. You know that, right?"

Of course I knew that.

Or, at least, I thought I knew that.

Hell, maybe I didn't think that I deserved to be happy at all. I'd made a promise to a dying man, and I was breaking that promise every single day. I deserved to be miserable, not happy.

When I didn't say anything, Ryan said, "The shit part of it is I feel like I'm only pushing you on this because of Claudia. If she hadn't walked in our bar, I'd still have my head in the sand, pretending your life was none of my business."

The mention of her name made my entire body warm, especially near the area of my pants that held her phone number. Her face flashed in my mind, the flush of embarrassment staining her cheeks as she gave me the scrap of paper. She couldn't get out of my bar quick enough. It was as adorable as it was infuriating.

Nick nodded. "I feel the same way."

I jerked my head up, unable to remember what the hell we were talking about.

"What way is that?" I pretended not to have just been in another Claudia-induced fog.

"That Claudia is the reason we're just now getting to the bottom of this. I knew you were unhappy, but I never knew why. I never thought about really pressing you for an answer. I always figured you'd kick my ass," Ryan said with a grin.

I wanted to be shocked and surprised that Claudia was the reason the two of them were suddenly on my case, but I wasn't. As much as I tried to deny it or pretend there was nothing between her and me, I was only lying to myself. And although I had no fucking clue *what* it was exactly, I did know that there was something.

"What is it about Claudia that has you both so invested in my love life all of a sudden?" I asked the question, hoping they'd give me some insight. It was like I couldn't see anything clearly anymore—everything was coated in a layer of fog I couldn't see my way out of.

"First of all," Ryan said, then pointedly tapped his empty glass on the bar top. Nick lifted the whiskey and poured us all another round of shots. "I've never, and I mean never, seen you look at someone the way you look at her. Your entire face lights up. You make fun of me for being a walking chick flick, but you're a fucking girly romance movie waiting to happen whenever she walks through our doors." He downed his shot and burst out laughing like he was the funniest fucking person in the room.

Nick joined in, laughing hard before he downed his own shot. "It's true. You actually smile when she comes in. And you flirt. *You*," he repeated, bursting out laughing again. "You actually flirt. It makes my night seeing that shit."

"It's like watching a baby deer on ice for the first time," Ryan added, tipping back his head as he swiped at his eyes.

I should have known he'd reference a fucking Disney movie. The two of them should have started a damn comedy tour with how hilarious they both thought they were.

I glared at each of them. "You both know I can kick your asses, right?"

"Worth it," they said in unison.

Assholes.

Ryan calmed himself down and looked at me sincerely. "Bro, seeing you with Claudia made me realize just how unhappy you've really been. You come to life when she's around. That's the only way I can explain it. You're not like that when you're with Shelby. It's like you're going through the motions, which makes complete sense now. Everything you do for her is out of obligation. I totally get it. I just don't want that for you."

"I refuse to throw away my relationship with Shelby for a woman I don't even know," I said, doing my best to think rationally.

Nick shook his head. "How you feel about Shelby has nothing to do with Claudia. One doesn't have anything to do with the other."

"It suddenly feels that way. Like I'm only now really wanting to end things with Shelby so that I can see if there's something there with Claudia. That's fucked up. I refuse to be that kind of man," I said with a snarl.

"What kind is that, exactly?" Nick asked.

"The kind who breaks up with his girl for another one. I could never live with myself."

"But it's not about that. You said yourself that you've been unhappy for years. Maybe you met Claudia so that you'd be forced to take action in your life. She's your catalyst," Ryan suggested, sounding like a self-help book.

"How do you feel about her? I get that you don't even know her, but there's a spark, right? A connection of some kind?"

That sounded so strange coming from Nick. I would have bet money that kind of question would only come out of Ryan's mouth.

How could I describe what I felt when I saw her? I wasn't sure. "Something's there. I don't know what it is, but it's more than just attraction."

Nick leaned toward me. "You feel pulled toward her? Drawn in some way?" He noticed my suspicious expression and held up his hands. "I'm not making fun of you or trying to be like Ryan. I'm sincerely asking."

I nodded because I did feel a pull toward Claudia. Anytime she was in the room, my body demanded to be closer to hers. It was like there was a cord tethering me to her, some sort of force, and I had to fight against it every moment she was in my vicinity. If either of us moved too far away, the cord yanked, drawing me back in.

"There's something you can't really explain," Nick said, "but you just know is different from anything else ever has been before, right?"

Discussing this kind of mushy stuff with my brothers was a huge mistake. I was basically handing them ammunition to use against me for years to come. One day, I'd regret admitting all this shit to them; I just knew it. But for now, I needed their help, their opinions, and their perspective.

I barked out an embarrassed laugh. "I haven't felt this drawn toward anyone, and we get a lot of women in here."

"You know, I felt that way about Jess when I first saw her," Nick said, his voice as sincere as I'd ever heard it. "There was something between us that I'd never felt before. I think there are just some people that you're drawn to, and you can't fight it or explain it. Which sucks because we're men, and we don't like emotions." He grinned and pounded his chest like Tarzan.

"I like emotions," Ryan said, and I swore right then and there that he had a vagina. "What? That's what I've been looking for. That's the kind of thing I want."

I scoffed at him. "That's why you dated every girl who came in our bar for months?"

Ryan had gone through a phase when it seemed like he gave pretty much every woman who wanted one a chance. It wasn't until he realized that he was creating a really bad situation for himself and our bar that he stopped.

Women constantly came in to flirt with Ryan, to beg him for another chance, to put him on the spot about what went wrong, or why he didn't like them. But what they didn't understand was that Ryan was working and they were coming into his place of business, basically harassing him anytime they pleased, and he couldn't do anything to stop it.

Ryan thought for a moment before answering. "It took me a long time to realize that having chemistry with someone wasn't the same as having a connection. Chemistry is all physical. Connection is spiritual. I want the connection."

"When you get married, will you wear the dress?" I teased, and Ryan narrowed his eyes at me.

"I won't apologize for knowing what I want. It's a hell of a lot better than the situation you're in and clearly never getting out of," he bit out.

Now that just pissed me right off. I could and would beat the hell out of my brother if he didn't shut up.

"Everyone calm down." Nick raised his hands in the air, playing the role of peacekeeper.

"He's just getting pissed because he knows I'm right." Ryan shoved back his stool and stood up.

I couldn't help but wonder if he was right. Instead, I said, "This isn't helping."

Nick shook his head. "On the contrary, I think we've accomplished more tonight than we have in the last five years. At least I have a way better understanding of you now. I just think it really sucks."

I wanted to ask them each what they would do if they were me, but it wouldn't matter. I knew they'd both say that they'd leave Shelby, but it was easy to say that when it wasn't your reality. It was easy to think you know how you'd react in a situation when it wasn't the one you were living.

Nick gave me a pointed look. "Remember how pissed you were when I told you what Dad was doing to me?"

I nodded, remembering how the overwhelming urge to protect him from the hell he was dragged into had surged through me. But his situation and mine weren't even close to the same thing.

"It's how I feel for you now. I want to stop this train you're on. I want you to be able to get off, or at least feel like you have a choice in the matter."

Damn. Nick made it sound so simple and easy when it was anything but. I didn't feel like I had a choice when it came to this . . . I felt like I had an obligation. I was required to stay put, no matter what, because I'd given a man my word. And I intended to keep it.

Calmer now, Ryan said, "Watching you live like this is really hard. Knowing the reasons behind it makes it even harder. I don't know why. It should make it easier, right? Because it all makes perfect sense, but it somehow makes it all worse."

I understood more than he knew. When you made a promise to a dead man, there was no negotiating. The words you said were written in blood, cast in stone, sent down a river made of his daughter's tears. They couldn't be taken back because there was no one to take them back from. Promises made to a dead man were permanent.

"What are you going to do?" Ryan asked as he went back to washing glasses.

"I don't know." I said it like it was my new fucking mantra. Those three words seemed to be my answer for every question these days. But if leaving Shelby had been an easy decision, I would have done it years ago.

"Can I have Claudia's number then, because she's—" Ryan let out an appreciative whistle, and I bristled at him. My jaw flexed and tightened before he lifted his hands from the soapy water in surrender. "Kidding! I'm just kidding. I'd never do that."

"But if you don't call her, Frank, someone else eventually will," Nick said. "And if you think there might really be something there between you and her, well . . . trust me. It's worth sacrificing all the other shit it takes to get there."

Was it worth my conscience? What if Nick was wrong?

And what if *I* was wrong and there was nothing between Claudia and me except mutual attraction? After all, I'd been out of the game a long time. What if everything I thought I was feeling was a lie? What if I ruined everything, crushing Shelby in the process, for what ended up being nothing, some sort of trick my mind played on me?

How did you decide what was worth the risk and what wasn't?

Fuck if I knew.

THE THREE-DAY RULE

Claudia

"**I** FEEL LIKE a fool," I said to Britney as she drove us to work Monday morning.

"Why? Because Frank hasn't called?"

It had been almost three days since I'd given him my phone number, and he still hadn't called or texted, hadn't done anything with it. Maybe I'd misread the signs. I probably should have taken my own advice, the wisdom I'd shared with Britney when she first talked to me about liking Ryan— bartenders were supposed to be flirty and make you feel special.

It didn't seem like Frank's MO to behave that way, but I didn't *really* know him. It could have all been an act, yet my gut instinct told me that wasn't true.

But if it was all real like my heart wanted to believe, then why hadn't he contacted me? My mind raced, trying to make sense of things that there was no making sense of.

"Maybe he's just busy. He does own and run one of the busiest bars in Santa Monica, you know," Britney said, turning down the volume on the radio. "He probably doesn't have a lot of downtime."

I scowled and crossed my arms. "Excuses."

It didn't matter how busy someone was. If they were interested in you, they made time. Plus, it took all of two seconds to type out a quick message, so I refused to believe that he was too busy to text. I refused to believe that *anyone* was too busy to text. Hell, if the president of the United States found the time to tweet, Frank Fisher could certainly type out a damn text message to me.

Britney gave me a quick glance before she returned her attention to the road. "I'm just saying. Maybe he didn't want to initiate conversation with you when he wasn't able to actually have one."

I shook my head as I tried to interpret her babble. "What are you trying to say?"

"He works all weekend, I assume. He probably doesn't have time to talk to you, so why text or call when he'd just have to end it after two seconds, or be constantly interrupted? I feel like that would piss Frank off, having to tell you to hold on all the time, or BRB," she said with a laugh. "I can't see Frank ever typing out 'BRB,' by the way."

"No," I said, refusing to accept that.

"No, what?"

"He can make time. It takes a second to text me *hello*. Text me and tell me *work sucks*. But text me something! I don't need some drawn-out hour-long conversation. I understand that we both have lives and are busy, but at least let me know you're thinking about me. It's not that hard." As I raised my voice, my accent came to life. Whenever I got riled up, it came out thicker, and Britney always found that amusing.

"Ooh, I love it when you get all feisty Colombian on me."

"I'm just saying—" I sucked in a deep breath, trying to calm down, but I was already too agitated. "I don't care how good-looking Frank Fisher is, I'm not giving him a pass to treat me like crap."

Britney slammed her fist on the steering wheel. "Girl power! I like it. Setting a precedent."

Was that what I was doing? Subconsciously, I probably was. My whole life had been spent making excuses for guys who didn't do things or treat me the way I expected them to. We women let them off way too easily, time and time again, and then we were the ones who ended up getting hurt in the end. I wanted a man who wasn't afraid to show me he liked me. I was tired of guessing how men felt, what they wanted, and where our relationship was headed. I was sick of the games. I craved authenticity, something real.

"What are you thinking about?" she asked.

"Just how much we settle when it comes to guys. I don't want to settle anymore. I want the kind of love I'm willing to give, and I don't want to feel bad about expecting that. I'm tired of lowering my expectations because guys can't seem to meet them." Frustrated, I stared unseeing out the passenger window as the world passed by in a blur. "I think we let men treat us like crap. We don't hold them accountable, almost like we're afraid they'll leave us if they don't like what we have to say."

Britney nodded. "It's a little deep for this time of the morning, but I smell what you're cooking."

"I really thought he'd call," I admitted, feeling more than a little vulnerable.

"So did I. I would have put money on it," she said, and it made me feel marginally better, like I hadn't made up the connection entirely in my mind.

"And now I've ruined our favorite bar for us. Because we

can't go back there." My mind was racing again. "You can, but I'm never stepping foot in there again. I can't face Frank after that rejection." I moaned and rubbed the heels of my hands into my eyes.

"It's only been a couple of days. Don't write him off yet," she said with a small shrug.

"I think if he was going to do something, he would have already."

I truly believed that. When a man wanted a woman, there was no sense in waiting. What would be the point?

"Maybe he's old-fashioned." She huffed out a breath. "Maybe he does that whole stupid three-day rule thing. Do guys still do that?"

"Oh God, I hope not."

I groaned, remembering when guys waited three days before they did anything. They waited three days before they called you the first time, then another three days before they asked you out, then another three days after that first date. It was like some unwritten rule in the guy-code handbook that they all followed. It was the worst, and we tolerated it. Expected it, even.

"I can't see Frank following any kind of rules," I said. "He strikes me as the kind of man who does what he wants, whenever he wants."

"That's what I thought too."

So then, what did it mean that he hadn't reached out to me yet? Even with my mind giving me the logical answer, my heart refused to accept it.

I still held out hope, even if I acted like I had given up.

*

I WENT THROUGH the majority of my day thankful for the distraction of work, but still disappointed. Anytime I had a free moment, my mind drifted to Frank, and I found myself wondering what he was doing and thinking. The sound of my cell phone pinging out a text notification grabbed my attention.

A phone number I didn't recognize appeared on the screen, and my heart thumped hard. When I clicked on the message, it read:

> UNKNOWN NUMBER: *I hope you're having a good day at work. Sorry it took me so long to reach out. Forgive me? It's Frank, by the way.*

My fingers flew, typing out a response before my brain could make them stop.

Should I force him to suffer and wait like I had all weekend? No. I hated games, and the last thing I wanted was to waste another second ignoring Frank when I could be talking to him, getting to know him.

After saving his number into my contacts, I pushed back from my desk and headed quickly to Britney's office. When I waved my phone at her from the doorway, her eyes widened and her mouth formed an *O* of surprise. She pointed at the telephone receiver held to her ear and flashed me one finger, so I walked back into my office and waited.

"Oh my God," Britney said as she ran into my office and shut the door a few moments later. "What did he say? I knew he would text you!"

"You did not," I insisted, because this morning we were both pretty sure he had ditched me, even if we hadn't said those exact words.

"Okay, fine. But I hoped. Now, read me the damn text."

I read it to her, and she swooned.

"It's not really swoon-worthy, Britney."

"It kinda is. *Forgive me?*" She started fanning herself. "Did you text him back?"

I leaned back in my chair and swiveled it back and forth. "Not yet. What should I say?"

"Yes, you'll marry him. You were thinking about two, maybe three kids, and you'll be over as soon as you get off work." She batted her eyelashes and I rolled my eyes.

"I was thinking more along the lines of this." I typed a short text and held out my phone so she could read it before I sent it. "Is it too much?"

She pressed a button on my screen before I could change my mind or even read my response over again to make sure it was okay. "It's perfect. And sent. You're welcome."

My jaw dropped as I grabbed the phone out of her grubby little hands. "You little . . . You can't be trusted!"

My phone pinged and we both squealed. Literally. I thanked the gods my door was shut because I was acting like a complete idiot, rather than a grown-ass woman with her act together.

"What does it say?"

Instead of handing Britney my phone, since she couldn't be trusted, I read Frank's text out loud.

FRANK: *Would you want to stop by the bar after you get off work? Mondays are usually pretty slow, and I'd love to see you.*

I read the text to myself twice more before I gathered the courage to look Britney in the eye, afraid of how much excitement might be reflected in mine. I didn't want to get my hopes up too high.

"What do I say to that?"

"Is that a real question? You say *yes* in all caps. With a thousand exclamation points after it," she demanded, completely serious.

Never in a million years would I type a text in that way. And especially not to Frank Fisher.

CLAUDIA: *I'd love to stop by. I'll text you when I'm on my way.*

"Boring." Britney glanced at my text and pretended to snore, and I pointed at the door behind her.

"Out."

"Fine. I'm leaving. But don't forget who drove you to work today, and who can forget how to get back to our apartment when we get off." She stuck her tongue out before disappearing from view. She'd never do anything to stop me from seeing a Fisher brother, and we both knew it.

Frank and I texted a couple more times throughout the day, but they were mostly polite messages in response to the others, which I appreciated.

I spent the next few hours swinging between being excited and wanting to throw up. It had been a long time since a guy had piqued my interest. But here I was, counting down the minutes until I could clock out, go home, and change into something comfortable.

There was no way I was showing up at Sam's in my work clothes.

NOT-SO-NICE GUY

Frank

WHAT THE HELL had I done? I'd successfully managed to get through the entire weekend without texting Claudia once. It hadn't been easy; I had fought off the urge to text her more times than I could count. Thankfully, the bar was packed on Saturday and we had a private party Sunday afternoon, so I could pretend my mind wasn't stuck on her as I distracted myself with work.

But when Monday rolled around, I couldn't resist anymore. Mondays were slow as it was, but when Ryan asked if I had talked to her or not, my mind went into overdrive. Once he mentioned her name, it was all over for me. I found myself texting her before I could talk myself out of it. And not only had I initiated conversation and given her my phone number in return, but I'd also asked her to stop by the damn bar. Tonight.

What the hell was I thinking?

At least it was Nick's night off, so I'd only have to deal with the wrath of Ryan, which wouldn't be too bad considering he was a Disney princess and all. I stood behind the bar, mentally scolding myself, when the door opened.

I knew Claudia was about to walk through it, sensed her

presence before I even saw her. Not wanting to read into that any more than was necessary, I buried the thought.

She walked in, wearing jeans slung low on her hips. The tight top she wore hugged her ample breasts, showcasing them like they were a work of art. Everything about this woman should be displayed; she was that beautiful. All rational thought, good sense, and logic escaped me with just one look at her.

Tamping down my inappropriate thoughts, I watched as Ryan greeted Claudia before turning to look me in the eye. He'd noticed that she was alone, and it didn't take long for him to put two and two together. Shaking his head, he looked away, pretending not to have an opinion on the matter, when I knew he damn well had one and I'd hear all about it later.

Claudia headed to my side of the bar, wearing a beautiful smile. "Hey," she said as she neared, her tone a little nervous. It was fucking adorable.

"Hey, yourself. I'm glad you made it. Do you want anything to drink?"

I knew I should care more about what the hell I was doing in this moment, but all I could think about was spending a little time with her. I wanted to get to know her better, and even though my head kept blaring warning signals, my heart was clearly taking the lead.

My heart. I was starting to sound like Ryan.

"Do you have soda? Like Sprite? Or are you going to force me to drink alcohol?" she asked with a laugh.

"I'd never force you to do anything," I said a little too seriously. "One Sprite coming up." I moved near Ryan to pour Claudia a Sprite and myself a Coke. If she wasn't drinking, then neither was I.

"Did you invite her?" Ryan whispered, and I nodded. "We are so discussing this later."

I looked at him. "I'm well aware."

"Good."

With the two drinks in hand, I walked back to Claudia before tipping my head toward the back of the bar, which was pretty much empty. She followed as I led her toward one of the high-top tables. I could have led us to the couch, but figured that sitting at a table might discourage my inappropriate behavior.

I pulled out a bar stool and sat down, placing Claudia's drink across from me. She sat and we stared at each other, grinning as we sipped our sodas.

"Can I ask you something?" She put her drink down, brushing her fingers across the moisture on the glass.

"Of course." Honestly, I was a little nervous at what might come out of her mouth. If she knew I had a girlfriend, she hadn't let on. But if she asked, I wouldn't lie to her. I knew I was already lying by keeping the truth from her, but I wouldn't outright lie if she asked. I couldn't.

"What took you so long to text?"

I laughed. I couldn't help it. She was straightforward, and I appreciated it.

"Why are you laughing at me?" she asked with a small frown.

"I'm not," I said, still grinning at her. "I like that you say what's on your mind."

She pursed her lips and narrowed her brown eyes at me. "So, what's your excuse, Fisher?"

"Which one will get me out of trouble?"

A loud *ha!* escaped before she covered her mouth, then lowered her hand. "Who says you're in trouble?"

"I just figure you wouldn't be asking me about it if I wasn't," I teased.

She stayed quiet for a minute. Hell, maybe it was longer. Reaching for her drink, she took a few sips, never pulling her soft brown gaze from mine. Finally, she lowered her glass and gave me a smile, signaling she was ready to talk again.

"I'm just trying to figure you out."

"I'm not really that difficult. I am a guy."

And that right there was the truth. Men aren't nearly as complicated as women. Women often have a thousand emotions, a million reasons, and a billion different scenarios going through their minds at any given time. We men usually have about three, maybe four, max. Any more and our circuits might short out.

"But you're a quiet kind of guy. Those are usually the most complicated. And dangerous."

"You think I'm dangerous?" I couldn't help but laugh again. I'd never been called dangerous in my life.

"I haven't decided yet."

"I think you might be the dangerous one," I said, and she had no idea just how much I meant it. I wasn't sure that even I had any idea how much I meant it.

Her cheeks flushed as she looked away for a second before bringing her attention back to me. "I *am* from Colombia," she said with a wink.

Jumping at the topic, I asked, "When did you move here?"

"My mom and I moved when I was seven."

"Why?" I sincerely wanted to know, curious about what it was like to be from another country and want to move to America.

Rather than answer, she sucked in a breath, making me wonder if she was weighing her options about how much to share with me. Instead of pushing, though, I waited. I wanted her to trust me.

"My dad had a girlfriend," Claudia finally said. "When my mom found out, she asked him to leave, and you know what he did?" She raised her voice, her heightened emotions telling me how much this story still affected her, all these years later.

"What?"

"He left," she said with a shrug. "He packed a single suit-case. It was brown and tattered, with a blue sticker on it. I don't know why I remember that, but I do. So vividly. I remember him giving me a kiss on the forehead and then walking out the front door and never coming back. I was four."

My heart sank, hurting for the little girl she once was and for the woman she had become.

"He didn't even say anything to my mom. He just left. She waited for years, thinking that he would come back, but he never did. So we came here. It was like once she made up her mind to leave for America, there was no stopping her. I don't even think my father could have talked her out of it by that point."

God, Claudia was honest. It was as refreshing as it was damning. Guilt stormed my heart, reminding me that I wasn't much better than her old man had been. How was what I was doing any better than what he'd did?

"Is she remarried now?"

"She is. And he's great. Bradley raised me like I was his own daughter. I'm thankful for all he's done for us."

I couldn't help but smile as she talked about her stepfather. It made me happy that she seemed happy. "Have you been back to Colombia since you left?"

She shook her head sharply. "Not once."

That shocked me. "Do you want to?"

"More than anything. I want to see where I came from, where I used to live, you know? I don't really remember any of it."

The conversation halted for a while, neither of us pressing the other to speak. There was a comfort in the silence, an easiness, that I couldn't remember ever feeling with anyone before. I wasn't the kind of guy to fill the air with noise that wasn't necessary, but I always sensed when people wanted to drown it out. Claudia seemed content in the silence between us.

What she'd said about Colombia sank in, and I rolled that around in my head as I waited. I had no idea what she was thinking, but I refused to interrupt her thoughts. I waited for her to come back to me, for her mind to return to where we were, but I didn't press. I could have stayed quiet for hours, if that was what she needed.

A few moments later, her gaze lifted from the table and found mine. "What about you? Are you from here?"

I nodded. "I am. We grew up in Laguna Beach."

"Fancy."

"It wasn't when Ryan and I were kids, but it is now. My dad's loaded," I admitted with a sheepish grin. The last thing I wanted was to throw my family's money in anyone's face. We might all be successful business owners, but I hated arrogance, and I knew she did too from what she told me the other night when those guys were hitting on her.

"What's your dad do?"

"He owns a marketing firm."

Her mouth dropped open like the gears spinning in her head had all connected together. "That makes so much sense."

"What does?"

"The marketing, and Nick being so good at it." She gave me a sheepish look. "I might know way more than I should about you and your brothers. That's a little weird, right? You can tell me it's weird."

I laughed, wanting to reassure her. "Used to it, honestly."

"Stop it. Now you're just being nice."

"I'm never nice if I don't mean it," I said, meaning every word, and she smiled.

"I like that."

"Oh, you do, do you?" I teased, and she looked away, her naturally olive-skinned cheeks turning pink. "What else do you know about me and my brothers?"

She shrugged. "Not much, I swear. Just that Nick does all the marketing, and he's a genius. Your own Snapchat filters? A wall just for Instagram pictures? Pretty brilliant."

I agreed, even though I didn't use either app. I had a Facebook page that I never checked, and that was it as far as social media was concerned. Everyone I cared about knew how to reach me if they needed me, and it damn well wasn't through a computer.

"What else do you know?" I pushed her for more. It embarrassed her, based on how my interest made her fidget, but I found it endearing.

"Ryan's a god at making drinks, and every woman who steps foot in the bar apparently falls in love with him," she said with a nonchalant shrug.

"Not you, though?"

"Not me, what?"

"You didn't fall in love with Ryan?" I asked with a cocky grin.

Claudia looked toward him working the bar. "Eh, I guess I could be persuaded," she said with a small smile, then cut a teasing glance back at me.

I wanted to hop across the table, grab her by the waist, and pull her against me. "Oh yeah?"

She laughed as she played with my emotions. "Nah. He's not my type."

"Poor Ryan. I thought he was everyone's type." I cast a quick glance at my brother, noting him smiling like always at one of our female patrons.

"Apparently, I prefer the more brooding, quiet type."

"Don't get too many of those in here."

"One's really enough."

When her gaze locked with mine, I couldn't fucking breathe. I wanted to tell her everything, hating the fact that I was keeping something so huge from her, but I couldn't. I knew instinctively that if I told Claudia about Shelby, she would leave, and I wasn't ready for that. Hell, it was the last thing I wanted—to lose the woman I couldn't stop thinking about, even though wasn't mine in the first place.

"Tell me about your job," I said, wanting to know everything there was to know about her.

"I work for a bank."

"Which one? I'm switching branches."

Claudia laughed at my lame joke, and I grinned back at her.

"I'm in charge of small business loans," she said with a smile that lit up her eyes.

"You love it."

She nodded. "I do."

"Tell me why."

Claudia sucked in a quick breath. "Because people come to me with their dreams in their hands, and I get to try to help them make those dreams a reality. Do you have any idea how many people want to start their own businesses and work for themselves?" She stopped short and shook her head. "Of course you do. You own your own business."

"You meet with people every day who are trying to get business loans?"

"Pretty much all day long."

"Wow." I had never given much thought to the number of people who needed to borrow money to make their dreams a reality. We'd been lucky enough to start ours with our own funds. "So, do you get the final say?"

"I wish. But then we'd probably be out of business, because I'd give everyone the money they wanted," she said before taking a sip of her drink.

"Everyone?"

"Why should one person be entitled to their dream more than someone else? I think everyone should get a shot at accomplishing the things they want." Her tone was matter-of-fact. She obviously believed in what she said, even if was a pipe dream, a fairy tale.

"I think it's a nice idea," I said carefully, "but probably not very practical."

"You apparently think like a computer and not a human," she said, her accent coming out with her words.

Apparently, I'd said the wrong thing. Trying to make peace, I held up my hands.

"I'm not trying to upset you. I get what you're saying from a sunshine-and-rainbows standpoint. But from a financial standpoint, you can't go around giving everyone who asks a bag full of money. It's just not smart business. You have to make sure that your investment will be returned; otherwise, you're taking a loss."

"But who are you to say what will or won't work based on some stupid business plan that you're required to provide?"

I laughed. I loved the way her mind worked. "That's what the business plan is for."

"You think I don't know what a business plan is for? I know that, Frank."

She'd spat out my name like it was sour on her tongue, and I hated to admit that seeing her get this fired up turned me on a little.

"But what you don't understand," she said, "is that not everyone has the means to have a well-written business plan. Do you have any idea the number of people who pay for someone to write them a plan that's pretty much guaranteed to get them the loan, versus the people who do it themselves? The people who write their own might not write it very well, or make it complete, but it's done with passion. They've done the best they can. They believe in their ideas, and I believe in them. It's not fair that because of some software program where I insert numbers into blank spaces, they can be approved or not. It's not fair because sometimes the idea is really good."

Claudia stopped for a second to suck in a breath, and when she continued, her accent was thicker than I'd ever heard it. "In fact, sometimes the idea is really good. But the computer says no. And I'm required to tell them no. It breaks my heart, actually hurts my feelings to tell good, hard-working people that we can't help them. When all they're trying to do is better themselves."

Her color high, she pressed her lips together tightly as she breathed through her nose, apparently waiting for me to respond. When my lips turned up into a smile, she narrowed her eyes.

"I have no argument," I said with a slight shrug.

Claudia glared at me. "Really? You have nothing to say to all that?"

"I have something to say, but it has nothing to do with your work." I thought about how turned on I was hearing her talk like that. How her good heart and passion for helping others ignited a fire inside me and fueled the connection between us.

"Ugh, you're so typical." She groaned.

"I can't help it. You're fucking hot when you're fired up. And this crazy thick accent comes out of nowhere. It's sexy as hell."

That got a laugh out of her. "Clearly, we need to change the topic." She cleared her throat, possibly trying to tone down her accent. "Tell me what you like to do in your spare time.

Shoot, do you even have time off?"

I thought for a second about letting her know that I usually had a standing day off on Thursdays, but then she'd expect me to ask her out. And I couldn't. I shouldn't even be sitting here talking to her like this, getting to know her better, but here I was, breaking all of society's rules. Not to mention my own.

"Not often, to be honest. I spend the majority of my time here. But I like to go for rides on my bike, clear my head, get away."

Her eyes flew open wide. "Your bike?"

"My motorcycle."

"Oh, thank God. For a second there, I thought you meant a bicycle. I'm sorry, but I can't see all this," she waved her hand toward me, "riding a bike around."

I glanced toward Ryan. "What about him?"

An adorable laugh bubbled out of her. "Definitely. Probably a beach cruiser. With a basket and a bell."

My own laughter burst free, matching hers. We sat there for a few seconds, both laughing at the thought. Knowing Ryan had no idea he was the butt of our joke made me laugh even harder.

When the laughter died down, I asked, "Do you like motorcycles?"

"I've never been on one before."

Of course, my mind instantly went there. I imagined Claudia's body pressed tightly against my back as I navigated us through the Hollywood Hills, or up the Pacific Coast Highway toward Malibu, my favorite spot to unwind.

Without thinking, I said, "I'll have to change that one day."

It was too late to take the words back, too late to stop them from tumbling from my stupid lips. I had no self-control when it came to this woman, and it was going to get me into trouble. Hell, it was already getting me into trouble. I was walking a dangerous line and I knew it, yet did nothing to stop it.

Claudia smiled at me. "I'd like that."

"The idea doesn't scare you?"

"Why would it scare me?"

"I don't know. Some women are scared of motorcycles."

Shelby hated my bike and refused to ride on it with me, no matter how hard I had begged her in the past. I'd stopped asking a long time ago, but also stubbornly refused to consider any other mode of transportation.

"Well, I'm not." Claudia leaned forward, her silky black hair falling over her shoulders. "And I trust you to keep me safe."

She trusted me.

She trusted me to keep her safe.

My stomach twisted at her confession. I'd do anything to keep her from harm, but I couldn't tell her that. Not when everything I did was the exact fucking opposite. Her emotions weren't safe with me. Her feelings weren't safe.

I should tell her about Shelby.

I need to tell her.

But at the sight of the softness of Claudia's brown eyes when she looked at me, I melted on the spot. If she knew the truth, she'd never look at me the same way again. Everything soft would turn hard, and I'd lose her forever.

So I kept my damn mouth shut.

MORE THAN A LITTLE CRUSH

Claudia

F RANK'S EXPRESSION CHANGED when I told him that I trusted him. Convinced that I'd scared him with my honesty, I tried to pull back. I was a little rusty when it came to dating, and had forgotten how easily guys could be scared off, even if Frank hadn't seemed like the type.

"Can I ask you something about the bar?" I scrambled for a subject change, hoping it would ease the tension radiating from him.

"Anything," he said, and the worry lines between his brows disappeared altogether.

Thank God.

"What's the plan? Do you eventually want to open more bars, or just keep this one?"

"That's a great question, actually," he said, sounding almost out of breath. "I'm honestly not sure what the future holds, but for now we're happy with just this one location. It keeps us all in one place, and we really like working together. If we had multiple bars, we'd spread out and never see each other, and none of us would like that idea. Does that sound stupid?"

It was completely endearing to see this tough-looking,

confident man be a little insecure and unsure.

"I like it when you think like a person instead of a computer," I teased. I couldn't help it. That had been too golden of an opportunity to pass up.

"Yeah, yeah. I know we could increase our income by opening more bars, but we're not really in it for the money."

"So he's human after all." I all but swooned, and Frank shook his head at me before raising his hand and making a tiny space between his finger and thumb.

"Only a little."

I reached across the table and parted the space between his fingers as wide as they would go. "I think it's sweet."

"Sweet?" He raised his eyebrows in challenge.

"Yeah. It's *sweet* that you boys like each other that much. You're lucky. I don't have any siblings." I'd always wanted a brother or sister, but eventually accepted the fact that my mom and Bradley were never going to give me one, even though I put it on my Christmas list in the number-one spot every year for at least a decade.

"Did you hate being an only child?"

"I didn't hate it, per se. It wasn't bad, just a little lonely sometimes. But I'd always been intrigued by the idea of having a built-in, forever kind of best friend. You know?"

He nodded. "I do know. We're pretty lucky. The five Fishers."

"Five? Oh, you three plus your mom and dad. I get it. Are you showing off your finance major?" I asked, not seriously because he didn't seem like the numbers type. I wasn't sure why, but Frank could have told me he majored in How to Make Walking Look Sexy and I would have believed him.

"I did, actually."

"You did not! I was only joking."

"I did."

I tilted my head and stared at his rugged jawline, longing to run my fingers along the scruff that lined it. "I guess I can see it. After all, you do handle the finances for the bar, don't you?"

"I thought you didn't know anything else about me and my brothers?"

"You never asked what I knew about you." I reached for my glass, which had been empty for a while, and Frank hopped up.

"I'll get us refills. Hold that thought."

As he walked away, I found myself watching him go. I knew without a shadow of a doubt that I could absolutely fall for Frank, and if I did, I was going to fall hard. I already liked him way more than I should, even though I barely knew him.

It was funny how life worked sometimes, how we were drawn to certain people for no good reason, logic be damned. Love wasn't logical, anyway. Not that I was falling in love with Frank, but I'd be lying if I didn't admit that I could picture it happening. Who the hell wouldn't fall for any of those brothers?

I smiled at him as he came back toward me, our drinks in hand. My eyes never left his, and we held that contact until he sat down again across from me. The air between us stirred, and my body buzzed with attraction.

"Now, what were you saying about me?" he asked with a cocky grin.

"I don't remember. I thought I was talking about Ryan." I

gave Frank a grin of my own, and his green eyes narrowed. He didn't like that. And I liked that he didn't like that. "Kidding. We were talking about you and your talent for finance."

"I am good at it," he admitted, but it didn't sound like bragging.

"Do you enjoy it?" I asked, wondering if he loved what he did as much as I loved what I did.

"I do. There's something about working with numbers that I enjoy, seeing how they come together. When I come up with a way we can make the bar more profitable, I get as excited as Ryan does when he creates a new drink. Or when Nick thinks of some new marketing gimmick."

Frank smiled at me, and it was so genuine that it made me smile in return. Seeing him happy made me happy.

"I love that so much," I said. "We're lucky, you know? You and me."

"How so?" His eyes were so green, so fierce in the way they watched me, it was almost unnerving.

"We both love what we do for work. How many people can say that?"

He nodded. "You're right."

"Always am. And the sooner you learn that, the better," I said, trying to sound tough, but failing.

"Typical woman," he said, narrowing one eye at me.

"It's not my fault that we're the superior gender." I didn't want to smile when I said it, but I couldn't stop grinning at Frank. He laughed, which only made me smile more.

"Did you always know you wanted to get into banking?"

I sat back into my chair. "I don't think so. I did study business in college, but only because it seemed like a useful degree, not because I knew what I wanted to do with my life." I stopped for a second to organize my thoughts. "That sounds crazy, but they make you choose a major, and I had no idea at that point what I wanted to be when I grew up."

"Most people don't know. I was supposed to be a baseball player."

His confession shocked me at first. But Frank had the build and natural grace of an athlete, and I wondered why I'd never put two and two together before.

"What happened?"

He pointed to his shoulder. "I got injured."

"I'm sorry." I twined my fingers in my lap, stifling the urge to reach for his hand.

"It was a long time ago."

"Still, it had to be hard." Even though Frank was running one of the most successful bars in the area, a loss like that had to sting. "What position did you play?"

"Catcher," he said, a tinge of sadness in his voice.

"Were you good enough to go pro?" I asked, not knowing much about baseball. It bored me, to be honest, and if I watched sports at all, I preferred soccer.

He smirked at me, and I found myself caught up with him all over again. Frank was a truly sexy man.

"I was."

"Then I really am sorry. Not that I wasn't sorry before, but now I'm even more sorry. That really had to suck." I felt bad for him, assuming that he would always wonder about what could have been.

"It got pretty dark there for a while," he admitted, swallowing hard.

I could tell that he wanted to change the topic, so I obliged him. "I think it all worked out. The bar is amazing. You get to work with your brothers and, like you said," I flashed him a smile, "you love what you do."

"You're right. Again." He winked at me, making my insides flutter.

"Speaking of . . ." I looked around and noticed the handful of people in the bar. "Do you need to get back to work?"

Following my lead, he glanced around. "I probably should."

I wanted to be disappointed, but told myself not to be. This was his job. "I understand."

"I'll walk you out."

Frank stood up, and I took one last sip of my soda before grabbing my purse. He placed his palm on the small of my back, instantly warming me. As we walked past Ryan, Frank told him he'd be right back.

Ryan grinned. "Night, Claudia."

"Night, Ryan." I smiled, knowing I was blushing as a few people turned to watch us leave.

We headed out into the cool coastal night, and I stopped and turned to Frank.

"I'm parked right around the corner. You really don't have to walk me," I said, trying to give him an out, but hoping he wouldn't take it.

"I'm walking you to your car, Claudia. It's late."

I liked this chivalrous side of Frank. It was just one more thing about him that I found attractive.

"Well, thank you. It's right there." I headed for the dark blue Jetta parked at the curb and he walked with me, apparently intending to walk me all the way to the door. I pulled out my keys and clicked the button to unlock the car.

"Thank you for coming tonight," he said as he pulled open my door for me, keeping an eye on oncoming traffic. "I had a really good time."

My cheeks warmed with yet another blush, and I looked away from his green eyes for a moment before meeting them again. "Thanks for the invite."

The street suddenly felt too small, closing in around us.

Is he going to kiss me? God, I really want him to kiss me.

Frank wrapped his arms around me and held me tight. We fell into each other easily, our bodies fitting together in puzzle-like perfection. It was as if my body was made for his, the way it molded to him.

When he slowly pulled away, my mind raced with the thoughts of *would he* or *wouldn't he.* Would his lips be soft? How would he taste? Frank looked like a man who could really own a kiss and, God, how I wanted to be owned by him.

Looking down at me, he reached for my chin and tilted my face up. This was it. He was going to press those gorgeous lips to mine. I held my breath in anticipation and waited for him to make the next move. Frank was completely in control, and for once in my life, I was perfectly fine letting him have it. He squeezed my chin before dipping his head toward my face.

"I'll talk to you later. Drive safe." Then he placed a soft kiss on my cheek.

My heart pounded as confusion overtook me. I forced a smile and tried to hide my disappointment. "Okay. Good night."

"Night, Claudia."

I lingered a moment longer, willing him to change his

mind about the kiss, but he stepped away and I gave up, reluctantly getting into my car. As I pulled away, Frank stood on the curb, one hand in the air and the other tucked in his front pocket. I gave him a small wave as I drove away.

What the hell had just happened? Had I imagined the connection between us? Did I do something wrong, say something offensive?

My mind spun, going over our evening together, but nothing popped out. Frank Fisher was an enigma, and I had no clue how to figure him out.

CROSSING LINES

Frank

CLAUDIA DROVE AWAY, and I knew she was confused. She had expected me to kiss her. Hell, even I hadn't known if I was going to or not until we were in the moment and it was happening.

At the last second, I'd gathered my wits and kissed her cheek instead of her gorgeous fucking lips, fighting against my wants and needs the entire time. Every step outside the bar with her was another step into a moral minefield, where mentally I knew I was doing the wrong thing, but emotionally I couldn't find the strength to stop it.

I wanted to kiss her.

I wanted to take her into my arms and feel her tongue on mine.

I daydreamed about what her beautiful mouth would taste like. And I knew it was wrong.

This entire situation was a ticking time bomb, waiting to explode. There was no way around that. Wrong and right existed in this world, and I was currently on the wrong side of things.

The only questions left were: How badly did I want to make things right? And more importantly, could I?

Walking back into the bar, I braced myself for Ryan. I figured he'd launch in on me the second I came through the front door, but he only gave me a questioning look before stacking some clean glasses. His silence unnerved me more than his blabbering ever could.

Sidling up next to him, I said, "You aren't even going to ask what happened?"

"You'll tell me later. After we close." He gave me a curt nod, and I was thankful for his discretion.

I washed the few glasses left in the sink as Ryan chatted up the handful of customers in the bar. When I finished, I fished my cell phone out of my pocket and fired off a quick text to Claudia, then stared at the screen, waiting for a response.

FRANK: *You get home safe?*

CLAUDIA: *Yep. Thanks again for a nice night.*

When her response came right away, I tried to decipher it.

What did *yep* mean, exactly? Was she pissed? Was she being sarcastic? Had she really had a nice night, or was she mad that I hadn't kissed her like any normal man would have?

She didn't know my situation, and if she did, she'd never speak to me again. That wasn't something I was willing to risk. Not while I felt the way I was feeling about her. Not while I was blatantly aware that there was some crazy connection between us that you didn't find every day.

Shaking my head, I told myself to stop wallowing in my emotions like Ryan, a fucking chick.

I refilled a guy's beer and made a Guy Hater for another as I tried to clear my damn head. It was no use. Nothing I did worked, because no resolution I came up with felt right.

In order to make myself happy, I had to hurt Shelby, and she didn't deserve it. But she also didn't deserve the way I was disrespecting her and our relationship. Guilt was quickly becoming my best friend, my closest acquaintance, my partner in crime.

After closing and locking the bar doors behind our last customers, I headed toward the tables to clear them off and wipe them down while Ryan worked on the rest of the remaining glassware and the bar. He eyed my every move, and I waited patiently for the inquisition to start. I knew he was dying to give me his input, or at least say something. But for whatever reason, he was holding back, maybe waiting for me.

"Just say it already," I yelled from across the bar.

Dishes clanked, and Ryan tossed a towel over his shoulder. "How are you?"

How was I? I stopped wiping the table, tossed the towel on its wood top, and shrugged.

"How am I? Fine, I guess. How are you?" I said in my best smart-ass tone.

He rolled his eyes and groaned out loud. "I'm fine. But I'm not the one inviting girls over to the bar while my girlfriend sits at home waiting for me to get there." When my hands fisted and I looked down to see them clenched, my knuckles white, he said, "Sorry, bro, I'm not trying to piss you off."

"Could have fooled me," I said, slowly unfurling my fingers.

"So, how was Claudia? Is she still cool?"

My eyes met his from across the bar as I steadied my breathing, thinking back to the night I'd just shared with her, getting to know her better. "She's great. Really great."

"I figured. She's really into you."

My heartbeat sped up with his words. "How do you know?"

"I'm a bartender, which makes me an expert at reading body language. She likes you a lot. You like her too, but you already know that."

Reaching for the discarded towel, I finished wiping down the table and moved on to the next. Of course I liked her. And I wasn't an idiot. I knew she liked me too; I just enjoyed hearing it from someone else.

Ryan called my name. "Did you kiss her?"

"No," I said a little too quickly.

"Did you want to?"

"Fuck yeah, I wanted to."

Ryan let out a small laugh. "What are you going to do?"

"I don't know."

God, I was so sick of those three fucking words—sick of feeling them, of saying them, of not having answers to fix the crazy-ass mess I'd gotten myself into.

"I've never been in this kind of situation before." God, what a coward I was. I hated the way it made me feel, the way it forced me to see myself.

"Just be careful," he warned as I finished wiping the last table.

I headed to the register. As I closed it out and printed the night's totals, I asked, "What would you do? Realistically, if you were me. How would you handle this?" I was desperate for some thoughtful feedback, needing something that would resonate with me, something that might help.

Ryan put away the last clean glass and turned his attention to the liquor bottles. He rearranged them, putting them back in their proper order and facing them the same way, cleaning the pourers as he went along. He didn't say anything as he worked, which told me he was giving my question serious thought. It made me feel less inept that the answer wasn't something simple.

He stopped and turned to face me, nodding as if he was having a silent conversation with himself. I clipped the receipts together and put them down, hoping some pearl of wisdom would fall from Cinderella's lips.

"I know you're in a bad position," he said slowly. "Or, at least, you feel like you're in a bad position. You feel like you have no real say in the matter, but the matter we're discussing is your life, Frank. So, in essence, you feel like you have no choice when it comes to your own life anymore."

I cleared my throat, determined to argue because my natural reaction was to get defensive and stand up for myself whenever someone challenged me, but Ryan saw it coming from a mile away and tossed his hand in the air to stop me.

"Just hear me out. Somewhere along the line, and we can probably narrow it down to Shelby's dad passing away and the promise you made to him, you stopped being the driver of your life. In that moment, you became the passenger, and I get it. Trust me, I wouldn't wish that on anyone. I know you feel guilty. I know you feel obligated. But it's not right. Hell, you were just a kid. You had no right making a promise like that to anyone. And to be honest, he had no right asking you to make it."

Those last two sentences stabbed me in the gut, and my

stomach twisted painfully.

Fuck. I'd never thought of it so bluntly before, but Ryan was right. I had no business agreeing to that kind of thing, but it had seemed so right at the time.

Before I could roll that thought around further, Ryan said, "I know that none of this makes it any easier. I can only imagine that trying to end a relationship that you've been in for years isn't simple, or you would've already done it. Leaving is the right thing to do, the hard thing to do. It's easier to stay, even if you're miserable. But, what if there's something real between you and Claudia, and you miss out on it?"

I bristled, and he noticed. It wasn't that I didn't like him bringing up her name, it was that I'd already thought about that fact more than once. What if I missed my chance with Claudia? What if this thing between us was a once-in-a-lifetime opportunity, and I let it go?

I'd struggled with those thoughts because I didn't want how I felt about Shelby and our relationship to have anything to do with Claudia. None of this was truly about her. How I felt about Shelby—my unhappiness, my feelings of obligation and guilt—none of it had anything to do with any other woman, and the last thing I wanted was for it to. I truly needed to keep a clear head, but the second Ryan brought Claudia up, my brain fogged up like a bathroom mirror.

"You invited her to the bar tonight," he said, his tone almost incredulous. "You're in no position to be doing things like that, but you did it anyway. I'm not judging you, because I want you to be happy, but I think this might get out of control if you're not careful. And then instead of no one getting hurt, everyone is going to."

I chewed on my bottom lip, letting his words swim around in my head, wondering why the hell I felt so stuck.

"Why can't I just break up with her? It's not like we're married or have kids. I mean, I look at her sometimes and I'm just sitting there staring at her, willing my mouth to say the things my mind is thinking, but the words never come out," I admitted, my frustration only growing.

"What is it thinking?" Ryan asked, and I shot him a confused glare. "You said you wanted to say what your mind was thinking."

"Oh, right. It tells me to just end things. Tell her that I don't want to be together anymore, or that I think we should break up. That I'm not happy, and I'm sure she isn't either. And I sit there yelling at myself to just say it out loud already, but I never do. It's like I can't get the words to actually leave my mouth." I closed my eyes, willing the frustration and emotions battering me to grant me a reprieve for one second.

"Frank, it's not in your nature to hurt people. You've got more integrity than anyone I've ever known. Remember when guys tried to step on your back to get ahead in baseball? You never acted like that. You always worked hard for the things you wanted, and you never took shortcuts. You've always been a stand-up guy in every aspect of your life. That's why this is so hard for you. Because it's making you feel less than stand-up. It's making you feel small and like you're in the wrong."

Ryan placed a hand on my shoulder and gave it a quick squeeze. "But there's nothing wrong with moving on. If you don't want to be with Shelby anymore, that doesn't make you a bad guy. I can tell you that a thousand times, but none of it'll matter unless you believe it yourself. You gotta cut yourself some slack, brother. I mean that."

He was right. Those were three words I'd never wanted to say out loud because I was certain Ryan would never let me live them down, but he was right.

"It helps hearing you say it. I've been beating myself up for years, but when you tell me I'm not a bad person, it makes me want to believe it."

"You're not a bad person. But I do think you'll hate yourself if you cross the line with Claudia while you're still with Shelby."

"I definitely would." I nodded. "But I can't stay away from her." Admitting that should have made me feel worse than it did.

"Like I said, I think there's a reason for all of it. If there was no Claudia tempting you, you'd still be content to stay miserable and live in your little duty-filled world. It's probably time to make a change in your life, and this is the only way to get you to really see it."

Sometimes I wondered how and when my brother got so damned enlightened. It was a highly spiritual concept, one I'd studied for a bit when I went through my post-baseball who-am-I-now phase. But what Ryan said made sense to me. It resonated.

"Thanks again. I really do appreciate you being here for me, and not judging."

"You'd do the same for me," he said with a stupid grin that made me want to hit him. Ryan had that effect on people.

I needed to figure my life out, and I needed to do it without bringing Claudia into the mix. The problem was that whenever I started to think about her, she was all I saw. My dying relationship had absolutely nothing to do with her, but it suddenly felt like she was the reason for everything.

CONFUSED

Claudia

I T WASN'T THAT I dreaded walking through the front door and filling Britney in, but I felt almost embarrassed at the way my night had ended with Frank. *Embarrassed* wasn't really the right word. I was confused. Sucking in a deep breath, I steadied myself for the barrage of questions sure to come as I opened the door.

Britney sat on the couch, pretending she wasn't waiting up for me, but we both knew exactly what she was doing. She clicked a button on the remote, and the TV fell silent as a wide grin appeared on her face. As she patted a spot on the couch next to her, her smile never faltered.

"Tell me everything. I've been dying all night. I half wondered if you'd even come home."

I laughed. "You wouldn't even think something like that if you had seen the way we said good-bye."

She squinted at me, obviously unsure what I meant. "What are you talking about? Wait, was the night bad?"

I snuggled into the couch, pulling my legs underneath me. "No. It was amazing. At least, I thought it was."

"But?" Britney waved a hand for to continue, like I was telling this story far too slowly.

"I don't know. He was weird when I left."

"Weird how? Did he kiss you? Oh, please tell me that one of us has been kissed by a Fisher brother." She fluttered her eyelashes and held a hand to her heart, practically swooning at the thought.

"Nope."

"No?" she squeaked out, her eyes wide.

"No," I said again.

"Wait. Before the good-bye, you guys were having a good time? Do you feel a connection with him?"

I nodded my head furiously. "There's definitely something there. I'm so attracted to him, but it's more than that, you know?"

She sighed out loud, her tone almost dreamlike as she said, "I wish I did."

Her reaction made me laugh. "What are you talking about?"

"I wish I knew what it felt like to have that connection, that spark, that thing we see in all the movies and read about in books. I want that, and you have it. And with a Fisher brother, no less!" She groaned as she threw her head back into the cushions.

I wanted to argue, to tell her that I didn't *have* anything, but it would have been a lie.

When a soul-deep connection exists between people, it can't be denied because it isn't in your control. You can't wish it away or pretend it's not there once you're aware of it. Soul connections bond people, whether you want them to or not.

"But what if he doesn't feel it? What if I'm sitting here thinking there's this big, beautiful connection between us, and he doesn't feel the same?" It terrified me to think that Frank would try to deny what was between us, or fight against it.

Britney shook her head. "Not a chance. He may not know what it is that he's feeling, but he definitely feels something for you. You can see it all over his face and in his eyes when he looks at you, Claudia."

"Really?" I hated how insecure I sounded, but putting your heart on the line was terrifying, and I scared easily when it came to love.

"I swear. I wouldn't lie to you about this."

I breathed deeply, forcing myself to calm down. "Thank God, because I'd really hate to feel like this alone."

"There's no way this is one-sided," she reassured me, and I believed her wholeheartedly because I wanted to. I needed to.

"So, how did you say good-bye? Did he walk you out? Did he hug you? What happened?"

"He walked me to my car and I thought he was going to kiss me, but then he kissed my cheek instead." I couldn't hide the disappointment in my voice.

Britney burst out laughing, and I swatted her arm to get her to stop. "I'm sorry. I don't mean to laugh," she tried to say through her laughter. "I don't even know why I'm laughing."

"You're not helping," I growled, but then my phone let out a beep. I pulled it out and found I had a text from Frank, asking if I'd gotten home safely.

"Is that him? Oh, please, let me text him back."

I turned away from her, holding my phone in a death grip as I composed a nonchalant response. Once I'd hit SEND, I dropped my phone into my lap and glared at my roommate.

"Are you going to tell me why you think my evening was

so funny? I'm dying here, Brit. Why the hell didn't he kiss me? Do you think he didn't like me after spending more time together?"

I hated to even think it, but it was the only possibility that made any sense. If Frank had lost interest after getting to know me better, then he wouldn't want to take things further.

But could that be possible when I felt the exact opposite?

"Did you say something super offensive? Did you hit on Ryan? Did you hurt Frank's precious ego?"

Frank's ego? What the hell was she talking about? "No," I said slowly as I frowned, amazed at the crazy way her mind worked. "I don't even know what you're talking about."

"You know how men are. Hurt their ego and pride, and they cry behind closed doors and hold it against you forever."

And there we had it. My roommate and best friend was officially crazy.

"I didn't do or say anything to hurt anyone. There weren't even any awkward pauses. It was all—" I shook my head, searching for the right word. "It was effortless and really, really nice."

"Oh my God. I know what it is," she said, punching the couch cushion with her fist.

I relaxed a little at her sudden enthusiasm and change of attitude. "Tell me."

"We both know Frank is quiet and reserved. We've talked about it before. He probably just chickened out at the last second. Do you think that's possible?"

I chewed on that for a moment. "Maybe, I guess. I don't really know." Thinking about Frank chickening out didn't seem possible, but maybe he had.

"It makes so much sense. He's probably scared of you."

"Scared of me?" The concept was beyond ridiculous. "Why the hell would he be scared of me?"

"Have you looked in the mirror lately? You're stupid-hot, confident, and opinionated. That's intimidating to men."

My first instinct was to argue with her, but I stopped myself. It wasn't that I agreed on the *stupid-hot* part, but I had been known to intimidate men in the past. I'd always hated that, and immediately lost interest in any guy who wasn't strong enough to deal with me.

"I don't think Frank's scared of anything," I said softly.

"But you don't know, right? Maybe when it comes to him, you're going to have to be the aggressor. If you want this to go further, you might have to initiate things. Maybe something bad happened to him in the past, and he's skittish when it comes to relationships."

I pondered her words, bristling internally at her suggestion that I be the aggressor. It wasn't the first time she had mentioned me having to be the one who took the lead when it came to Frank.

"What's with the face?" Britney asked.

"I really don't like the idea of being the stronger one. I don't want to be the guy in the relationship. And to be honest, I get it that Frank's quieter than Nick and Ryan, but he's not insecure. He's not one of those guys who *needs* the girl to take the lead. I think the problem is something else; I just don't have any idea what."

"Well, you know him better than I do. But I wouldn't rule out attacking him with your mouth the next time you see him." She puckered her lips and kissed the air.

Was she right?

Was I completely wrong in the way I read him?

I longed to latch on to anything that made sense when it came to our night and how it ended, but I failed. I tried to convince myself that Frank being shy was the answer, but I knew in my heart that it wasn't the truth. There was no way Frank had chickened out at the last second because he was scared like Britney had suggested. It didn't add up, didn't feel right at all.

"Maybe he's just the kind of guy who likes to take things really slow," I said, and Britney gave me a halfhearted shrug.

"Maybe."

Defeated, I sighed. "I just have no idea what else it could be. Actually taking the time to get to know someone before getting physical with them does seem like something he'd do. He has integrity."

"I can see that now you that you mention it," Britney said, and my thoughts settled. "Maybe you should play hard-to-get. Make him crazed with want."

"I don't want to play games. I just want to be gotten. Oh God, I'm so into him already. I'm just like all the other girls who fall for a Fisher brother!" I groaned.

"You are not. Frank actually likes you back. He's just . . . cautious," Britney said with a shrug. "Yeah, he's cautious."

"Cautious." I repeated her word, liking the way it felt.

She nodded. "Do you think you'll see him again?"

"I want to," I admitted without shame.

"You might have to ask him." She laughed. "And then attack him with your mouth."

"I am not doing that. I'm just not." I shook my head,

refusing to be the one who asked to see him again, or took the lead in whatever this was that we had started. I wasn't sure why I was so adamant about letting him take control, but I refused to budge on it.

Britney stood up from the couch, reaching over her head as she stretched. "All right, then. We'll play it by ear."

"*We* will?"

"Yes, we will. I'm invested. But first, I'm going to bed. Unless you want to talk more?"

"Nothing to say, really."

"See you in the morning then. Try not to overthink it. We'll figure this Fisher dilemma out."

"Thank you." I smiled, feeling significantly better than I had before, even though nothing had actually been resolved. Sometimes just having your best friend's ear was all you needed to feel less crazy and alone.

*

I WOKE UP the next morning to find a message waiting for me from Frank. When I saw his name on my phone's screen, my heart skipped a beat. I pressed the button to read the text, and his words filled me with warmth.

> FRANK: Good morning. I had a really nice time last night. I hope to see you again soon.

"He wants to see me again!" I shouted from my bed, hoping Britney would hear me.

"What are you yelling about?" she shouted back.

I laughed and tossed the covers off, then ran into her

room, waving my phone. "He wants to see me again!"

"Who does?" she asked through a yawn.

"Frank, dummy."

Her eyes lit up and she sat up, tucking pillows behind her back. "Ooh! Let me see the text." She grabbed my phone and when she read the text, a smile appeared. "That's sweet."

"Right?"

"What are you going to say back? That you're coming over right now? That you'd prefer him to be naked the next time you see him?"

I giggled. "Probably none of that."

"Of course. You should play it cool," she said, sounding completely serious.

I typed out a quick response and waited.

"Wait, what did you say? You didn't even consult with me before you pressed SEND." Britney gave me a pout.

"I asked him if I could come by later."

She swatted my arm. "You little vixen. I like your style. Now, get out of my room so I can get dressed."

I practically skipped out of her room and down the hall to my bathroom. Whatever weirdness I'd thought was there last night had evaporated in the morning with a single text message. If all it took was a few words from Frank to completely set me at ease and change my mood, I was in deeper than I thought.

On the drive to work, Britney asked no less than twenty times if he had responded yet. I kept telling her that he hadn't even read it, but that tidbit of information seemed lost on her.

"He's probably still sleeping, Brit. He gets home at like three in the morning, so I'm sure he sleeps half the day away."

"You're right. Has he responded yet?"

I rolled my eyes as I navigated my Jetta through the parking garage. "I promise I'll tell you as soon as he does."

It took Frank more than a few hours to finally respond, but when he did, it made me smile from ear to ear.

FRANK: Hell yes. Come by anytime. Can't wait to see you.

If I'd thought the text from this morning had made my day, then this one made my week. Everything inside me softened. Frank took all my sharp edges and rounded them without even trying.

I dialed Britney's extension on my office phone to let her know that he'd finally texted and exactly what he said, which set her off about my outfit for *round two*, as she'd started calling it. It had either been that or date *numero dos*, and hearing her try to speak Spanish, even if it was only a couple of words, was more than a little painful. Round two, it was. I'd deal with her suggestion later about wearing a super-slutty outfit, an idea I wasn't even remotely entertaining.

"So, are you excited for round two?" Britney asked with a smile as we drove home.

"I am."

Nerves fluttered in my stomach. Seeing Frank was all I could think about. Not even telling Mrs. Schilling that I couldn't approve her loan for the second time had soured my mood. The possibility of what could be and the hope I felt blooming about something special beginning between Frank and me made everything better. Everything.

"This one better end in a kiss this time. Or even better, start with one." She waggled her eyebrows like some old creeper.

"Please never make that face again." I gave her a teasing glance before focusing back on the road.

"Fine. But I still think you should attack him with your mouth the second you see him."

"Noted." I smiled, but knew I would never do it.

Britney frowned at me and let out a sigh. "You won't do it."

"You're right. I won't."

She made a sound that was somewhere between a groan and an annoyed huff. "Knowing Frank, he'd probably be turned off if you attacked him. Or it's exactly what he's waiting for. I wish he was easier to figure out!"

"*You* wish?" I let out a laugh. "How do you think I feel?"

"Lucky. Because you like a Fisher brother, and he actually likes you back."

Her tone wasn't resentful or angry, but it was tinged with a hint of sadness. It wasn't easy to forget that the whole reason I'd even met Frank in the first place was because of Britney's crush on Ryan. I glanced at her, noting she'd turned almost wistful as she looked out the passenger window, and neither of us said anything more.

She was right, though. I was lucky.

And I knew it.

LOSING CONTROL

Frank

WHEN CLAUDIA HAD mentioned coming by the bar again, I couldn't tell her no.

I'd wanted to.

But I couldn't.

No, that wasn't true at all. Because I hadn't *wanted* to tell her no; I simply knew that I should have.

Just the idea of seeing her beautiful smile spurred me on. The thought of getting to know her better fueled me. So when Claudia asked if she could stop by the bar after work, my fingers were typing out the *hell yes* response quicker than my brain could stop them.

I realized in that moment, if I hadn't realized it before, that my willpower wasn't strong enough to keep her at a distance, especially when she tried to close it. All my carefully laid-out thoughts and plans halted the second anything with her became a possibility. I tossed everything out the proverbial fucking window the moment I spotted her reflection in it. My heart was in the lead. Or maybe it was my dick? An image of her body sprang to my mind, and I instantly hardened.

Shit.

My brain had definitely gone on hiatus, taken a vacation,

filed for an extended leave. And since Nick's girlfriend, Jess, was sick and he'd asked if he could take the night off to stay with her, Ryan would be here again to witness my failure at keeping my distance from Claudia. So here we were, about to have a repeat of the night before.

"She's coming in again?" Ryan asked as he mixed a new concoction for me to try.

I'd given him a heads-up about Claudia so he wouldn't be surprised. Or maybe I'd simply wanted him to know. Either way, I'd filled him in.

I nodded and waited for him to finish my drink. He topped it off with a spritz of something, then zested an orange and ran the peel along the rim of the glass before sliding it over.

Breathing in the citrus mixed with whiskey, I was intoxicated. It smelled amazing but tasted even better. "I don't know how the hell you do this. You have a gift."

"It's good, right?"

"It's really fucking good."

Ryan grinned. He scribbled a note into his Moleskin before folding it and tucking it into his back pocket. "I can't believe she's coming here again."

I didn't really want to talk about Claudia, about my fucked-up priorities and decision-making skills since meeting her. We'd already said everything there was to say last night. My telling him before she arrived tonight had been a courtesy. Or a warning.

"You're going to get in trouble. Seriously, how long do you think you can put off kissing a woman like that?"

It wasn't as if those thoughts didn't run through my mind

constantly. They did. I imagined her long, lean legs and all the ways I could wrap them around my body as I slid inside her. I wanted to plant kisses all over her tanned skin as I made her moan my name over and over again.

"Probably not very long."

"No shit. So, what the hell are you going to do?" When I merely shrugged my shoulders, he said, "Just tell her. Tell her you're in a relationship, but it's over. It's been over."

A cough bubbled up and escaped, and I pounded at my chest. "You want me to tell Claudia that I have a girlfriend? But not to worry, because it will be over soon? She'd probably rip off my head with her bare hands and spit on my corpse. Both pieces."

Ryan laughed. "I was just thinking that a little honesty might be your best option at this point, but you might be right. Maybe it's too late to tell the truth."

His words struck me like a sucker punch. Was it ever too late to tell the truth? Was there a line you crossed where the truth was no longer relevant, or no longer mattered? Or was honesty always your best option, your best bet?

I downed the rest of the new drink he had made as the door swung open and Claudia walked in. When my eyes met hers, she gave me the most genuine and beautiful smile as her long legs propelled her toward the bar. She was wearing a pair of skinny jeans and a fitted white tank top. Her outfit might be simple, yet the woman wearing it was anything but.

The moment I saw her face, I forgot what I'd been thinking about. I swear, I might not have been able to remember my own name if anyone asked.

"You look gorgeous," I said as she took a seat in front of

me, resting her elbows on top of the bar.

Her face crinkled for only a moment before she thanked me. "You look all right," she said, her lips lifting into a half smile.

"What about me?" Ryan jutted out his hip and struck a ridiculous pose like a runway model.

"Oh yes, Ryan. You look magnificent. Utterly perfect." She brought her fingers to her lips and kissed them with European flair.

"I knew it," he said in a horrible British accent. "Can I get you something to drink, milady?"

She glanced at me, almost as if she was waiting for a sign as to whether she should order something, and my stomach rumbled. It was in that moment when I wished our bar had a kitchen.

Food was pretty much the only thing missing from Sam's, but we'd decided it wasn't worth the hassle. Yes, people did leave the bar when they were hungry, but they always came back. Plus, not having food hadn't hurt our sales in the slightest, so there wasn't any real incentive to add a kitchen, to get licensed and deal with additional staff and food. It would only add a whole new level of things to manage, and the three of us weren't very interested in the dining side of things.

Except apparently my stomach. It growled again, and Claudia laughed.

"Hungry?" she asked.

"A little."

"I'll hold off on that drink, Ryan. We should probably get some food into this guy's tummy," she teased, batting her eyelashes at me.

Ryan immediately perked up. "Pizza. Definitely pizza. And bring me back some."

I turned toward Claudia. "Do you eat pizza?"

She scoffed at me, offended. "Do I eat pizza? Oh, because I'm Colombian, I don't eat Italian food? Is that what you think?"

I held my hands in the air and grinned. "Calm down, feisty. I was just asking. Maybe you hate cheese? Maybe you have a gluten allergy?"

"No and no. I love cheese. I could live off pizza. Feed me pizza or lose me forever." She gave her long black hair a dramatic toss, and I couldn't get around the bar and over to her quick enough.

"I was serious about bringing me back some. Don't forget," Ryan called out as we headed toward the exit. "Don't forget!" he shouted again, and I stopped and turned back.

"Jesus, Ryan, we won't," I told him as I placed my hand on the small of Claudia's back.

God, it felt good to touch her, to feel her warmth underneath my palm. She leaned into my touch, pressing harder into me than she had a second earlier, and I wasn't sure if she even realized she was doing it.

Once we were outside and in public, I dropped my hand. I wanted to lace my fingers with hers but stopped myself from being that forward, from crossing that particular line.

Smiling at her, I pointed toward the pizza place across the street, and we walked there side by side. Every few steps, her hip would brush against my leg, making my dick twitch. My mind ran wild with want, my body hummed with desire, but some sliver of self-control remained. Thank God we only had a few feet left to go, or I was certain I would have lost my mind and mauled her up against the brick wall beside us.

I held the door open as she walked through it, and we stopped to check out the chalkboard menu just inside the entrance.

"Are we taking it to go?" Claudia asked absentmindedly as she stared at the menu.

"Let's eat here."

She ducked her head, her hair dropping into a curtain that nearly hid her smile. "Are you going to make fun of me if I order a salad?"

I tried to keep my face serious. "I thought you ate pizza? Loved cheese? Could live off pizza alone? Told me to feed it to you or lose you forever?" I poked at her shoulder.

She swatted my arm. "I meant *with* the pizza."

"Order whatever you want, babe," I said, then froze when I realized I'd just responded as if she were my girlfriend. Her cheeks flushed, and I knew I was screwed. It wasn't like I could take it back, but I could pretend it had never happened. *Stupid fucking mouth.*

We ordered more food than we could possibly eat, and I paid, not wanting to let Claudia buy anything when we were together. She tried to argue with me, reminding me how I always paid for her drinks at the bar, but in the end, I won. Her wallet stayed in her purse, and her purse stayed on her shoulder.

Looking around the small space, I was glad it wasn't busy, and urged her toward a small table in the back.

Claudia sat down across from me and smiled. "Thank you for dinner."

"You're welcome."

"Next time I'm treating you," she insisted, and I knew better than to fight her on it. I simply nodded and wondered how the hell I'd pull off a next time with her.

When we finished eating, I grabbed Ryan's pizza and our leftovers before we headed out into the chilly evening air. Claudia wrapped her arms around herself as we hustled back to the bar. I'd left Ryan alone for way too long, losing track of time as Claudia and I ate and chatted like we'd been doing it for years. Even though Sam's would be all but empty on a Tuesday night, none of us liked working alone. Not to mention the fact that there was safety in numbers, and being the lone person tending bar wasn't all that smart.

I was glad when we walked inside to see only a small handful of patrons. Ryan seemed to have everything under control, laughing easily with them as he prepared a drink.

"Let me put this in the back," I said to Claudia, and she smiled and gave me a quick nod. I left the pizza on the desk in my office, then returned to the bar.

"Pizza's in the office. Go eat. I'll take care of things out here," I said before giving Ryan a slight shove. Before I knew it, he had the pizza box in hand, and rather than eating in the office, was headed toward where Claudia gone to sit in the back of the bar, at the same table we'd sat at last night.

I bit back a scowl, wanting to strangle my brother as I answered nonstop questions from two guys who wanted to know how long we'd been open, what our plans were for the future, and why we didn't serve food. Jesus, I wanted them to shut the hell up. I kept my responses short, my tone gruff, and they eventually stopped being so damn chatty. If they wanted a bartender best friend, they'd have to wait for Ryan to come back.

Claudia's laugh filled the room. I jerked my head around to find she and Ryan were laughing so hard, they looked like they each might fall off their chairs. Jealousy ripped through me. As irrational and immature as it was, the emotion still seared my every fiber. I wanted to make her laugh like that. I wanted to do so many things both to and with Claudia.

Needing a distraction, I reached for the empty beer tumblers and started washing them. I kept my head down and scrubbed furiously, letting out all my pent-up emotions on the poor glass cylinders.

Ryan's voice startled me. "Whoa, bro, what'd those glasses ever do to you?"

I had no idea how long I'd been standing there, my hands moving furiously, my knuckles white from my grip.

"She's really cool," he said in a low voice as he gently removed the glass from my hand.

"I know she is," I bit back before casting a glance at her direction. She sat at our table alone, her eyes on me. Not on Ryan, but me. I couldn't wait to get back over to her.

The door opened and several loud female voices floated into the bar. I looked up, immediately recognizing one in particular, and froze in shock as Shelby and three of her coworkers stepped inside the bar. The group had clearly already been drinking, and Shelby was apparently more than simply buzzed, based on the way she carried herself and the higher-than-normal volume of her voice.

Ryan stomped on my foot. "What's she doing here?" he asked behind a smile meant for my girlfriend and her friends.

"I don't know," I ground out behind a plastered-on smile of my own, trying not to freak the fuck out.

"Hey, baby!" Shelby hopped onto a stool, reaching over the bar to loop an arm around my neck and plant a kiss right on my mouth.

With my eyes still open, I met Claudia's confused gaze, then looked back at Shelby.

She frowned. "Did you forget we were coming? I told you this morning."

My mind sifted through foggy memories for a conversation where Shelby had mentioned coming by the bar tonight, but came up empty. With my luck, she had probably told me while I was still half asleep.

I mumbled something in response that she assumed was my recognition. Obviously, I had no idea she'd be stopping by the bar tonight.

She gave me a big smile and waved it off. "Anyway, it's Suzi's last day, so we're out celebrating and saying 'bye." She faked a pout in Suzi's direction, or in what I assumed was the direction of whoever the hell Suzi was. I didn't know any of the females currently drooling over Ryan.

"Where were you ladies before this?" Ryan asked them.

Thankful for the distraction, I tried to pull myself together and failed miserably. I shifted my weight from foot to foot, unable to breathe, every second feeling like the life was being choked out of me.

How the hell was I going to get out of this? How could I explain this to Claudia? This wasn't how I wanted her to find out.

When Shelby said, "We were at Don Tequila's, the Mexican place down the street," I almost lost my dinner. She and her friends had just been three doors down from where Claudia and I had been eating dinner.

What the hell had I been thinking? My heart made me careless, foolish even.

"Let me guess. Pitchers of margaritas?" Ryan winked, his tone flirty as he chatted with the group. They all laughed as Shelby made her way behind the bar and tugged on my arm.

I looked down at her and forced a smile. "You okay?"

"Yeah, but I might be a little drunk," she admitted before covering her face with her hands.

"That's okay, babe," I said as she fell into me, wrapping her arms around my middle and pulling me tight against her.

"I still love you, you know," she said, her breath warm against my chest. She tightened her grip and I hugged her harder in response, but didn't say anything. "I know things are weird between us, but I still want to be with you." Her tone was desperate, as though she knew I didn't want this anymore, as if she'd sensed it somehow but had been keeping it all inside.

I swallowed hard, everything around me blurring. I didn't want to say the words back to her, fought them from coming out of my mouth, the lie bitter on my tongue. So I kissed the top of her head, absentmindedly rubbing the length of her back as I stayed silent.

"You don't." She pulled back slightly to look me in the eye. "You don't feel the same anymore, do you?"

Her slightly unfocused eyes reflected her sadness, and my stomach twisted. This was a worst-case scenario, not at all how I wanted any of this to go down. Yes, a conversation about our future needed to be had, but not in the bar, and not while she was drunk. And most certainly not with an audience.

I opened my mouth to say something, but I had no idea what.

From the corner of my eye, I caught Claudia moving toward us. I hadn't looked at her since that first time, too scared that her hurt expression might tear me apart. But I couldn't stop myself this time. She was too close. And while I worried for only a second that she might cause a scene, something inside me trusted that she wouldn't.

I looked directly at Claudia, and my breath caught. I half wondered if Shelby felt me stiffen as she followed suit, staring at the woman I'd been secretly falling for behind her back. Claudia's eyes were tear-filled but furious, shooting daggers. She paused for only a moment before she all but sprinted from the bar.

Shelby looked up at me. "Who was that?"

Thank God, Ryan immediately jumped in.

"Be right back." He slapped me on the back and handed me the drink shaker before bolting out after Claudia to handle what I so clearly couldn't. If there was a Brother of the Year award, he should win it for how he handled that moment.

"Another of Ryan's groupies, I guess? She looked really upset. I wonder why?"

I didn't respond. I couldn't.

A GIRLFRIEND?!

Claudia

SQUEEZING MY EYES shut, I repeated the word *no* in my head at least twenty times. This couldn't be happening. There was no way that I had fallen for a guy who wasn't available. Frank hadn't just deceived me. There was no way he had a girlfriend . . . *was there?* Everything had been going so well, until . . .

I shook my head and wiped at my eyes as I stumbled through the night in search of my car. Alone. Because that woman who had come into the bar with her friends had definitely been Frank's girlfriend.

I'd watched as she wrapped her arms around his waist like he belonged to her. Seen her press her lips against his like they were hers to claim. And I'd definitely taken note of how Frank had refused to look at me after she arrived, knowing that he'd been caught, knowing that I'd need answers.

I fought off the sickness that threatened to rise from my stomach at the memory of it all. Had it been cowardly of me to race out of the bar instead of confronting him? The thought had only crossed my mind before I realized that I'd only be making a fool of myself. And Frank had done that enough for both of us already.

"Claudia!"

The voice tore through me and stopped me in my tracks. I froze and was devastated when I turned around to see the wrong Fisher brother chasing after me. I felt so stupid for even thinking that it might be Frank coming for me, to right his wrong or to apologize.

"Ryan?" I choked out his name as I waited for him to catch up to me. "Ryan, was that Frank's . . ." I couldn't even say it, couldn't bear to have my fear verified, even though I already knew the truth.

"I'm really sorry, Claudia. It's not what it looks like." His expression was pained as he gripped the back of his neck briefly before dropping his hand and looking away.

"How the hell could it not be what it looked like?" I spat out. I knew exactly what it looked like, exactly what it was.

"I mean, it is," Ryan said, stumbling over his words, clearly uncomfortable. "But it's not that black and white."

I figured he was trying to cover for his brother. Of course he'd cover for him. Those brothers seemed to be the very definition of loyal, at least when it came to each other. I stifled a sick laugh at the idea of Frank being loyal to any other person.

"What are you talking about? That's his girlfriend, though, right? Frank has a girlfriend?" My throat tightened as I finally choked out the words, but everything started to make sense as things that had seemed odd to me before clicked together like a puzzle.

"Yeah, but it's complicated."

I shook my head at his crappy reasoning. "No. It's really not."

Frank having a girlfriend was a deal breaker. If I hadn't seen it with my own eyes, I probably wouldn't have believed it. Frank didn't seem like the kind of guy who would lie and cheat, but it just went to prove that you couldn't always trust your heart in these matters.

"Claudia, it's not my story to tell, otherwise I'd tell you everything," Ryan said, obviously trying to make me feel better.

That wasn't going to happen. I was done. Whatever had sparked to life between Frank and me now needed to die. I'd stomp on it until only embers remained, and throw water on the rest.

"Please trust me when I tell you that there's more to this than you think," Ryan pleaded as if he could read my mind and see the defeat there.

"No, there's not more to this. There's nothing to tell. Frank has a girlfriend, and he lied to me. He lied! I feel so stupid," I blurted, confessing all the thoughts running through my head. They kept spilling out of my mouth without a filter. "Make sure you tell him to lose my number. And not to ever fucking contact me again."

"Claudia!"

Ryan shouted after me as I stalked away, a million thoughts running through my head as my heart broke into a million jagged pieces. He kept talking, but I didn't stop or turn around. There was nothing left to say.

Frank was a liar and a cheater.

Just like my father.

*

"HE HAS A girlfriend?" Britney asked for the fifth time as she placed a quart of mint-chocolate-chip ice cream with two spoons between us on the couch.

I'd walked through our front door fully composed, my anger keeping me from falling apart until I spotted Britney's face. One look at her and all my resolve went out the window. I started to cry, confessing the ugly truth to her as I collapsed onto the couch and tried to pull myself together.

"He has a girlfriend," I repeated, my tone swinging between sadness and anger. My emotions were all over the place. One second I was mad, and then devastated, and then mad all over again. It was a relentless merry-go-round, one I apparently had little control over.

Britney shook her head in disbelief. "You're sure? A hundred percent certain?"

I glared at her. She now knew every detail from this past evening as well as I did. "She kissed him." I scooped a spoonful of ice cream into my mouth. It melted instantly, the cold creaminess turning into warm liquid before I added, "Like he was familiar to her. It wasn't something new. They were comfortable together." Seeing her press her body against Frank's she'd done it a million times before played in my mind on a loop.

"I just can't believe it." Britney shook her head, echoing my own thoughts.

"Ryan could have said something to me. He could have clued me in, given me a hint, anything," I spat out.

"It wasn't Ryan's place to say something to you. Can you imagine him telling you something like that behind Frank's back? Frank would murder him."

I hated agreeing with her, but she was right. I squeezed my eyes shut and forced out a breath through my nose. "No, you're right. I just feel like such a fool. There I was, falling for Frank, and Ryan knew the whole time that he wasn't available. I must have looked so stupid."

"You're not stupid. And you didn't do anything wrong. But I guess now everything sorta makes sense."

"Like what? What exactly makes sense?" I choked back a sob, trying to keep my emotions in check, but it was a losing battle. I was a wreck.

"Why he was so weird with you. It wasn't because he was shy or wanted to take things slow. He had a girlfriend the whole time."

I cringed as she said the words, wishing this was all just a nightmare I could wake up from. "Then why pursue me? Why see me at all? I don't understand. If he had a girlfriend, what the hell was he doing with me?"

My mind spun as I tried to make sense of things, searching for logical answers, but it kept coming up empty. Why had Frank continued talking with me, paying me attention, when there was never a future there? Did he honestly think I was the type of girl who could or would be someone's side piece?

"You're not going to like my answer," Britney said.

I looked up, waiting for her to continue her thought. When she didn't, I raised my eyebrows and waved my hand in a circle, urging her to go on.

"He likes you. Frank likes you. And Ryan said his situation wasn't black and white, right?"

I huffed out an annoyed breath. "He isn't allowed to like me. If he has a girlfriend, then he isn't allowed to like anyone else but her."

Britney laughed. She fucking laughed. "You can't put parameters on someone's heart. You can't tell them how to feel. It's not like he was looking to meet you. It just . . . happened."

I clenched my jaw, grinding my teeth. I hadn't wanted to justify anything Frank had done and think it was okay, regardless of how I felt about him. "No. There's right and wrong, and what he did was wrong. He should have never made me a part of it. I would never have hung out with him if I knew he had a girlfriend."

"I know that. Frank probably knows that too. Which is why he didn't tell you."

I threw my head back and groaned. "Stop defending him."

"I'm not. I'm just trying to see it from both sides."

"You can't see it from both sides. You don't have all the information."

"Neither do you," she snapped back, and when I flinched, she placed a hand on my leg. "Hey, I'm sorry. I don't want you to think that I'm not pissed off at him, because I am. I'm on your side, truly. I'm just trying to understand his motivation. Frank doesn't seem like the dirtbag type, you know?"

"I do know," I said, my eyes brimming with tears. It made me feel better that Britney hadn't thought Frank was the kind of man to do this either. It made me feel a little less stupid, a little less naive in my assessment of him and my willingness to give him my heart. Or, at least, my desire to.

"He's not like your dad, Claudia," she said out of no-where.

The hurt of that old betrayal soured the air between us,

cutting me straight to the core. My head shot up and I practically snarled at her.

"We don't know that, though, do we? My mom said that my dad was really charming too. And that she didn't see it coming. Not when he cheated, and not when he left."

My dad was definitely a sore subject for me. When I thought about him, emotions bubbled to the surface that I could usually push aside and pretend didn't exist. But right now, I was brought low by disappointment and betrayal, and felt once again like that little girl left behind without a backward glance.

"Frank knew about it too," I said softly.

Britney's eyebrows shot up. "You told him about your dad?"

"Yeah." I sucked in a breath, hating how the old anger rose inside me.

"Well, hell, Claudia," Britney breathed out. "He definitely wasn't telling you he had a girlfriend after hearing that story."

"Knowing about my dad should have kept him away from me. It should have made him want to do the right thing, not keep doing the wrong one."

"But maybe you are his right thing? It's obvious he likes you. I don't think this was some game to him, or anything sinister like that."

"Britney, stop."

"Sorry, but I can't stop thinking about the things Ryan said. I don't think Ryan would lie. I think there's more to the story. Don't you?"

"It doesn't matter. I don't want to understand why Frank did what he did. I don't want to give him an excuse or a reason that makes what he did all right," I admitted as I searched for the real reason behind my apprehension. "I think it's because I don't want to understand why my dad did what he did to us. I don't want it to be okay. It wasn't okay." Tears rolled down my cheeks as the pain I'd once felt as a child clawed its way to the surface, tearing me apart.

Britney moved the now-melted ice cream onto the coffee table and scooted next to me, then leaned her head on my shoulder. I wiped at my cheeks, brushing away the tears.

"You're right," she said. "Frank should have told you. He should have been honest. And when you told him about your dad, you gave him the perfect opportunity to come clean."

"Right? Thank you."

"But I bet he was scared shitless," she added with a slight giggle that for some reason made me smile through my tears.

"Good. I hope he was scared. And I hope he is now," I said, my tone a little more vindictive than I'd intended.

Britney pulled her head from my shoulder and squared to face me. "Wait, what does that mean? Are you going to do something psycho?" She rubbed her palms together. "Don't you dare go off the deep end without me. If you plan some kind of revenge, I want in!"

I narrowed my eyes and pulled back from her. "Whoever said white girls weren't crazy, clearly never met you."

"Damn straight," she said with a proud grin.

"For the record, I'm not doing anything psycho. I just like the idea of him being scared or worried. Of him feeling . . ." I paused, searching for the right words. "He needs to feel something because I'm hurting, and I want him to hurt too."

I stopped for a second, realizing how awful and immature

my words sounded, but I refused to take them back. They were the truth.

"And I know it's probably dumb. Like I shouldn't feel like this over someone I barely know," I admitted, hating how weak I sounded and felt. "I feel like I'm mourning a loss or something."

"It's not dumb. You liked him. You wanted to date him. Of course you're hurting and grieving. You did lose something tonight."

Once again, Britney was right. I had liked Frank, and I had wanted to date him. Until tonight, he'd represented possibility and hope, two things I hadn't had with a man in a really long time.

"You know, I never even asked if he had a girlfriend, but I assumed that if he was spending time with me that he didn't have one. It didn't even occur to me. And it's not like we were hiding. We hung out in his bar. Anyone could have seen us." I replayed in my head the moments we'd spent together, even though there were only a few, and I felt so foolish.

"It's all of those reasons why I think there really might be more to the story. You should talk to him."

"I don't want to talk to him," I insisted, and I meant it. I didn't want to hear Frank's explanation or reasons. None of it changed the truth or altered the situation in any way. "I don't want to talk to any of them." I pushed up from the couch and stretched my arms over my head.

"There's no way Frank just disappears on you and doesn't explain things. Not a chance in hell that he ghosts you," Britney insisted, referring to the way guys would stop returning texts and phone calls like they had never existed in the first place.

"Does it really matter? He has a girlfriend, Britney. I don't care what he does."

"There isn't any part of you that wants an explanation from him? Because I do, and it wasn't even me he was dating."

"He wasn't dating me either," I said softly before shaking my head, too many thoughts racing through my mind, refusing to cut me any slack. They were exhausting. "I need to sleep so I can stop thinking about all of this."

"Okay. For the record, I'm really sorry. I didn't see this coming at all."

I swallowed hard as her face became blurry. "Me either."

I felt so vulnerable and naive. Should I have seen it coming? Was there something I missed that was so blaringly obvious that I had simply overlooked it?

No. I refused to take the blame for this. Frank was the one in the wrong here, not me.

Then why did I feel like I was the only one paying the price?

THE UGLY TRUTH

Claudia

WHEN I WOKE up early the next morning after a restless night, the reality of what had happened with Frank crashed back into me at full force. My alarm went off and I smacked it into silence, half wishing that I could call in sick to work today, but knowing that I wouldn't. Not for something like this.

Reaching for my cell phone, I was surprised to see that it was off. I never turned my phone completely off at night, and I searched my mind trying to remember exactly when I'd done it. I came up empty as I waited for it to turn back on, the screen practically blinding me with its brightness as it did. When it had fully come to life, it was devoid of any new text messages or voice-mail notifications.

Frank hadn't even attempted to reach out to me. Last night I'd said I hadn't wanted him to, but this morning I found myself bitterly disappointed that I wasn't worthy of an explanation or an apology.

Don't I deserve one?

Hell, don't I deserve both?

Kicking at the covers with my feet, I pulled myself out of bed and rubbed my hands over my face and through my hair. I stumbled into my bathroom and stared at my reflection in the mirror, my swollen eyes revealing the truth of just how much I'd cried last night. As I splashed cold water onto my face, I reveled in the relief that it momentarily brought before it turned lukewarm.

Last night I'd been angry and hurt, the two emotions warring for first place in my mind and my heart, but this morning brought about a whole new level of emotion. The anger had dissipated slightly, and I found myself swimming in a sea of sadness. I had really liked Frank and thought we were in the beginning stages of something good between us, albeit at a snail's pace. Regardless, I had been invested.

When I glanced at my phone again and saw the notification screen was still blank, I turned it facedown and hopped into the shower to get ready for work. I was suddenly thankful that it was a weekday and that I could focus my attention on something other than Frank and his jerk-like behavior. A distraction would be good, and work was the best kind of distraction because I got paid for it.

"Hey, I know it's your turn to drive, but I'm driving today," Britney said as I headed into the living room with my car keys in my hand. "No arguments."

I nodded, thankful for her offer. It was a simple gesture, but it was that type of kindness that made all the difference in moments like these. She knew I wasn't all there mentally today, and that was no way to operate a vehicle in the heavy Los Angeles traffic.

"No word from him?" she finally asked as we drove. She'd probably been holding the question in since she'd woken up.

"Nothing." Even I could hear how disappointed I sounded. My tone mirrored my heart.

"He'll reach out today. I know it." Her tone was certain, but I wasn't so sure. I wasn't sure of anything anymore.

"I checked my phone this morning—Never mind. It's stupid."

Britney shot me a frustrated glance. "Say it."

I let out a long sigh. "I expected there to at least be a text from him, if not a voice mail. I didn't hope or want there to be one; I *knew* that there would be. Because there was no way that Frank would go all night without checking on me, or seeing if I was okay, or apologizing, right? But I was wrong. So wrong."

Voicing all those thoughts out loud, admitting them to someone else, it forced me to realize more than I wanted to. I had expected Frank to reach out to me because I assumed that he had more than friendly feelings for me. I still had more than friendly feelings for him. Right now, in this moment, after everything, I *still* liked him.

She nodded, keeping her eyes on the road. "I would think the same thing if I was in your position."

"You would?"

"Hell yes! Are you kidding? Of course I'd expect a text message from him. Of course I'd expect him to check on me and give a shit about my feelings and my general well-being. It's awful that he hasn't apologized or tried to talk to you, and it's making me not like him, if you want to know the truth." She glanced at me, her expression fierce.

"I wish it made me not like him," I whispered at the passenger window, but Britney heard me.

"Come again?"

"I still like him. Don't get me wrong, I'm pissed and I'm

hurt, but I still like him. And I hate myself for it. Why can't I hate him?"

"Because our hearts don't work like that. Our heads do, but our hearts are never on board with our heads. That's why they're always at war, and we're always torn between the two."

Isn't that the damn truth. Life would be so much easier if our heads and our hearts were on the same page, but they so rarely were.

"I'll get it together. I'll be fine eventually," I said, not knowing who I was trying to convince, myself or Britney.

"I know you will. But it's okay to feel everything you're feeling. It just happened. And I still think there's no way he goes another twenty-four hours without contacting you."

I pursed my lips and kept quiet. My heart wanted to believe Britney, but I couldn't let myself go there. Believing in things that ended up not happening would only hurt me, and I was hurting enough already.

When we walked through the doors at work, I was thankful for the reprieve of thinking about Frank. Pushing aside my emotions, I settled into my office and pulled up my calendar for the day. I planned to keep myself far too busy over the next several hours to even think about him, what he'd done, or the fact that he wasn't trying to contact me.

Briefly, I considered turning off my phone again like I'd apparently done the night before, but decided against it. My willpower wasn't strong enough to go quite that far. The moment Frank did contact me, if ever, I wanted to know about it.

I hated that he hadn't reached out.

I hated that the hours continued to tick by without a

single word from him.

And I definitely hated that I cared so much and couldn't stop checking my damn phone.

*

HOURS TURNED INTO days, then a week, and it became clear that Frank had done the unthinkable. He'd ghosted me, disappeared without a trace.

Of course, I knew exactly where to find him, but I couldn't bring myself to face him if he didn't want to talk to me. Britney had tried to convince me to show up at the bar and demand an explanation, to put him on the spot and make him uncomfortable, but I couldn't do it.

Forcing Frank to be uncomfortable meant making myself uncomfortable as well. I cared about him so much that any pain I might inflict upon him would cause the same pain in me.

Why the hell would I want to do that?

And what if the answers I demanded from him weren't the ones I wanted to hear? What if he said that I was a mistake, or that he had no feelings for me? I wasn't ready to hear any of that. As weak and pathetic as it sounded, I simply wasn't ready, even though I knew I should be. My pride was wounded, my ego sulking.

"Stop wallowing," Britney said one night as we binge-watched a television series everyone had been talking about.

"I'm not wallowing," I insisted, but it was a lie. "Ah, hell. I am wallowing."

"I know. It's annoying. And completely unlike you." She

kicked her feet on top of the coffee table and settled deeper into our couch.

"I don't know where my anger went. I was so pissed, but it was short lived. Now I'm just so sad. And a little pissed off when I start thinking about it all, but I've gotten pretty good at compartmentalizing."

And I had. I didn't realize how good I could be at tucking Frank into a corner of my mind and locking him there. I still thought about him every single day, though, and it still hurt that he hadn't tried to talk to me. But the second the pain started to kick in, I turned it off and went about my business. I convinced myself that I was fine, moving on, and didn't need Frank Fisher in my life.

Britney shook her head. "You shut it off, all right, but it still affects your emotions. You wouldn't be wallowing if you were as fine as you acted."

"I miss him. And it's stupid, I know. I shouldn't miss him. I should be plotting his demise and wishing his dick would fall off."

"Yes, you should be. I hope it falls off in small pieces and takes a really, really long time." Britney gave me a wicked grin, and I laughed.

"You're evil." I tossed one of our small throw pillows at her but she blocked it, knocking it onto the floor.

"Yup."

"I can't believe he's never called. I wouldn't have thought that he would be like that, you know? He seemed like such a together guy. And mature, a real man. The way he's acting now, though, is cowardly. And what the heck?" My blood pounded in my ears as my irritation rose. "I am *not* attracted to cowards."

When I thought about Frank in that way, disgust multiplied inside me like a virus, poisoning everything in its path. Frank didn't deserve my thoughts to be only of him as the kind of man I wanted him to be when he was proving to be anything but.

"He is a coward," Britney said. "And a jerk. It almost feels wrong to describe him that way, but his actions say everything. Or his lack of actions, anyway."

Something deep inside me that felt a lot like self-respect stirred to life.

"You know what? I deserve an explanation." I sat up straighter on the couch as a door in the back of my mind flew wide open, allowing new realizations to pour out of it. "I've made this so easy on him by going away. He hasn't had to deal with me, or what he did to me, at all."

Maybe my emotions did have a switch, after all. It might not have been the on-off kind, but there was definitely now an array of feelings to choose from. One simply replaced the other in the space of a heartbeat.

Britney turned toward me, narrowing her eyes. "Nope. You've let him sweep it under the rug like you never happened. Like you didn't even exist. He's had absolutely no consequences for his actions."

I bristled at that comment, but she was right. In all my self-imposed pity, anger, embarrassment, and sadness, I'd left Frank alone, thinking I was doing myself a favor, but I wasn't. Not having any answers made the situation even harder on me. I'd willingly walked away as my pride hoped he'd chase me, and my heart silently cried out, begging to be healed.

My staying in the background had given him an easy out, and that wasn't fair to me. I deserved so much more.

Abruptly, I stood up. "All that ends today."

"Today?" she asked, leaning forward and plucking the pillow from the floor.

"Yeah. Right now."

I reached for my phone to send Frank a text. It was time to start the conversation I'd been so clearly avoiding.

SILENT TREATMENT

Frank

THE PAST SEVEN days had been absolute torture. Between the weight of my guilt, which only multiplied by a thousand tons after the night Shelby arrived at the bar, and Claudia not responding to my texts or voice mails, I was a fucking wreck.

All I wanted to do was explain things to Claudia. I needed her to understand the situation I was in, and how sorry I was for involving her in it. It was wrong of me, I knew that, but I couldn't help myself when it came to her. Everything I felt for her was genuine, and she was probably sitting at home thinking it was all some sort of game for me, or a lie. It killed me to think about the suspicions that might be going through her head when I knew they weren't true.

I needed to tell her everything, but I couldn't tell her anything at all because she refused to talk to me.

I didn't blame her, but I didn't want to give up. I just didn't know what the hell else to do.

"You look like shit," Nick said when he walked through the office door. I had been sitting there with my head in my hands, staring at the same inventory sheet for the last forty-five minutes.

"I know."

"Frank, this isn't you."

"Which part?" Honestly, I didn't know who the hell I was anymore. When had things gotten so far gone that I failed to recognize who I was supposed to be?

"When you heard about everything that was going on in my life, you told me to man up. You were pissed for me, pissed at me. You wanted me to take control of my situation and stand up for myself." Nick's voice rose, and I suspected he was getting emotional at the memory of his not-so-distant past.

"What's your point?" I demanded, but my tone sounded more defeated than anything.

He walked around the desk and clapped a hand on my shoulder, giving it a hard squeeze. "I've got to give you the same advice, bro. You need to stand the fuck up for yourself. You can't keep living like this. Do you really want to spend the rest of your life miserable and unhappy? Why? Who benefits from that? I promise you that everyone will be better off—and I do mean *everyone*—if you would just end things with Shelby. I know it's not easy. But sometimes you have to make the unpopular decision and do the hard thing because you're the only one who will."

I wanted to shout that he didn't know what the hell he was talking about, wanted to grab his hand and throw it the fuck off my shoulder. But I didn't do either of those things.

Because he was right; my baby brother couldn't have been more right. And I was only pissed off at him for it because I was mad at myself. I had let things go too far and for too long, and I had no one to blame but myself.

I had done this. I had created the life I was currently living, and it was up to me to either get out of it once and for all, or to shut the fuck up and be happy. The decision was the easy part. It was the follow-through that was painfully difficult.

Defeated, I dropped my head in my hands and mumbled, "You're right."

"I know. Can I ask you one more question without you wanting to kill me?"

"Depends," I said cautiously, glancing up at him.

Nick dropped his hand and leaned against the edge of my desk. "On what exactly?"

"Just ask already," I said on a huff, and he cleared his throat.

"Have you called Claudia?"

My stomach dropped at the sound of her name. "Only about a hundred times."

"And?"

"She doesn't answer."

"Try texting?"

"Try texting." I mimicked him like I was some idiot who didn't know how to get in touch with a woman. "Obviously. She's not responding to those either."

"Go to her house then," he said with a shrug.

"I don't know where she lives. And I can't pull that kind of shit while I'm still not available."

He nodded. "True. No grand gestures until you're single," he said with a grin. "But when that time comes, make sure you ask me what to do, because apparently I'm pretty good at them. I got my girl back."

His tone was cocky and annoying, and his shit-eating grin made me want to hit him or hug him. I wasn't sure which.

"Get out of my office," I growled before staring at my phone, wondering what the hell else I could do to get Claudia to talk to me before I completely fell apart.

I dialed her number one last time and waited.

MESSAGES AND CONFESSIONS
Claudia

I PULLED UP Frank's contact in my cell phone as I prepared to send him a well-worded, albeit pissed-off, text message. As I wrote it, the words flew from my fingertips like magic, but then a notice popped up when I hit SEND.

"You didn't even let me see what you wrote before sending it," Britney complained as I stared at my phone in confusion. "You should always get approval first."

My cell phone informed me that in order to send the text message, I needed to unblock Frank's contact. It wasn't until then that I noticed the small circle with a line through it next to his name, and my throat instantly thickened.

"Britney," I choked out, hardly able to speak through my surprise and confusion.

"What? What's wrong with you?" She leaned closer so she could see what I was staring at.

"His number's blocked."

Her jaw dropped. "What? When did you block him?"

My head spun, my thoughts swimming around before drowning. "Did you block it?"

"Me?" she sputtered. "Why the heck would I block his phone number? Give it to me." She grabbed the phone from my hand and stared at it. "Crap. It's definitely blocked."

Duh. I searched my memory, trying to remember when I could have possibly blocked him. I couldn't remember doing it, the same way I hadn't remembered shutting my phone completely off that first night. Maybe I'd done it then in some sort of angry, sad, sleep-deprived haze?

Then it hit me. I *had* blocked him quickly in the moments after I left the bar, but once I was in my car, I'd unblocked him just as fast.

"Oh my God, I did it. I blocked him, but I thought I undid it right afterward. I must not have." I shook my head in disbelief. "He's been blocked this whole time."

"You know what this means, right?" Britney tossed my phone back and I glanced at his name, noticing that she had unblocked him.

"That if he has tried to reach me, I'd never know it," I said.

When you block a contact, all their text messages are sent into a void in the universe, never to be delivered or read. Their phone calls never get through either. But someone could leave you a voice mail, and although you'd never be notified that one was left, it still existed on the server and could be accessed.

I frantically dialed my voice mail, putting my cell on speaker so Britney could hear the messages, if any even existed. Sending up a silent prayer to the relationship gods that there would be at least one message from Frank, I waited. After everything he'd done, I still held out hope. I still wanted Frank to care that he had hurt me, and I still wanted him to want to fix things between us, or at least explain just what the hell he was thinking.

What kind of person does that make me?

"You have eight new messages," the robotic voice finally said, and I did nothing to hide my shock as my jaw dropped.

"Eight!" Britney shouted as the first message started to play.

"Claudia," Frank said as a breath escaped into the phone. *"I'm so sorry. It's not what it looks like. Well, it is, but there's more to it than that. It's complicated. My situation is just really complicated. Fuck. This isn't coming out right at all. Please, please, call me back. I know you probably hate me and never want to see me again, but please give me a chance to explain. I really am sorry."*

I looked at Britney as she covered her mouth with her hand, waiting in silence as I pressed SAVE on the message and the next one played.

"Claudia." When he said my name again, my entire body chilled. He said nothing more for a moment, and I almost thought he'd hung up until he spoke again. *"There's so much I need to tell you. Please call me back."*

Saving that message as well, I let the next one play as Britney and I both stared wide-eyed at the device in my hand like it was magic.

"Your silence is killing me." He took an audible breath and I waited, holding mine. *"And I get it, I do. I just really want to talk to you. Can you at least text me back if you don't want to call?"*

Everything shifted inside me as I listened to the messages.

Frank sounded so desperate, so sad. Normally, that would have turned me off, but when it came to him, I was anything but.

It hurt me to hear him pleading with me in this way, regardless of whether he deserved my pity. My heartbeat quickened with his words, taking pleasure in the fact that he wanted to talk to me, wanted to explain things.

God, this entire time I'd thought he hadn't tried to get in touch with me at all. I'd been so angry that he could walk away from me and treat me with such blatant disrespect and disregard.

But I'd been wrong. He'd been trying to reach out the whole time.

"So he *has* been texting you," Britney said, her words mirroring my thoughts.

"Guess so." I wished I had the ability to pull those texts from the void and bring them back to me. I really wanted to know what they said.

"Play the next one. I'm dying to hear the rest," she insisted.

"I don't know how else to reach you. I don't know what else to do."

That one was short, almost abrupt in its desperation, then the next message played.

"Claudia, I know that you must be hurting and angry, and you're probably disgusted with me. I deserve all of that, but I never meant to hurt you. If you don't believe anything else I say, please believe that."

Pressing SAVE again, I held my breath as I waited for the

next one to begin.

"It's stupid, but I miss you." His tone was so sincere that my eyes immediately filled with tears. I believed him.

"I miss the way your accent would come out whenever you got all riled up or excited about something. I miss our conversations and the way just being with you made me feel more alive than I've felt in years." I could hear the smile in his voice, and felt myself smiling along with him. I missed him too.

"I know I shouldn't be telling you any of this, but if you're not going to call me back, then I need to tell you these things here, on your voice mail, because they need to be said and you need to hear them. I know you hate cheating and cheaters, and you probably think I'm no better than your dad." Frank sucked in a breath as if saying the words caused him physical pain, and I felt my heart catch.

"And maybe I'm not, but I'd like to think that I am. I'd like to think that if you knew everything about my situation, you might not hate me as much as you do right now. Maybe you'd . . ." He paused for three heartbeats before ending the message with, *"Maybe you'd understand and actually be able to forgive me."*

He sounded so choked up at the end, it almost broke me to hear him lose it.

Forgive him? How could I ever forgive him?

"Please tell me you're dying to know everything," Britney asked between the brief lull in messages. "Because I sure am. This is like a soap opera, and I'm completely invested."

"This is my life, Britney," I snapped, and her expression fell. "Sorry. I'm just not enjoying this as much as you are."

She gave me a quick one-armed hug. "I'm not enjoying this. I just really want to know the whole story. My curiosity is killing me. Play the next one."

Without a word, I saved the last message and played the next.

"It's been six days. It should be getting easier by now, right? But it's not. I can't get you out of my head. I can't stop thinking about you. I should have told you about Shelby, but I didn't know how." Shelby. My insides clenched as he gave me a name to go with his girlfriend's face.

"I know that's not an excuse. I'm starting to understand that maybe I've messed things up so badly that they can't be fixed. I really am sorry. I know I keep saying it, but there's no other word. If there was, I'd overuse it too."

I found myself laughing a little at that, even though his tone was filled with anything but laughter. Pressing SAVE, I waited for the next message to play, and frantically looked around for a clock when it said the date and time that this last message had been left.

"He *just* left this," Britney said, checking the time for me on her own phone. "About ten minutes ago."

It was one thing listening to the messages knowing that they had been left days ago. But waiting for this last one to start, realizing that he had just left it only ten short minutes earlier, caused my heart to punch against my chest like a defiant beast wanting out of its cage. If Britney had told me that she could see it beating through my clothes, I would have believed her.

"*Claudia.*" He sounded so defeated, my pounding heart ached with each beat. "*I have no idea how many messages I've left you, or how many texts I've sent. But since you aren't responding to me, you've left me no choice. I won't go another day without explaining myself to you. I wanted to do this in person. I wanted to look you in the eyes and tell you everything. But I guess I'm doing it in a voice mail instead.*" He huffed out something between an uncomfortable breath and a small laugh before continuing as my chest tightened.

"*I've been with Shelby for years. Too many, if you want to know the truth. I haven't been happy in a really long time, and meeting you only magnified my situation a thousand times over. I've wanted to end things for so long, but... I've been a coward.*" A bitter laugh escaped him as his tone changed. It sounded like he was realizing something for the first time as he began speaking again.

"*Yeah, I've been scared. That's the only real excuse I have. I guess the truth of the matter is that I haven't been strong enough to leave her, even though I know that I should. You see, I made her dad a promise. I promised him I'd always take care of his daughter. And when he died, I didn't know how to take it back without feeling like it was a betrayal of some sort. I had no idea when I made that promise that I'd eventually stop wanting to be with her, that I'd fall out of love. I sure as hell never knew I'd meet someone like you. I know I've let you down. I know you're probably disappointed in me. Trust me, I feel the same way about myself, so I get it. I know I have a lot of changes I need to make in my life. I know that every day that passes is another day I've wasted. And I know that I hate myself for what I've done to you. I really am sorry for hurting you. I'm sorry for lying. Maybe someday you'll forgive me? Maybe one day you'll give me another chance to make things right. I know I don't deserve it, but maybe one day you'll change your mind."*

When the messages ended, I found myself at a loss for words, trying to process all the things that Frank had said. Never in my life had a man said the things that Frank had just said to me, and part of me was filled with joy at the way he claimed to want me. The rest of me couldn't imagine the guilt he must have felt after making a promise like that. My heart actually hurt for him and for Shelby both.

"That wasn't at all what I was expecting," Britney said, her mouth still agape like it had been during half of Frank's last message.

Swallowing hard, I nodded. "Me either."

Britney's eyes looked suspiciously glassy as she cried out, "I can't believe he made a promise to her dad, and then her dad died!"

"I know. Can you even imagine being in a situation like that?" I tried to put myself in Frank's shoes, and all I could think of was how obligated I would feel. It made me sympathize with him, and feel sorry for his girlfriend.

Britney turned away and swiped at her face before facing me again, her expression all business. "So, what are you thinking?"

"Just that the whole thing is really sad, you know? I feel bad for him and for her," I admitted with a small shrug.

I didn't wish unhappiness on anyone, and knowing that two people were in a relationship that wasn't filled with love made me physically ache. I knew I was projecting my own fears of being in a passionless relationship onto Frank's situation. It was the last thing I wanted, for myself or for anyone else. And even though I knew that my feelings for

Frank clouded my judgment, I still wanted him to be happy, even if it wasn't with me.

I hated knowing that he wasn't.

"It's really messed up," Britney said. "No wonder Ryan said it was complicated."

I had almost forgotten all about Ryan chasing me out of the bar that night and the things he had said. He wasn't lying or trying to cover up for his brother; he was being sincere when he told me that things weren't black and white. I had been too devastated at the time to listen.

"What do I do?" I begged her, so conflicted I couldn't think straight.

"What do you want to do? Does any of this change things for you? It would for me."

"I don't know. I understand the predicament that Frank's in, but it also kind of pisses me off. Who settles and stays miserable for years? Why doesn't he want more for himself? Or if not for him, then for her? It's not like they're married and have kids. He should be less selfish, or maybe more selfish. I just don't know."

I hated seeing Frank in a light that was anything but flattering, but right now all I could think about was his ability to settle. And while I understood his feelings of guilt and obligation, I couldn't wrap my head around the fact that he would choose to stay in a relationship that didn't bring him joy . . . *for years.* Or that he would do that to his girlfriend, as if he was doing her some kind of favor by staying for so long. They both deserved better.

"Jesus, Claudia, he just told you why. The dude's racked with guilt. He's a man, and in my experience, they tend to do a lot of stupid things for reasons they think are the right ones. They're constantly making decisions based on their ego and pride instead of their hearts."

"You're right. I know that, but still."

I shook my head, trying to get my thoughts and feelings into order, but they refused. One part of me wanted to run into Frank's arms and tell him everything would be okay, while the other part warned me to keep my distance until he got his life in order, if he ever did. I refused to be in the middle of this sort of situation. I couldn't—and wouldn't—be the reason someone left their longtime partner.

"Think about how many people stay in their marriages 'for the kids.'" Britney did air quotes with her fingers. "They think they're doing their children a favor, but they're actually doing the opposite. The kids know their parents hate each other, but Mom and Dad think they should win medals for hiding the truth. In the end, all they've done is given their kids a really screwed-up example of what love is supposed to look and sound like, and wasted years of their lives being miserable when they could have moved on and been happy."

"I've never understood why people do that," I said with a sigh. "Stay together for the kids and stuff. It's never made sense to me, but then again, I've never been married, and I don't have kids."

Britney rolled her eyes. "Well, as a product of two parents who could barely stand to be in the same room together but thought they hid it well, trust me when I tell you that it doesn't work. I can't tell you how many times my brother and I wished they would just get divorced already. Growing up in a house like that was exhausting, and it messed with my head."

"I can't imagine," I said honestly.

"No, you can't. But then again, I can't imagine my dad walking out and never looking back. Don't get me wrong, I wanted my dad to leave a hundred times, but I never wanted him to stay gone. I never wanted to not see him again."

The mention of my dad's abandonment still stung, and I felt myself physically recoil with her comparison. I sat on the couch in silence, thinking about everything and nothing, my mind spinning like a hamster wheel.

"Will you go see Frank and talk to him face-to-face?" Britney asked, her question bringing the wheel to a screeching halt.

I met her gaze. "Should I?"

"After that last voice mail, don't you want to?" Her tone was almost incredulous, like my considering this was the most asinine idea ever.

"Yes and no. I'm a little afraid to see him in person."

"Why?"

I let out a quick breath before biting at my lip, hating the ugly truth that I was about to reveal. "Because I know I'll still want him. What's between us is more than just attraction or lust. There's something else there, and I don't know that I could say no to him if I was looking him in the eye."

Britney folded her arms over her chest and narrowed her eyes. "True or false?"

"True," I admitted, practically wincing. I wasn't a home-wrecker, and I'd never considered myself a weak woman. If a man was married or had a girlfriend, he was off-limits. No questions asked, end of story.

But this had been different. I hadn't known that Frank was

unavailable when I started to fall for him. I knew now, yes, but that didn't stop my heart from wanting him. It didn't stop my body from reacting to thoughts of his. And it didn't stop my mind from thinking about him all day long. After hearing his story through his voice mails, I was sympathetic to him and his situation.

But Frank didn't belong to me.

He wasn't mine.

He belonged to someone else.

And the last thing in the world I wanted to consider was that I could be the type of woman who could still want a man who wasn't single.

I was afraid that if I saw him, I'd still want him, and that went against everything I believed in, everything I stood for as a person. I'd spent my entire life deploring cheating and those who cheated, so what would that make me if I still wanted Frank when I knew for a fact he wasn't single? Would that mean I had to hate myself?

"So you'll just never see him again? That's it?" Britney waved a hand in the air. "Good-bye forever, Frank Fisher?"

"I don't know, Britney."

"Would you be able to do that? Act like you never met him?" She continued to push, like the concept was too insane for her to comprehend.

"Britney . . ." I breathed out her name in defeat. "I don't know, okay? I don't know."

And it was the truth. My mind was a mess of jumbled thoughts, ideas, and feelings that I refused to sort out in that moment. I didn't have all the answers, and trying to figure it out right now was exhausting.

"What if he broke up with her?" she asked, her tone softer.

Frank actually breaking it off after all this time seemed like a long shot, a fantasy only a stupid girl would cling to and hope for. Why would he do it now? Because of me? No. I knew better than to think that guys left the security and comfort of their relationships for someone else. My dad might have done it, but he was definitely the exception, not the rule. Most men led women on, made promises they couldn't keep, and kept up affairs for as long as they could get away with them.

"I don't want to think about what-ifs."

"Why not?"

"Because they aren't real."

I offered her a slight smile before pushing up from the couch. I needed the kind of clarity and peace that only a good night's sleep could provide.

As I walked down the hallway toward my room, I hoped I would get at least that much.

PARENTAL ADVICE

Frank

A QUICK KNOCK sounded on the office door before it flew open.

"Nick, I told you to leave me the fuck alone," I growled without looking up from my paperwork.

"That's no way to greet your old man," a familiar deep voice said, and my head shot up.

"Dad!" I jumped from my chair to give him a hug. It seemed like forever since I'd last seen him.

He hitched a thumb toward the bar. "Please tell me why I just watched your brother take his shirt off for a herd of screaming women."

Was it closing time already?

"You don't want to know." When I rolled my eyes, Dad laughed. "What are you doing here? It's late. Is everything okay?"

He waved his hand before settling into the chair in front of my desk. "Everything's fine. Your mother and I had a work party tonight, and we wanted to stop by on our way home."

"Is Mom here?"

"She's with Nick. He's showing her around while your other dumb brother is tending bar with no shirt on. Is that even legal? Doesn't it violate health codes?"

I laughed, then moved the conversation away from Ryan and his inability to stay clothed. "Haven't seen you guys lately."

After everything that had gone on between Nick and our father, we had all been trying to spend more time together as a family. We shot for Sundays, but even those get-togethers had become further and further apart the past few months. Dad was extra busy with work, and Mom had various charities she was always coordinating events for. Not to mention the three of us were slammed with the bar.

But we needed to do better, to try harder. Seeing him now only reinforced that for me. I missed my parents.

"Work has been killing me, and your mother has taken on more projects than one person can possibly handle. She's a machine who refuses to say no to people."

I smiled, realizing that both my parents were workaholics in their own way. It made me happy to know that it was in my genes, my very DNA, to want to be successful and be willing to work harder than most to make that happen.

"You look like hell, Frank. Is the bar okay? Do you need money?" Dad leaned forward, resting his elbows on the arms of his chair, looking into my eyes with sincerity.

I winced slightly, knowing that I must look like absolute crap if he was offering money. The past week had taken its toll on me, and I knew I couldn't hide the fact that sleep had all but eluded me for days.

"The bar's fine, Dad, but thanks."

"Girl trouble then?" He settled back into the chair, rubbing his chin.

"What?"

"If it's not business, then it's love. Is everything all right with Shelby?"

Narrowing my eyes, I wondered just what the hell my dad could possibly know on the subject. It hadn't been that long ago that he'd almost forced Nick to marry someone he didn't even like. There was more to it than that, but my dad had let things go too far and Nick almost paid the price for it.

"Dad, not to be a dick, but I'm not sure you're the best person to talk with about my relationship problems," I admitted honestly.

He smiled, nodding. "You're right. I know I'm probably the last person who should be doling out advice on the subject, but I'd still like to know what's going on, if you'd tell me. Fill your old man in, son. I know you're not happy. Why?"

I considered lying to him for all of two seconds before I gave him the CliffNotes version of my relationship with Shelby and my feelings for Claudia.

His expression changed, and I hated the sympathy I saw in his eyes. I hadn't confessed everything to get him to feel sorry for me. It was the last thing I wanted. I'd been a very active participant in bringing my love life to its current sorry state, so I had no one to blame but myself. This was on me.

"Don't look at me like that, Dad."

"I'm just processing it all. Letting it sink in."

"Well, can you let it sink in without that look in your eye, please?" I sounded like a child, but then again, I was *his* child.

Silence hung between us. I knew quite well that my father, a man who had built a multi-million-dollar company from nothing, would think over carefully all I'd just told him before he shared his opinion on it. He processed first, and acted second. I waited, wondering exactly what he would say.

"I'm going to tell you something that no one else knows, Frank," he said, and surprised, I sat up straighter in my chair. "After everything that happened with Nicholas, your mother was extremely upset. I'd never seen her so angry before. She had no idea what I'd been up to, what I'd been pushing him to do."

That was something I'd wondered about when the shit hit the fan with my youngest brother—how much my mother had known, and whether she'd been involved. I had suspected that she was in the dark, but none of us had worked up the courage to ask. I was starting to see how we Fishers swept things under the rug and moved on when we should have been slicing the issue open and talking about it.

"She actually kicked me out of the house."

"What? When?" That surprised me.

"It doesn't matter. But she told me to leave and that I couldn't come back until she could stomach looking at me. She wasn't sure when that would be, if ever."

I couldn't hide my shock. "Holy shit, Dad. I had no idea. None of us did."

"I know. Now, listen because I'm actually getting to my point. When she did that, your mother, it devastated me. Devastated." He emphasized the word, conveying the intensity of the emotion behind it before continuing. "The idea of losing her was unimaginable to me. It knocked me straight on my ass, threw me for a loop, and I never saw it coming. I fought like hell to get her back. Apologized, went to counseling on more than one occasion, anything she wanted I would have done because I couldn't lose her. I couldn't live the rest of my life without her in it. I didn't realize how off track I'd gotten until I almost lost everything."

I sat there stunned at my father's confession. He wasn't the emotional type, so this was a side of him that I'd never seen. Especially since he'd tried over the years to convince Nick that love didn't matter, that it wasn't real, and a bunch of other crap. My dad had definitely turned a corner since he'd tried to ruin Nick's life.

Then pride rolled through me at the thought of my mom's strength and determination to stand up for herself and for my baby brother. I was so damn proud of her for doing what was obviously right, and found myself inspired.

"I can't believe all of this happened and none of us knew."

"You boys are a bit busy running a successful business." He gave me a sheepish grin. "And I didn't want you to know. I was pretty embarrassed."

I was nodding in understanding as my mom poked her head through the doorway.

"Can I come in?"

I stood up and swept her into a bear hug, pride still surging inside me. "Mom."

Her green eyes, so like mine, shone brightly as she cupped my cheek with her hand. "My sweet Frank. How are things?"

I cast a wary glance at my dad, and he cleared his throat.

"I'll give you two a minute alone," he said before placing a soft kiss on my mom's cheek and peeking out the door. "You'll be happy to know that your brother's shirt is back where it belongs," he called out before closing the door behind him.

I laughed, and my mom's face lit up. She looked genuinely

happy before focusing her attention on me, her expression shifting to reveal the concern she so clearly felt.

"If your dad left us, then I'm a bit worried."

Curious what her opinion might be, and knowing she'd never let me get away with not coming clean at this point, I filled her in. Her face softened as she listened intently, tucking a strand of her sandy-blond hair behind her ear.

"Oh, honey, I'm so sorry you're in this situation, and I know how hard it must be for you. I want all my boys to be happy. It kills me to think of how long you haven't been, and that I had no idea." She pressed a hand to her heart and sighed. "And while I would never suggest leaving one relationship for another, that's not what this is. So, before you go beating yourself up over that notion, because I know how you are, listen to me."

She motioned for us to sit, and I moved back behind the desk while she took the chair Dad had just left.

"I like Shelby. She's a nice girl, but if she's not the one for you, then it's time to move on. For your sake *and* hers. It's not fair to either of you to continue living like this. It's not about the other woman you met either, and you need to know that. She will probably need to know that as well at some point, since she was the push you needed to finally put things in perspective. I'm convinced that if you'd never met this girl, you'd probably stay with Shelby as long as she allowed it. But I promise you that eventually Shelby would have left you. A woman can only take things not going well for so long before we snap. And once we walk away, there's usually no coming back."

Everything Mom said made so much sense, and I nodded.

"I've just been so afraid to make a mistake or make the wrong decision. I've been afraid that leaving would somehow ruin Shelby, or break her, or make me a bad person."

Mom gave me a stern look. "You're not a bad person, but you are being selfish and inconsiderate. You're not being fair. And more importantly, you're wasting time. Life is short, sweetie. It's too damn short to live with regrets. Or to spend years in a relationship when you've grown apart and the love has shifted. Not one of us is guaranteed a tomorrow. Everything can change in an instant," she said, snapping her fingers. "We all think that our time is infinite, but it's not. It's limited, and you're throwing it away. True love brings true happiness, and you deserve to have both. So does Shelby. You need to set her free, and you need to free yourself. Her dad would understand, honey. I promise you, he would want that for you both as well."

My eyes stung, and I almost started bawling like a baby. I'd never realized how much I needed the support and encouragement from my parents. Hearing them both tell me that what I wanted to do was the right thing, and that wanting it didn't make me a bad person, made a difference in how I felt about myself and the situation I'd put myself in.

"Are you okay?" she asked.

"I am," I said, feeling stronger and more resolute than I had five minutes before.

"I love you." She stood up and hugged me, and I squeezed her extra tight.

"Thank you."

She looked up at me, her gaze pleading. "I'm always here for you, Frank. Please don't keep things like this to yourself from now on. Talk to me. Or, at least, talk to your brothers."

"I will," I promised, and she turned for the door. It opened before she reached it, and my dad stepped through.

"I was just coming to get you. I'm exhausted, woman."

My mom laughed. "Me too."

"I'll be right out," he said as she slipped past him, and my heart felt full.

"I thought of something while I was out there talking to your brothers," he said, and I nodded for him to continue. "If you were to go home to Shelby right now and she asked you to leave, told you it was over, how would you feel?"

That was a question I hadn't expected. My answer was a gut-level response that came out before I could stop it. "Relieved."

"And the idea of never seeing this other woman again . . . how does that make you feel?"

Using the same tone he had earlier, I said, "Devastated." My throat and stomach clenched at the thought of never seeing Claudia again, of not getting the chance to explore what was between us. "Shit, Dad, I'd be devastated."

He gave me a knowing smile and gripped my shoulder, giving it a squeeze before walking out without saying another word. And just like that, in the span of a heartbeat, everything was crystal fucking clear.

Saying the things out loud that I had kept locked up so tight inside was like opening up a vault and finding out the door couldn't be closed anymore. I inhaled a long, deep breath before I released it just as slowly, my resolve strengthening.

I couldn't deny the truth any longer. I knew what I needed to do, what I'd been putting off for far too long. It was going to hurt like hell and would be really hard, but this cowardly version of myself sickened me.

It was time to do the right thing once and for all. It was time to grow the fuck up and act like the man I knew I was.

I'M BACK

Frank

ONCE I STARTED the conversation with Shelby when I got home that night, ending things hadn't gone at all like I'd expected. It had actually been . . . *easier.*

I'd dreaded saying the words for so many years, but once they were out of my mouth, I couldn't take them back. And I hadn't wanted to, not even for a second. That's how I knew without a doubt that I was doing the right thing, even if Shelby hadn't agreed.

I tried to get her to stay in our condo, insisting that I could move in with Ryan, but she refused, saying she didn't want to live with the memory of us or the ghost of me. I couldn't blame her, but I wanted to make things as easy as possible on her since I felt responsible for shifting her entire life's plan.

That only angered her more, my insistence on making sure she was comfortable and taken care of. She told me that she didn't want my sympathy, my comfort, my friendship, or anything else that had to do with me.

Three days later, she loaded the last of her things into her friend's waiting SUV. As they drove off, the driver's side window rolled down and Lauren, Shelby's coworker and new roommate, flipped me the bird.

Stunned, I simply stood there for a minute.

As I watched them drive away, several emotions ran through me—sadness, guilt, and relief—one right after the other. Then I got excited, refusing to feel like an asshole for finally gaining control of my life and my future.

Heading to the bar that afternoon, I felt free. The weight that I hadn't realized had become a part of me was suddenly lifted. My breaths seemed deeper as my lungs expanded. I could truly breathe for the first time in years. The cost of listening to my head over my heart had taken a heavy toll, but everything changed today.

Everything.

My new life began, and the old Frank was back.

"So, she moved out already?" Nick asked as I stepped behind the bar.

"She left today, gave me her keys and everything."

"Wow. She wasted no time."

I couldn't help but agree. Shelby had packed her things, found a new place to live, and was completely moved out three days after I'd ended things. The last few nights, I'd come home to an empty bed and boxes half-packed on the floor, the only signs that Shelby had even been there at all.

"Yeah, I know. It was kind of the perfect storm as far as timing. Her friend had just broken up with her fiancé, so she was looking for a roommate."

"I still can't believe you actually did it," Nick added as he mixed a drink for a woman with collagen-plumped lips and fake lashes. "I'm glad that you did, but I still can't believe it."

I glanced at him, wanting to smack him upside the head just because I could. "Do you and Ryan want to keep cheerleading about it, or are you ever going to shut the hell up?"

Ryan scowled at me. "Hey, I didn't even say anything."

I threw a towel at his head, annoyed when he ducked out of the way and it fell to the floor. "Yet. You haven't said anything yet."

"How did she take it? What did you say? Give us all the details, man," Nick asked.

"When did you turn into Ryan? I swore I only had one sister, but now I apparently have two," I fired back, knowing I was being a dick. My brothers were nosy fuckers, but if our situations were reversed, I'd want details too. I'd just be more of a man about it.

Nick handed the drink to the woman, who batted those fake eyelashes at him repeatedly before sipping the concoction and letting loose a sensual hum of appreciation. A lot of the women who came here tended to do that after trying a drink—purring like kittens, moaning like they were having an orgasm, or groaning like they were on a porn set, all for nothing.

"You know your efforts are wasted on that one, right?" I hooked a thumb toward Nick and gave her a quick grin.

"Can't hurt to try," she said with a coy smile, and it took everything in me to tell her that yes, it could hurt her to try. Because Nick saw no one other than Jess.

Moving to the corner where Ryan stood, I reached over his shoulder and grabbed a bottle of whiskey. Nick followed me like my shadow.

"Just give us the rundown," Ryan said.

I thought back to arriving home that night and being surprised to find Shelby still awake and in the kitchen. Even thought it was an ungodly hour, I'd taken it as a sign and had started the conversation by asking her if she was happy. She tried to insist she was, but I knew she was lying, both to me and to herself.

Keeping my voice low, I said, "She was pissed. She said pretty much everything I thought she would. How I'd wasted her life and led her on. I was an asshole who wouldn't know a good thing if it hit me in the face. Then she threw her coffee mug at me."

"What? No way." Nick laughed. "I can't imagine Shelby doing that."

"She was mad. And she was hurt. Don't worry, I ducked." I mimicked the movement, and both my brothers laughed.

"Did you tell her about Claudia," Ryan asked.

"Why the hell would I do that?"

"Figured she'd ask if there was someone else. Girls *always* ask if there's someone else," he said with conviction.

I nodded. "She did ask me that, and she asked me why now. She wanted to know if there was someone else, and if there wasn't, what exactly had changed between us."

"What did you tell her?" Nick leaned in closer as he waited for my answer.

"I told her nothing had changed, but I just couldn't keep doing this anymore. That we were both settling, and I wasn't the right guy for her."

"Jesus. That was harsh." Ryan blew out a breath.

Blinking hard, I said, "Then I told her about the promise I made to her dad."

"Shit! Was she shocked?" Nick said at the same moment Ryan blurted, "What'd she say?"

So I told them exactly what had gone down . . .

*

"DID YOU KNOW I made a promise to your dad right before he died?" I'd said, wanting Shelby to know what I'd done, what I'd promised to do.

"My dad? What kind of promise?"

"He made me promise to always take care of you. He said that you were mine now and he couldn't imagine a better guy with his daughter." My voice broke as I relayed the information to her for the first time.

"He did that to me too."

Shocked, I blurted, "He did?"

Shelby nodded. "He said he couldn't imagine me with anyone else. Told me how lucky we were to have found each other, and that we should always remember that. Relationships were about compromise and love wasn't easy, he said, but when it got hard, you stuck it out and didn't give up. He told me not to give up on you, even when you were hard to love. Dad promised me that you would get hard to love; he said that's what men did."

She gave me a sad smile. "He also said that what we had was worth fighting for, and that true love stood the test of time. He hoped we'd get married one day, and said he'd be watching over us when we did."

*

RYAN GAVE ME a sad look when he heard that part. "Wow, her

dad really did a number on both of you."

I agreed. Shelby's dad had obviously meant well, but he'd put more pressure on us than we could handle.

"So she probably stayed with you for all these years because of the conversation she had with her dad," Nick said softly. "That's messed up."

"I know. That's how I saw it too, but Shelby didn't see it that way."

I thought about how convinced she was that we shouldn't give up. She tried to get me to see reason, to stay and fight for what we had, but I didn't want to. She made me say that to her out loud, and it killed me to hurt her in that way, but she refused to listen.

I'd had to be mean to make her accept that I was serious . . .

*

"I THINK WE should break up," I'd said, not knowing any other way to word it so she'd believe me. I hadn't wanted there to be any doubt about my intentions, so I'd added, "I want to break up."

"You're serious? Frank, no. No, we're not breaking up." Her voice quavered as her eyes filled with tears.

"It's the right thing, Shelby," I insisted, refusing to change my mind. I'd lived this way for far too long. I couldn't do it a second longer without feeling like I was going to stop breathing. "I can't do this anymore."

"No. I stood by you when no one else did."

"I know," I said, feeling my heart break a little at how

much I was hurting her.

"I gave you everything."

"I know."

"I moved here for you," she reminded me, and I winced a little, knowing that I'd never asked her to.

"I know," I repeated.

"Stop agreeing with me!" she yelled before changing course. "You don't want to work on things, try to fix them? We shouldn't just quit."

"I don't want to keep hurting you, Shelby." I hated saying anything that would cause her further pain, but she wouldn't listen and I needed this to end. "But I don't think this is fixable."

She rose to her feet, her face turned to stone. "It's not fixable because you don't want to fix it. Everything is fixable if both people want to work at it. You're not even trying. You have to want to try."

"I don't," I said, snapping her last thread of hope and wrecking her composure.

Stunned, she stared at me with wide eyes, her mouth agape. "You don't even want to try?"

"No."

*

"WOW. LIKE I said, harsh," Ryan said again after I'd finished.

"I know," I admitted, refusing to feel bad about it anymore. I was done feeling bad.

Nick circled his hand in the air, impatient all of a sudden. "When can we get to the good stuff?"

"What the hell are you babbling about?" I asked with a groan.

Ryan chuckled. "You know he's talking about Claudia."

I shot them both a look that told them to mind their own damn business when it came to her, even though I knew they wouldn't. Now that I was officially single and on the market, these knuckleheads would meddle in my social life until that status changed.

"Can't a guy be single for ten minutes before you two set him up?" I said, not meaning the words at all. I still hadn't heard from Claudia, and it drove me crazy. She hadn't responded to a single text message or voice mail, and hadn't set foot in the bar since she found out about Shelby.

"Oh, so you don't mind if I ask her out then, right?" Ryan asked, sounding serious.

Just like when he'd mentioned that idea before, my temper flared. Jealousy tore through me at the thought of any other man touching her, let alone my own flesh and blood.

"Fuck yes, I mind. I mind a whole hell of a lot," I growled, and the asshole laughed.

"Yeah, I know you do." Ryan continued laughing while I wished I could shoot arrows from my eyes at his stupid mug.

"So, wait." Nick leaned back, his brow furrowed. "Do you want to be single? After all, this is the first time you've been alone in ten years. Maybe you want to play the field before settling down again?"

I don't.

At all.

Even though I'd been paired up with Shelby for the last decade, it hadn't always felt that way, especially the last few years. It was weird to think about how alone you could feel when you technically weren't alone; how you felt like you were missing a teammate, a partner, when one was sleeping next to you night after night. I supposed that was what being with the wrong person eventually started to feel like. You stopped seeing the person standing right in front of you because you no longer wanted what they had to offer.

"It makes sense," Ryan added, now that his laughter had stopped. "No one would blame you if you wanted to take some time to be alone."

Annoyed, I shook my head. "No. I don't want to play the field. I don't want to be single. I don't care about any of that, okay?" Damn, I wished they'd shut up and get back to work. I should have known better.

"You're going to win her back then, right? You have a plan?" Nick lit up like a toddler with a new toy.

I smirked. "Yeah. I'm going to get her."

Nick whistled as Ryan asked, "How?"

I closed my eyes and willed myself to count to ten. "I don't have to fill you two in on every single detail, you know?"

"He doesn't have a plan," Ryan said with certainty as he looked at Nick with disapproving eyes.

"After we close tonight, he will." Nick rubbed his palms together and I bit my tongue, not wanting to argue any further with the two lunkheads.

I did have a plan, sort of, but I was being honest when I said I didn't want to tell them every little thing about it. I had been biding my time, waiting for Shelby to move out before I did anything else in regard to Claudia. Refusing to push her further when my life hadn't yet changed wasn't something I was willing to do. I wouldn't put her in a no-win situation again.

But now that Shelby was gone, all bets were off.

I couldn't tell my brothers that, though. Not yet. They would want up-to-the-second details, and this was something I needed to do on my own, without anyone's interference or opinion. After we closed the bar for the evening, I'd tell them exactly that. It was my job to go get the girl, not theirs.

The front door flew open, and I was relieved at the interruption as Jess and Rachel walked inside. They were just the distraction I needed. I pointed toward them, and Nick's whole damn face lit up.

"Dear God, woman, do you walk around Santa Monica looking like that?" Nick shouted toward Jess, who instantly blushed and stumbled to a halt. "Rachel, you just let her walk around looking beautiful?"

Nick made his way from behind the bar and stalked toward his girl, talking the whole time. "This woman right here is what dreams are made of. I'm so damn lucky," he said when he reached her, lifting her into his arms and planting a Hollywood-worthy kiss onto her lips as Rachel wrinkled her nose and moved a respectful distance away.

As usual, the entire bar watched transfixed. Some sighed at the sight, and a few people even clapped.

"Making us all look bad, man!" a guy called out.

Nick didn't even look up. "Nah. You just gotta do better." He kissed Jess one more time before setting her on her feet and smacking her on the ass.

The truth was, Nick really was making the entire male population look bad. But most people had no idea what Nick and Jess had been through as a couple, and how he never stopped making up for lost time. He hadn't forgiven himself for what he'd put Jess through, and ever since, he spent every single day making sure she knew how thankful he was for the second chance she'd given him.

And now, I was able to relate to that concept more than I had ever thought possible.

DREAM FRANK

Claudia

FRANK HAD HAUNTED my dreams the past few nights.

Haunted wasn't really the right word, not when the dreams were lust-filled, sex-riddled, and most definitely enjoyable. Frank visited me in my sleep, his hands roaming over every part of my body that I'd always wanted him to touch. In my dreams, I forgave him and fell into the taste of his kiss and the feel of his tongue on mine without question. Dream Frank was one hell of an attentive lover, and I woke up aroused on more than one occasion with a pillow between my legs.

Embarrassed for no good reason on this particular morning, I kicked the pillow away and lay there a minute longer, reveling in all that Dream Frank had done to me and my body.

Then, I got pissed at myself. How could my subconscious continually betray me? I wasn't sure how I felt about Frank Fisher, and every part of me—my subconscious and all my girly parts—needed to be on board.

But that was the problem. I didn't know exactly how I felt, how I was supposed to feel, or what the right way to feel even was.

"Are you ever going to call him back?" Britney called out

from the kitchen table. "Or even better, let's go to Sam's. I miss Ryan's hot face."

It was the same question I'd been asking myself on repeat for days.

As I entered the kitchen, she was spooning Greek yogurt into her mouth. "I thought I'd have a clear answer by now," I muttered as I searched the fridge for something to eat. "But I'm not any closer than I was yesterday. Or the day before that."

I vacillated between completely understanding Frank and the situation he was in, and not *wanting* to understand Frank and his situation. My emotional side longed for me to go talk to him, but my logical side kept reminding me that he had lied and misled me easily, and more than once.

Part of me thought that I'd stop thinking about Frank as the days passed, but so far, that hadn't been the case. He was my last thought at night before I closed my eyes, and the first thought in the morning when I opened them. It was annoying, the hold he had on me, and I sensed it meant more than I was willing to admit. The connection I'd felt with him the first time I looked at him was real and it still existed, even when I tried to push it away. We were bonded by an invisible thread, and you couldn't cut the ties of something you couldn't see.

"I think you should talk to him. It's been days since his last message. He hasn't called or texted since, right?"

I closed the refrigerator door, holding a Greek yogurt of my own, and my heart sank. "No, he hasn't."

Saying those words out loud made me nervous as a realization hit me hard. What if Frank had changed his mind about me? What if he no longer meant the things he'd said in his voice mails? Maybe he and his girlfriend had worked things out since we'd last talked, and were happy again?

My mind fed me scenarios that involved Frank forgetting about me and being perfectly fine with that decision. Why else would he stop calling and disappear completely? He had to be trying to fix his relationship.

"What's the matter?" Britney tilted her head, studying me, which reminded me how well she actually knew me. She could always tell when I was about to lose it.

"I just . . . what if they're happy now? What if he realized that I was a mistake? A fantasy of some kind that he'd built up in his mind?"

More fears I never knew I even had bubbled up from deep within me. If I had been an escape for Frank, an oasis in the middle of his relationship desert, then maybe nothing he thought he felt for me had been real. Maybe everything about me, about us, had been something to hold on to, a life raft when his world was falling apart.

"You think his feelings for you weren't real?" Britney barked out a disbelieving laugh.

I braced myself on the kitchen counter and shrugged. "It's totally possible. He hasn't called in days. If he couldn't live without me, or was so sorry like he seemed to be, then why did he stop calling? Why did he give up when he said he wasn't going to?"

"Maybe because you never called him back," she said with an exaggerated eye roll. "A guy can only fight for so long before he has to stop. Frank wouldn't like it, but if he thought it was the best thing for you, or what you really wanted, he'd do it. He'd walk away. I don't really know the guy, but I'd bet money that he's the type who would eventually listen. And your silence told him everything."

The air ripped out of my lungs, deflating me with a single breath. "Shit." I tried to pull it together, willed my heart to slow down its rapid beating, and pressed a hand to my stomach. "You're right."

"I know." She grinned before spooning up more yogurt. "So, what are you gonna do about it?"

"I don't know what I'm supposed to do when nothing's changed."

"You're seriously the most infuriating woman on the planet," she said with a groan.

I narrowed my eyes at her. "What the hell did I do?"

"You won't even talk to the guy! I know you like him, Claudia. Even though he has a girlfriend, you still like him. And that's killing you, tearing you up inside. You're beating yourself up, but to what end?"

Shaking my head, I grabbed a spoon, then pulled out the chair next to hers and sat down. "What would you do? Seriously, if you were me, what would you do?"

"Talk to him. Have an actual conversation. Let him explain himself, and hear him out. All these things you refuse to do," she said slowly, enunciating each word as if I were a child.

I hated how confused I still was. Conflicting emotions warred within me, none of them letting up their relentless persistence. The battle between my mind and heart was exhausting.

Maybe love wasn't always black and white, no matter how hard we tried to force it to be. Maybe connections weren't always easy and uncomplicated. Maybe love was filled with challenges sometimes, only to see how hard you'd fight to overcome them. I didn't have the answers, but I sure seemed to have a lot of questions.

"Can I ask you something else?" Britney asked. When I nodded, opening my own yogurt and digging in, she said, "What are you so afraid of?"

I swallowed quickly, hoping I wouldn't choke. "I'm afraid to feel more for someone when I shouldn't be feeling anything at all."

"No." She shook her head. "I mean, what's your biggest fear? What are you the most afraid of?"

Britney, the brat, was trying to get me to admit more that I wanted to. She wanted me to dig out the things I longed to shove deep inside and pretend weren't a part of me.

"Just tell me," she said with an exasperated huff. "You know I won't judge you."

It wasn't her judging me that I was worried about. I was my own worst judge and jury.

Staring at my yogurt, I focused on my spoon circling in the creaminess rather than meet her eyes. "I'm afraid I won't care that he has a girlfriend. That I'll give in and take him any way I can have him, in bits and pieces, if that's all he could give me, because I like the way I feel when we're together. Because I feel so much when I'm around him. He makes me so happy. Or, at least, he did when I thought he was single."

God, I hated what a weak person I was being right now. I wanted to throw up as the words left my lips. As always, I wanted to do the right thing, but for once in my life, I wasn't entirely sure what that was. Of course, the right thing would be to let Frank go, but my heart ached at the idea in a way I'd never experienced before.

Stupid hearts are fickle creatures, demanding to be heard. They crush you with pain one minute before completely shutting off and feeling absolutely nothing the next.

Which was exactly why I had to keep my distance from Frank until I was strong enough to refuse to settle for scraps. Not to mention the fact that I didn't like how this entire situation was bringing out sides of my character that I didn't particularly like. I'd never considered myself this weak woman, or the type who would settle for anything in life, especially not in matters of the heart.

I was better than that.

Stronger than that.

And I deserved more than that.

"I just need more time," I said to Britney, who had been uncharacteristically quiet.

"For what?"

"To figure out what exactly I want to do and say. I need to have a plan when it comes to Frank, and I can't waver from it. Not even for a second when he looks at me with those stupid green eyes."

"But you will talk to him?" she asked with a hopeful lilt in her voice.

I nodded. "I will."

"Promise?"

"I promise," I said, not knowing exactly when I'd do it.

The betrayal was still too fresh, and the connection between Frank and me only existed to the point that it still affected me, obviously. I needed time and space to allow both those things to simmer, but at some point, I'd need closure for my heart to heal. I just wasn't entirely sure when that would be.

And maybe by the time I was ready to face him, I wouldn't feel the need to anymore.

TEAMWORK

Frank

NICK LOCKED THE door when the last of our customers left, and Ryan put his shirt back on without even being asked. Apparently, there was a first time for everything.

"I know you don't want to talk about this because you're all broody and Frank-like," Nick said, scowling as he waved a hand in my direction. "But I want to hear your Claudia plan."

"*Cloud-ee-ah*," I said, and he repeated her name properly, but in a mocking tone. "And I don't want to talk about it. Not yet."

"Why not?" Ryan and Nick asked in unison, and instead of getting annoyed, I tried to understand. It took almost all my patience.

"Can I keep this to myself for now, and if I need your help—which I very well might—I'll let you guys know?" It was my version of a compromise. I might need them on board if I ended up not being able to track Claudia down, or figure out a way to get to her, which I was struggling with, to be honest.

Ryan and Nick glanced at each other in silent communication before giving me begrudging nods.

"I'm just throwing this out there," Ryan said as he rotated the bottles on the shelf, ensuring the labels faced outward and were aligned. "But Britney gave me her number, and I'm pretty sure I could find it if you hit a dead end."

For once, I found myself thankful that Ryan got hit on by every single female that entered our bar. "Thanks. I might just need that."

I really had intended to keep my crappy plans closely guarded, but that was my pride talking. My heart was on the line here, and it wasn't like Nick and Ryan were rooting against me. They actually wanted me to end up with the girl. Maybe I could use their help instead of trying to do everything on my own.

Nick gave me an exasperated look. "I know we said we'd butt out, but I can't. Just tell me what the hell you're planning. You guys helped me when I needed you." He grimaced. "Well, you both yelled at me was more like it."

And just like that, I gave in. All my resolve and bravado vanished as I stared at the two people I trusted most in my life.

"To be honest, I've been going over and over this all night long." My head had been spinning the entire night, trying to think of ways to find Claudia so I could talk to her, and hopefully get her to listen to me.

"Have you tried Facebook?" Nick asked like the social-media marketing guru he was, which didn't surprise me at all.

I shook my head. "I need to see her in person. Texting and calling her haven't worked so far, so the whole social-media angle isn't going to work. What am I going to do when I find her, anyway? Send her a friend request and another email for her to ignore? No, it's got to be face-to-face."

When it came to Claudia, being passive wasn't going to get the job done. I needed to physically see her and make her listen. I wasn't above begging, if necessary.

"He's right." Ryan reached beneath the bar and pulled out an old oversized mason jar filled with scraps of paper of all shapes and sizes. He dumped them onto the bar top and sorted through them, clearly searching for one in particular.

"What are you doing?" I asked.

He scoffed at me as if I'd asked the stupidest question in the world. "Finding Britney's number."

"You seriously think you're going to find her number in that mess?" I pointed at the pile of paper scraps, shocked by how many phone numbers my brother had accumulated, and kept.

"You have little faith, brother. She gave it to me on off-white paper. I'll find it," Ryan said with a grin.

"How the hell do you even remember that?" Nick asked, echoing my own thoughts.

Ryan stopped sorting and looked up with a sheepish grin. "I have no fucking idea."

The three of us laughed, and Ryan went back to digging through pile. A few moments later, he let out a whoop.

"Got it! Found it!" He waved a cream-colored slip of paper in the air. "Told you," he said with a smug smile.

"All right, Romeo, now what?" I asked.

"We need to get Claudia to come here," Ryan said matter-of-factly.

My face twisted into a grimace. That idea hadn't sat right with me when I'd first considered it, and it didn't feel any better now.

Ryan glanced at my expression and seemed to deflate. "What? I'll just text Britney and get her to bring Claudia here.

I'm sure she'll do it."

"And then what?" I threw my hands up in frustration. "Claudia and I discuss all of our private business in public, in front of you and anyone else who wants to watch and listen?"

I couldn't stomach the thought of people witnessing our private moments, when so much about my brothers and our business was already in the public eye. I also couldn't in good conscience trick Claudia into coming here if she had no desire to see me.

Quickly running through the possible scenarios, I shook my head. "Not to mention the fact that having Claudia come here would put her on edge. This is my turf, and if we were all waiting for her to show up, she'd feel ganged up on and would be defensive instead of willing to listen. Not to mention pissed off. I can't have Claudia pissed when I'm trying to reason with her."

I imagined her feisty attitude and couldn't help how it turned me on, but I needed to focus on getting her to hear me out first before I thought about all the things I wanted to do to her body. And the list was growing by the day.

"Then I'll ask Britney for their home address. You can show up there like a proper stalker," Ryan said, and Nick laughed.

I hated that idea as well. It felt like an ambush, so I shook my head again. "I can't do that either. It's too personal, showing up at her home. Not to mention it's a little creepy." Going to Claudia's place uninvited would be invading a very private space that I hadn't been invited into yet. It would be one thing if I'd been over there before, but I hadn't.

"It's only creepy if she doesn't like you," Nick said with a smile. "Otherwise, girls think it's romantic."

Ryan frowned at him. "Since you have all the answers, little brother, why don't you tell us what you think he should do."

"If you won't reach out to her online, get her to come here, or go to her house," Nick said, "then what do you want to do? How are you going to talk to her if you won't do anything that puts you with her in the same place at the same time?"

Nick was probably thinking back to what he had done to win back Jess. But that had been different. They had been dating and had a history when he showed up on her doorstep.

Claudia and I barely had anything together yet; we didn't have a foundation. I still needed to build all of that, if she'd let me, and she definitely wouldn't talk to me in a situation where I had the advantage. So, if I wanted to give her the high ground, I needed to go where she ruled, where she was queen. Where she wouldn't want to kick me in the nuts the second she saw me, if only because it would get her into trouble.

"Do you think you can find out where they work?"

Ryan laughed and tapped furiously on his phone. "Easily. They might be asleep, so we probably—" He stopped mid-sentence as his phone buzzed in his hand. "Never mind," he said, shoving his phone toward me so I could read the name of the bank and the branch they worked at.

I glanced over and committed it to memory. "That was too easy."

Ryan's phone vibrated again, and he laughed. "Britney says that better have been about Frank and the fact that he's getting his shit together to win back her friend."

I forced a half smile as Ryan typed something back to her. "What are you telling her?" I watched as he typed again, then stopped for a second before starting again. "Jesus, Ryan, you even text like a girl. Are you sure you're a guy?"

He glanced up and stopped typing. "Do you want me to pull out my dick?" Before I could answer, he reached for the zipper on his jeans.

"No, thanks, I'm good."

He typed away again and cleared his throat. "Anyway, I'm telling her that it is about you and Claudia, but not to say anything. She said good, and I told her we might need her help. She said she's in. Whatever we need that she can do, she'll do it. And she said it's about time."

That made me smile, knowing that Britney was on my side.

As if Nick could read my mind, he said, "That's a good sign. If she's willing to help, then you know Claudia doesn't hate you."

"I was just thinking the same thing. Ryan, ask her if I need an appointment to see Claudia for a business loan."

He gave me a wary look but was typing before I'd even finished talking. "A business loan?"

"That's what she does at the bank. She's in charge of small-business loans."

Nick blew out a breath. "Good idea, getting on her schedule. Smooth."

Ryan looked up from his phone. "She says it's best if you do, and she'll make one for you tomorrow when she gets to the office. She'll text me and let me know the day and time."

My throat tightened as I imagined waiting another day, or

days, to make things right. I didn't want to waste any more time. "Tell her to make the appointment for tomorrow, or I'm showing up without one."

Ryan chuckled as he paused from typing to read Britney's response. "She says you're bossy. But she'll text me tomorrow. She doesn't think it should be a problem."

"Tell her I said thanks."

For the first time in days, I felt like smiling. I had a plan, and I was going to get the girl.

*

THE NEXT DAY, I showed up at the bank fifteen minutes early. Not wanting to alert Claudia to my presence, I stayed outside until exactly one minute before my two o'clock appointment time.

Britney had blocked off an hour on Claudia's calendar and booked me as "Mr. Trout," knowing that Claudia would freak out if she saw a Mr. Fisher on her schedule. I had laughed at the alias before worry set in, and prayed that Claudia wouldn't figure out the ploy and suddenly call in sick for the rest of the afternoon. I knew I owed Britney big-time if this worked out in my favor.

My heart pounding, I pulled open the door and headed toward the small reception area in the center of the bank where Britney had told me to wait. I looked around, searching the private-banker offices on the periphery for my girl when I caught sight of Britney in hers. She waved and I smirked, continuing my search for Claudia.

When I spotted her, my heart leaped into my throat. She

hadn't noticed me yet, but watching her, it was like I hadn't seen her in years. I took in her silky black hair pulled up into a ponytail, the ends brushing her shoulders bared by her sleeveless blue dress as she turned her head to glance at her computer screen.

My entire body perked up, reacting to the sight of her. I was like a starved man in need of food, and Claudia was my next meal. She was like a breath of fresh air after you'd been trapped underground for years without windows or sunlight. She was a drink of water after you'd been lost in the sandy desert, parched and dreaming of something cool to sip. Claudia was a fucking dream.

She grabbed a clipboard from her desk and walked toward the reception area.

"Mr. Tr—" The name stopped on her lips as I pushed to my feet. Her eyes locked onto mine, and I swore I saw her breath catch. "Frank. What are you doing here?"

"I'm your two o'clock," I said, willing my nerves to shut down and pull it together.

"You're serious?" She cast a glance toward Britney, who buried her face in a file folder, pretending not to be watching our every move.

I wasted no time. Without a word, I took the clipboard from Claudia's hand as I rested my other hand on the small of her back and guided her toward her office.

"I'm serious. We have business to discuss," I whispered into her ear, thrilling at the sight of tiny goose bumps appearing on her bare shoulder. *Another good sign*, I thought, even if her reaction had been involuntary.

She looked stunned but moved willingly with me, and

closed the door behind us as I took a seat in the guest chair across from her desk. God, she looked sexy as hell, all professional and in charge.

"Why are you here? I'm pretty sure you don't need a business loan." She tried to sound tough as she sat down, keeping her spine ramrod straight, but I sensed the hurt underneath her businesslike tone.

"I needed to see you so I could apologize in person. You wouldn't return my calls or my texts. You left me no choice."

Her expression hardened before I could explain. *Shit.* I'd said something wrong.

"No choice? I left you no choice? That's rich," she spat out at me. "What about me and the fact that you neglected to tell me that you had a girlfriend the entire time you were"—she sucked in a breath, waving one hand in the air—"whatever it was you were trying to do with me. What was I, Frank? A conquest? A notch on your belt?"

Like the fool I so clearly was, I hadn't been prepared for this level of anger. I knew she'd be upset, but hadn't anticipated how deep that anger might run. The only way to counter her heightened emotions was to stay calm, keep my responses measured and even, and be honest. I had to be more honest that I'd ever been in my life.

"You were unexpected," I said, the words spilling straight from my heart. "I've never felt this way about anyone before. I know I messed up, okay? I should have told you about Shelby, but I couldn't."

"You *could* have, but you *didn't.*" She glared at me. "There's a difference. I didn't have a choice, but you did. You chose not to tell me, and I want to know why. Do you do this all the time? Is this some sort of sick MO for you? Is leading women on just a game?"

I shook my head, hating that she could think so little of me, but knowing deep down that I deserved it. I'd expected her to see me as the stand-up guy I had always tried to be, but when it came to Claudia, I hadn't acted like one.

"No. God, no. I've never done this before. Not one time. I swear it."

Her expression softened briefly before she hardened it again. She had the upper hand, and I needed to swing the pendulum in my favor somehow. I wouldn't give up this easily.

Her lips pressed into a firm line. "Why should I believe you?"

Hell, I didn't have a good answer to that question. Why would she believe anything I said to her? If I were in her shoes, I wouldn't believe me either.

"Because it's the truth." I reached across the desk for her hand, but she pulled it away, refusing to let me touch her.

"So you expect me to believe that in all the years you were with your girlfriend and not happy, you never wanted to cheat on her until I came into the picture?" Her accent thickened as she continued. "That's what you're telling me?"

My jaw tightened as I worked it. I didn't like what Claudia was insinuating or how she was thinking. "Yes. That's what I'm telling you. I'm not a cheater," I ground out, even though technically it was a lie. "Yes, I crossed an emotional line with you. And, hell yes, I wanted to kiss you every fucking time you were near me, but I didn't. And yes, Claudia, I do expect you to believe me."

I was frustrated, even though I knew I had no right. I had dug this hole I was in all on my own, but that didn't stop me from wanting this woman to send down a rope and help me climb out. Instead, it felt like she kept kicking me back down as soon as I neared the top.

Claudia crossed her arms over her chest and leaned back in her chair. "Why me? What makes me so special?"

Why her? Didn't she have any idea the kind of effect she had on me, the sheer pull that her existence held on my soul? *Fuck.* How could I put this connection into words so she'd understand? How did you explain the unexplainable?

I stared at my hands in my lap for a moment, digging deep for the right words to express the crazy feelings I'd had for this woman since I first laid eyes on her. Everything I came up with seemed stupid or crazy, but when I glanced up and found her unexpectedly looking at me with yearning in her eyes before she masked it, the words came easily.

"I've never had my world so shaken up from a single look before, okay? But that's what it felt like the moment I saw you. The very foundation that I stood on split and cracked in two. I knew I could never be the same again. It sounds cheesy as hell and like something Ryan would say, but I swear it's the truth, Claudia. Meeting you was like looking up at the stars and realizing there was an entire galaxy up there that you never knew existed. And then, every time you walked outside and looked up, it would be all you could see. And now, *you're* all I can see."

"Jesus, Frank," she said low, her voice breaking. "You can't run around saying things like that to a girl unless you mean it."

I stared into her warm brown eyes. "I mean it. I've never

meant anything more."

She swallowed and looked away for a moment, obviously trying to pull herself together. I prayed that meant she was trying to repair the cracks in her armor that I hoped I'd inflicted.

Her tone was stronger, but still a little shaky when she responded. "If I'm a galaxy, then what is your girlfriend?"

"I broke up with Shelby."

Claudia's mouth dropped open slightly before she closed it. "You did? When?"

"Last week."

"So you're single?" Her voice rose on the last word, and I bit back my smile.

"I am."

I HAVE QUESTIONS

Claudia

*H*OLY CRAP. FRANK wasn't only sitting in my office right now, but he had just dropped the most unexpected bomb in my lap.

He was single.

It was something I hadn't wanted to hope for since it seemed like wishing for the impossible. Plus, it was selfish to hope for someone else's relationship to end, even though I had wanted it to.

And now here he was, sitting across from me in all of his Frank Fisher glory, telling me that he was available and comparing me to the night sky.

I had to keep my legs crossed to stop myself from jumping into his lap and straddling him the way I'd done numerous times lately in my dreams. No, there were still a lot of unanswered questions I needed answers to, and unresolved feelings I needed to work through. This was an overload of information hitting me all at once, much like his voice mails had been.

"Say something," he said softly, his tone pleading.

I didn't know what to say or where to start. I was over-whelmed, my thoughts in a jumble, all mixed up and out of order. I couldn't have sorted them out in that moment if I tried.

"Can we talk about all of this later? Preferably not where I work," I said as I noticed my next appointment already waiting in the lobby.

"How about where I work instead? Tonight. Come by. It doesn't matter what time." When I didn't respond right away, he firmed his voice. "Tonight, Claudia. Come." It wasn't a request.

"We'll see." I tried to be strong, to resist, but he knew better. It was as though he could sense my vulnerability when it came to him and my newfound information about his relationship status.

Frank stood up, his muscular body seeming enormous in my tiny office. "If you don't show up, I'll come here every day until you do." He flashed that fabulous Fisher smile at me, the one that slayed women every night of the week, and my heart raced. "I'm not giving up."

Looking down, I swallowed my smile. "I still have questions."

"Bring 'em. Hell, make a list if you need to. I'll tell you anything you want to know."

"Anything?" I glanced up at him through my lashes, unable to stop the teasing tone that came out.

"Yes. After tonight, I don't want there to be anything between us. Except maybe some sheets," he said with a laugh. "But probably not even those."

As he turned and walked out of my office, I found myself staring at his ass and broad shoulders. He paused before he reached the front doors and glanced back, giving me a small smile.

Dammit, he knew I'd been watching him walk away.

I attempted to catch my breath as I headed to the lobby to greet my next appointment. Britney caught my eye through the glass wall of her office, practically bouncing in her seat with frustration. I held up a finger in her direction, telling her to wait, and then extended my hand to the customer waiting for me.

*

As soon as my next appointment left, Britney shot through my open door and closed it behind her before she plopped into my guest chair.

"Tell me everything. And don't leave out a single detail."

After I filled her in, she insisted she'd be going to Sam's with me that night. "To make sure you don't wimp out," she said.

When she confessed that Ryan had texted her and that she had set up the meeting today for Frank, I could only pretend to be mad for so long when I wasn't. At all. I was more shocked at how good she was at keeping me in the dark, pretending through breakfast and our whole commute to work that nothing out of the ordinary would be happening later that day. She was a skilled liar, and I'd never even known it.

"I wouldn't have been able to keep it up for very long. I only had to last about twelve hours, just so you know. If it was any longer, I would have caved," she admitted with a grin as she stood up to head back to her office, and I believed her.

As I sat at my desk pretending to work for the last hour of

the day, I was a mess inside, my emotions running in high gear. I couldn't believe that Frank had actually broken up with his girlfriend. But why had he done it? Why now? Was I part of the reason? And could I live with myself if I was? What did this mean for us? Did he want there to be an us?

The second we walked through our front door at home, Britney grabbed a pen and one of our bank notepads that she'd accidentally on purpose brought home. "I'll help you write the list."

Confused, I squinted at her. Had I somehow missed a portion of our conversation?

"The list?"

"Of all the things we want to know," she said matter-of-factly.

Then it dawned on me. "Oh, the list of questions for Frank."

"What other list would there be?"

"Groceries?" I said, trying not to grin.

She laughed and waved her phone toward me. "Why would I make a grocery list when we shop from our app?"

I hadn't really considered making a list, even after Frank had suggested it. He'd probably been kidding when he mentioned it, but it might be a good idea. It would be way too easy to be distracted and forget what I wanted to ask once we were together at the bar. Plus, my mind tended to wander, and I could jump from topic to topic without stopping to breathe. A list would be a good idea, a smart way to keep me on track.

"Anyway, I need to take a shower," I told her. "I'll think about my questions while I'm in there."

I thought for a second that Britney might suggest writing

the list together while I showered, and was grateful when she agreed to wait and headed into her room.

∗

"YOU READY FOR this?" Britney asked with a smile that brightened her whole face as we walked toward the entrance to Sam's. "I feel like we haven't been here in years."

I rolled my eyes. "It's been two weeks. Not even that long."

"I know, but I love it here."

"You just love looking at Ryan," I said, calling her out, and she waggled her eyebrows.

"Can't blame a girl for having a fish wish," she said as she threw open the door and held it for me.

I scanned the room, searching for Frank in the sea of people. Knowing that he usually hung out in the back office, I was a little surprised when I saw him behind the bar, mixing a drink. His body language looked more confident than usual, his presence more commanding.

"Claudia!" Nick and Ryan both shouted at the same time.

When everyone in the bar turned their heads to look at me, my entire face flamed. I prayed my cheeks weren't anywhere near as red as they felt.

Frank's head shot up, his gorgeous green eyes meeting mine with a possessiveness I'd never seen from him before. Trying to keep my cheeks a normal color tonight was a moot point. If he looked at me like that all night, I'd probably spontaneously combust at some point. My entire body would go up in flames with the heat of that stare, and there wouldn't be a damn thing I could do to stop it.

Britney nudged my shoulder with hers. "I'll be at the bar making googly eyes at Ryan. Have fun with Frank. And don't forget about the list." She hurried over and grabbed the only available seat at the bar. Luckily for her, it was between a pair of good-looking guys.

Thank God she mentioned the list. I'd already forgotten all about it. *Questions? What questions?* This was exactly why I needed to write everything down. Frank and his sexy green eyes were more than a little distracting.

Not to mention the way he was currently carrying himself as he stalked toward me. This was a man on a mission. And from the look of him, I was said mission.

"You look beautiful. Thank you for coming." He leaned down and pressed a kiss to my temple before placing his hand on the small of my back, leading me away from the bar and toward the tables.

A few whispers swirled in our wake, but I drowned them out with the mantra I was repeating in my head. *Answers first, answers first, answers first.*

A reserved sign held the table that Frank and I had sat at before, and he steered me toward it. He pulled out a chair for me and motioned for me to sit. As I situated myself, I looked around and frowned, realizing that it was a little more crowded than I would have liked. The conversation we needed to have was a private one, and there was no privacy here.

As if reading my mind, Frank popped back up from his chair and extended his hand. "Let's go in the office. Everyone will hear us out here, and I'm not into discussing my personal life in public."

Once inside the office and behind the closed door, I let out a small breath of relief. "This is much better."

"Really?"

"Absolutely."

He indicated I should sit in his guest chair, then dragged his own chair from around the desk and placed it next to mine. After turning it to face me, he sat down and ran a hand through his hair with a sigh.

"Good. There was no way we could have this conversation out there. I'm sorry. I didn't realize it would be so crowded tonight. Mondays are usually a lot slower."

"It's okay. Crowded is good." I gave him a small smile. "For business, I mean."

"I knew what you meant," he said, sounding as if he was assuring me.

Frank seemed to sense my nervousness, although I wasn't sure why I was the nervous one. I wasn't the one who had done anything wrong. Maybe I was apprehensive for what was to come, or what was at stake. If I didn't like the things that Frank had to say, then I wouldn't be able to entertain the idea of dating him. But if it was the opposite . . .

"Claudia, I want to get right into it. We've wasted enough time, and I don't want to waste any more."

I swallowed around the small lump in my throat. "Okay. Hold on." I leaned to one side and pulled the folded piece of paper from my back pocket.

Frank laughed. "You actually made a list?"

"I had to," I said honestly.

"Why did you have to?"

"I was afraid I might forget something."

He smiled again. "Okay. But first, I need you to know

how sorry I am. I know I've said it on your voice mail and in text messages a thousand times, but I haven't said it enough to you in person. I am so sorry for everything. I'm sorry I lied, and I have no excuse that would ever be good enough for you, but I hope that you understand. Or maybe you will after tonight."

"That's why we're here, right?" I softened my tone. "To see if I can understand why you lied to me?"

He shifted in his seat, clearly uncomfortable. Frank obviously didn't like the idea of my possibly not being able to understand or forgive him, but he'd accept my decision if it went down that way. "Should we have a rapid-fire question round, or . . ." He paused as he waited for me to respond.

"I can just go down the list, if you don't mind. Start at the top?" I suddenly felt a little foolish for not only having a list, but for wanting to read from it like a child who couldn't simply speak from her heart.

Again, Frank seemed to be clearly in tune with my emotions. He reached for my hand. "Ask me anything. Ask me everything. I'll tell you whatever you want to know." He brought my hand to his lips and pressed a soft kiss on my knuckles. "I like that you have a list."

"You do?" I asked, hating that I sounded a little breathless.

"I do." He cleared his throat and released my hand, giving me my space. "I'm ready. Ask away."

And just like that, he'd eased any potential tension I had previously had. He'd calmed me down, leaving me ready to grill him until I had every answer that I needed.

"Why did you lie to me?"

A breath whooshed out of Frank like I'd sucker-punched

him. He probably hadn't expected such a hardball question right off the bat, but I needed to know. Frank hadn't owed me anything when we first met, so telling me that he had a girlfriend shouldn't have been that big of a deal. But for some reason, he had turned it into one, and I wanted to know why.

Firming his lips, he looked me straight in the eye. "Meeting you wasn't something I ever expected. The first time I saw you, I was completely shaken up from the inside out, but also calmer than I'd ever been before. It was a complete contradiction of emotions, and before I knew it, I was bringing you drinks and doing damn near anything I could to get close to you."

My gaze dropped to those gorgeous lips of his, which twisted into a half smile as he continued.

"I wanted to talk to you. I needed to be near you. I'd never felt that way about anyone, like I was drawn to them. Every time I looked in your eyes, I felt like I was home. I feel a pull when it comes to you that I can't explain, even though the logical part of me really wants to be able to."

He drew in a breath. "Each time I was with you, or saw you, I wanted more. I should have told you about Shelby, but telling you meant that you'd walk away. If you knew I had a girlfriend, you'd never talk to me again, and I couldn't stand the thought of that. So I kept quiet. You deserved the truth, but I was too fucking scared to tell you. That's why I lied. Because I knew you'd leave."

It was barely audible, but his voice cracked when he mentioned my leaving, and that little vulnerability from him caused my eyes to instantly fill.

But he was right. I would have left, and I wouldn't have

looked back. I would have chalked Frank Fisher up to being just another LA douchebag with no morals.

"Were you ever going to tell me?"

He nodded. "I was. I knew I couldn't keep lying to you, but the more time we spent together, the deeper I fell. For you, and into the lie. I wanted to tell you, but I didn't know how."

"So, when were you going to? There was never going to be a good time. What was your plan? Eventually, I was going to wonder why you weren't making a move on me," I said, remembering how he'd avoided kissing me at the car that night after walking me out, and how confused and insecure it had made me feel.

Frank sighed. "I know, and I thought about that a lot too. But I didn't have a plan. Like I said before, I didn't plan on meeting someone like you. I'd been unhappy for so long that I'd just sort of accepted it. It's hard to explain, but I felt like all my decisions about my future had already been made, and all that was left was for me to follow through. Obligation and guilt made me feel powerless in my own life, and I hated being in that position, but didn't know how to change it."

It was clear that I could keep pushing Frank about when exactly he was going to tell me about Shelby, but I'd probably never get a definitive answer. Not because he didn't want to give me one, but because he simply didn't know when he would have told me, or how. We were guessing right now after the fact, playing a game of what-if. We could run in circles around the question all night, or I could choose to move on.

"You said that you felt powerless about your life and your future. What changed?"

"You," he said, his gaze boring into mine. "You made me

want more. You woke me up. I didn't even realize that I'd been sleepwalking through my life until you came and opened my eyes. You made me feel, Claudia. I haven't felt anything for so long, and I didn't even realize it," he explained with passion in his voice.

I glanced at my list and squirmed in my seat before meeting his eyes again. "Did you break up with her because of me?"

Frank shook his head. "No. Not *because* of you. So much was already wrong and broken, and I knew that I didn't want to fix it. I realized that I was wasting time living a life I didn't want anymore. Even if you hadn't come along, we would have eventually ended. But I'd been doing both myself and Shelby a huge disservice by staying as long as I did because of the promise I'd made to her dad."

"Did she know about the promise?"

"She had no idea."

"I figured." I'd been wondering, and had assumed there was no way she could have known. If it had been me in that situation, I wouldn't have wanted any man to stay because of a promise they'd made.

Frank tilted his head, studying me. "How so?"

"It's just that most women want to be loved. We want to be your choice, not your obligation. We don't want to be the person you settle for; we want to be the person you can't live without. I would never want the man I loved to stay with me if he didn't love me back, no matter how noble the reason."

Frank said nothing for a moment. Since I wasn't sure what was running through his head, I asked another question, one that wasn't on my list.

"Have you talked to her since your breakup?" Since I'd

learned they weren't together anymore, I'd wondered if this woman wanted to stay in his life as friends. I wasn't sure how that would make me feel.

He looked away and then dropped his head, his voice sad. "No. She said she doesn't want to talk to me."

"Are you okay with that?"

Shelby had been a part of his life for a really long time. I wasn't sure anyone could come out of a long-term relationship like that unscathed, regardless of who ended things. What if her cutting him off completely made Frank realize that he wanted her back?

"I'm fine with it. It makes things easier, and I think it's better for both of us in the long run. But I hate that I hurt her," he said slowly, "that I let it go on for so long."

"You don't miss her?"

His eyes met mine as his jaw flexed. "I don't. Is that awful?"

I shrugged. "I just think it means you did the right thing."

"That's what I think it means too." He offered me a slight smile before it faded.

"Does she know about me?"

His shoulders squared. "No."

It was my turn to stay quiet as my thoughts swirled.

"Does that upset you?" he asked. "Do you think I should have told her I met someone?"

"God, no." The words tumbled out. "I just wondered."

"The breakup wasn't about you, Claudia. I wasn't breaking up with her *for* you," he said, and I knew that, so why did those words feel like a punch in the gut? "If I would have mentioned you, that's all Shelby would have heard. She would've been convinced that I was breaking up with her for another woman, instead of all the other reasons why it was really happening. I didn't want that."

"You're right. She would have." It was true. If my boyfriend gave me a list of twenty reasons why he was dumping me, and another woman was number twenty on that list, it would be the only thing I would focus on.

"And this is why women are crazy," he said with a laugh.

Pretending to be offended, I said, "Because guys are assholes," but my tone was more serious than I'd intended, and he stopped laughing.

"Present company excluded?"

"Yet to be determined," I said, and found myself smiling.

As if my smile gave him permission to relax, Frank's chest heaved and his expression softened. "What other questions are on your list?"

"So impatient," I teased.

His green eyes seemed to darken. "Do you know how long I've waited to kiss you?"

I found myself staring at his beautiful mouth, wondering how his lips would taste and feel. I'd imagined kissing Frank more times than I could count. "You're pretty confident on the whole kissing thing for a guy I haven't forgiven yet."

"What can I say?" He gave me a grin that turned my bones to liquid. "I'm hopeful."

Stupid charming Frank Fisher. I was hopeful too, but I still needed a few more questions answered before I could be sure.

"I'm almost done," I said, waving my list at him, "but I have to ask you these first."

"Ask."

"Obviously, I have feelings for you, or I wouldn't be here right now," I admitted. "But I'm a little worried."

"About what, exactly?"

"I—" I stopped and sucked in a deep breath, trying to figure out how to word my fears. "I'm worried that if we start dating and you become unhappy, that I won't know because you won't tell me. That you'll pretend everything is okay when you're really dying inside."

His Adam's apple bobbed and his eyebrows pinched together. "All I can tell you is that I don't want to ever live like that again. It wasn't fun, and it didn't feel good."

"But how do I know you won't fall into that habit? Feel like you somehow owe me to stay together?"

"I can't imagine growing tired of you, Claudia, or ever wanting out."

I grimaced at that. Everyone was happy at the beginning of a relationship.

He held up a hand. "Just hear me out. I don't want to go backward. I really don't ever want to be in the position that I was just in ever again. I refuse to live my life like that anymore. I know these are just words, but they're all I have. Trust takes time to build, and I want to put in the work with you. And for the record, I think Shelby knew I wasn't happy, but was afraid to rock a sinking boat. If I know anything about you, it's that you'll never be afraid to put me on the spot and toss my ass right off the boat, if need be."

A laugh escaped as I pictured myself hurling Frank off a small fishing boat and into the water. "You're right. If I thought something was wrong, I'd ask you straight out. But you also have to know that I'd believe the answer you gave me, so you can't lie to me about it."

"I know. And I don't ever want to." He clasped the arms of his chair tightly and leaned toward me. "Listen, I know we started off on a rocky foundation and that's all my fault. But if you're okay with it, I'd like to start over. Start fresh."

"How?"

"I'd like to take you on an actual date, for starters." His confident smile lit up the whole room. "But I'm kissing you first."

"Wh-what?" I stumbled on the words. "I haven't even said that I forgive you yet."

He released the arms of his chair and leaned in close, his mouth mere inches from mine. "Do you forgive me?"

When I couldn't respond, he leaned even closer, closing the space between us. His breath was warm and smelled of cinnamon as it feathered across my lips. My heart thundered inside my chest with a victory cry I hadn't yet approved.

"Say you forgive me, Claudia," he whispered, and my breath caught in my throat. "Say it."

I wanted him so much, I was nearly bursting out of my skin, but didn't want to give in so easily. "You're not the boss of me."

Frank laughed, reaching out to clasp the back of my neck, holding me in place. "I might be the boss a little bit." His fingers tangled in my hair, and his gaze dropped to my lips as he growled my name.

And that was all it took. I caved.

"I forgive y—"

My words died on my lips as his mouth crushed against

mine. I opened to him, wanting to feel his tongue, longing to taste every inch of him. He kissed me like he owned me, like I belonged to him, like he'd done it a hundred times before, and I let him. There was no way in hell I planned on stopping what was easily the most passionate kiss of my life.

This was definitely worth waiting for.

Maybe Frank was the boss of me after all.

SHE OWNS ME

Frank

THE SECOND MY mouth found Claudia's, it went to work claiming her. Her soft lips belonged to me. The tongue she darted in and out of my mouth also belonged to me. The sweet moan that escaped from within her as we kissed belonged to me as well.

She stood up quickly and without warning, never breaking our kiss as she brought me with her, her hands pulling at my hair, tugging me closer. Her tits pressed against my chest, her body flush with mine as she ground her hips into me.

I was half certain she didn't even realize that she was doing it, but it was driving me fucking crazy. I'd waited so long to have any part of Claudia, and now I wanted it all. I wanted to rip every piece of clothing from her body and take her right here on my fucking desk at work, but I couldn't do that to her.

At least, not tonight. Maybe tomorrow.

Breaking the kiss took all of my self-control; it was last thing I wanted to do. I pulled away from her slowly and admired the flush of her face, the way her hands gripped me tightly, not wanting me to stop, and the way her chest heaved in and out. I'd done that to my girl, made her breathless.

"Can we go on that date now?" I asked.

Her lips widened into a smile. "Now?"

"I don't want to waste any more time, Claudia. I want to be with you, and I plan on starting right this very minute if you'll have me." I held out my hand and waited for her to take it.

I'd already planned to take her to Malibu for dinner, followed by a walk along the beach. The optimist in me had hoped that tonight would end well. I hadn't considered any other outcome, hadn't even wanted to.

Claudia accepted my hand and squeezed tight. "Who knew you were so bossy?"

"There's a lot we don't know about each other, but I plan on finding out." I leaned down and pressed a kiss to those gorgeous lips. *My lips.*

"Are we taking your motorcycle?" she asked before I pulled the office door open.

"Is that okay? I can borrow Ryan's car instead," I offered, knowing that he would be fine with it.

She shook her head. "I'm excited to ride on your bike. I get a helmet, right?"

"Yep. I bought you one earlier today," I said with a smug grin, and she swatted my shoulder.

"You bought me a helmet? You really were quite presumptuous, Mr. Fisher."

"Told you I was hopeful."

I left out the fact that I'd also bought a new mattress set and had it delivered. I didn't want Claudia to feel insecure or uncomfortable when I finally had her in my space. I wanted everything to be perfect for that night, and a bed I used to share with my ex-girlfriend was anything but.

When I opened the door, Ryan and Nick both turned around and focused on our clasped hands.

"Thank the fucking Lord," Nick shouted. "Who wants a round on me?"

The bar erupted into cheers as Ryan walked toward us. "So you two worked it out?"

I glanced at Claudia, waiting for her approval, and she nodded. "I'm still working on it. I'm going to buy her forgiveness in the form of seafood, and then I'll be back for closing, okay?"

Ryan gave me a huge grin. "Don't come back, come back married, I don't care. Just have a good time. You both deserve it. I'm really happy for you guys."

His happiness for me was so damn genuine, and I was so appreciative, that it never occurred to me to want to kill him when he took Claudia into his arms and gave her a hug. He whispered something in her ear that I couldn't hear, but planned to ask her about later.

"I'll be back." I clasped his shoulder briefly before walking through a congratulatory crowd, who had no idea what they were congratulating us for.

"One sec."

Claudia squeezed my arm and stepped away from me, headed for Britney, who was sitting at the bar surrounded by guys. The two talked quickly, hugged, and then my girl was back at my side before I knew it. We walked outside and into the warm night air.

It felt right, having this woman on my arm. Even though part of me felt like I didn't deserve to be this happy, the rest of me clamored for every ounce of it. Genuine happiness had eluded me for so many years, I wanted to drown in a pool of it and never come up for air. I had been starving—all my own doing, of course, but still starving nonetheless.

We stopped at my bike, and I pulled out the new helmet for Claudia.

"What's the matter?" she asked, her beautiful face frowning with concern.

How had she so easily read my mind?

"Just beating myself up a little bit," I admitted honestly.

She caressed my cheek, her finger rubbing the scruff along my jaw. "What for?"

I set the helmet on the seat of the bike and took her hands in mine, then fell into her soft brown eyes. "I was thinking that maybe I don't deserve to be this happy after what I did to Shelby. That I don't deserve to feel this good. And I sure as hell don't deserve you or your forgiveness." As the words spilled from my lips, the truth of them filled me up inside. It felt really fucking good to say what I meant and to speak without holding back.

"Oh, Frank." She rose to her tiptoes and planted a kiss on my lips that I never wanted to end. "You can't undo what's already been done. There's no point wasting energy on the things you can't change. The past is over, but the future is wide open. You deserve to be happy as much as anyone."

I pulled Claudia against me, needing the physical comfort she provided. Her words struck a chord with me, resonated, felt right. "You're amazing, you know that? Thank you for giving me a chance to make this right."

She huffed against my chest. "I knew that if I didn't, I'd regret it."

"Yeah?"

"I was having a really hard time getting over you," she said, looking up at me through her eyelashes. "I couldn't stop thinking about you, no matter how hard I tried. I never believed in second chances before. I never thought that people deserved them, but I was wrong. No one's perfect. We all make mistakes. We all do shitty things sometimes. But the most important thing is that we learn and grow from them. You taught me that," she said with a soft smile that I loved.

"I won't let you down," I promised, meaning every word.

"You don't think less of me, right?"

Surprised, I pulled back. "Less of you? For what?"

"For forgiving you," she said softly, not meeting my eyes. "You don't think I'm a doormat, do you, someone you can walk all over? Maybe I should have stood my ground longer, or fought against you harder."

I hated how sad and unsure of herself she sounded, like she was letting herself down in some way, and I was the cause for it. Running my thumb down her cheek, I stopped at her chin and tilted her face up to meet mine.

"Claudia, the last thing in the world I would ever consider you is a doormat. I'm thankful that you gave me a second chance, but I don't think less of you for it. Hell, I want to worship you even more because of it." Little did she know, I was willing to fall at her damn feet if she wanted me to. "I completely understand what you're saying, but I'm never going to tell you that you should have stood your ground longer or pushed me away harder. Because I didn't want that. I never wanted that. I would have understood if you did, but I wouldn't have given up. I wouldn't have stopped fighting for this chance to be with you. And in the end, we'd be right where we are now, going on our first date."

"You would have fought for me?" she asked so softly I almost didn't hear her.

"I am fighting for you. But, yes, I would have fought until you gave in. I wouldn't have stopped, Claudia, I can promise you that." And I meant every word. One of these days, she had to believe that I wasn't just saying nice things to get another chance with her.

"Frank . . ." She huffed out a small breath. "It's like every woman's fantasy. We all want to be fought for. Hell, we all want to feel like we're *worth* fighting for."

"You *are* worth fighting for. That's why we're here. We always would have ended up here."

She gave me a curious look. "So, the end result would still be the same, no matter what I would have done? Is that what you're telling me?"

"Damn straight, that's what I'm telling you."

I smiled before picking her up and swinging her around. The sound of her giggle thrilled me, making me want to keep doing it. When she begged me to stop, I placed her gently on her feet and extended my hand.

"Hi, I'm Frank. I own this bar here, and I think I started falling for you the second I saw you. I really hope you're single, because I'd like to take you out to dinner."

Her cheeks reddened, but she took my hand and gave it a firm shake. "I'm Claudia, and it's your lucky night. I just happen to be single, and my night's wide open."

"Not for long." I pressed my lips to hers, claiming her again. I didn't want there to be any question as to whom those lips belonged to.

I helped her with her helmet, gave her my jacket to wear, and drove us down the Pacific Coast Highway to my favorite seafood restaurant in Malibu. Claudia gripped my waist the entire ride, pressing her body against my back, and I had to keep my excitement in check.

Focus on the road.

The restaurant was perfect, even though it was too dark to see the water. Claudia told me she'd never been here before, and I made a mental note to bring her back when she could appreciate the view.

I had forgotten how fun it was to take a person somewhere that was new to them. Claudia was appreciative and excited, her face lighting up as she took in every detail. It made me want to take her to every single place in Los Angeles that she'd never been to before, just to see her face as she experienced it. She made me feel young and alive, two things that I hadn't felt in a long time. And when we flipped through our menus and came up with the exact same appetizer and dinner selections, I took it as another sign that I had done the right thing. Not that I needed any more signs, but still.

"We can't order the same meals," she insisted, pinning me with her stare.

"Why not?" The reason didn't matter. I'd do whatever she asked me to.

"Because I want to try whatever you get. Don't worry, I'll share mine with you. But that's why we need different things, so we can eat more," she said with an excited smile, and I agreed.

I couldn't remember the last time I laughed so much, or

enjoyed someone's company as much as I genuinely enjoyed hers. Being with Claudia was effortless and comfortable.

∗

AFTER EATING WAY more than I should have, I patted my stomach. "Probably not going to be able to fit you on the bike now with this belly."

Claudia clutched her own stomach and groaned. "Why'd you let me order so much food?"

"Oh, that's how this is going to go, huh?" I laughed.

"I'm so full."

"I know."

"Come on." I pulled her chair back to help her out after paying the bill. She stood up slowly, rubbing her nonexistent pot belly.

We walked outside, our arms around each other. As I led her toward the bike, she asked, "Is the date over already?"

I wanted to take her to my favorite beach spot, but it was late. The coastal breeze had kicked in, cooling the night air.

I stopped and turned to face her. "I'd love for the night to never end, but it's late and it's cold, and I'm a gentleman." I said the last part with a small laugh. "As much as I don't want to, I'm going to take you home."

Her bottom lip jutted out in a pout that I found adorable and far too inviting. I leaned down, taking her lip between my teeth and biting gently before sucking it into my mouth. She moaned, gluing her body to mine as I deepened the kiss and fisted her hair. There was something about Claudia's long, dark hair that made me always want to get tangled up in it.

My tongue explored her mouth, loving the taste of her, wanting more. I moved to her neck, licking the parts of her I'd yet to explore, and she moaned softly. If she didn't stop making those noises, I was going to rip off all her clothes and take her in the damn restaurant parking lot. This was one of those moments I wished I had a car rather than a motorcycle.

The feel of her nails digging into my back both fueled my need for her and crashed me back to reality. I pulled away, panting. "We have to stop."

Her eyes were wild, her lips swollen and wet. I had to look anywhere but at her, or I'd never calm down.

She put a hand to her chest, her breathing choppy and fast. "Good God, Frank."

I swallowed hard and tried to pull myself together. "I don't have much self-control when it comes to you," I admitted, showing her my weakness.

"I beg to differ." She lifted one brow in disbelief.

"I want you. I've dreamed about this moment, but it was never like this."

I glanced around us at the nearly empty parking lot and the orange glow of the streetlights. Then I closed the space between us, not wanting her to mistake my meaning, or my desire for her.

"Our first time isn't happening in a parking lot. I don't care if it is my favorite restaurant." I took her hand and kissed it, like I always seemed to do with her. "Plus, it's only our first date. I don't think sex is supposed to happen until date three." I gave her a cocky grin, and she laughed.

"Who made up that stupid rule, anyway?"

"I think you women did."

She shook her head. "That's definitely something a man would do." Mimicking a man's voice, she said, "It's been three whole dates. I've paid my dues, put in enough time. I'll die if I go one more date without having sex."

"We definitely start dying if we have to go longer than three dates," I said jokingly, and she shook her head in mock disgust. "Honestly, though, I don't care if it's on date three or date fifty-three. I'll wait however long you want."

Her eyes widened. "You mean that?"

She was so serious, I almost felt bad for women for having to deal with us men and our excuses for our penises. But then I remembered that women were a little crazy, so I considered us even.

"Of course I do."

"Such a gentleman."

"I am, but my dick's another story. He might start crying if we really wait until date fifty-three."

Claudia grinned up at me. "Aw, I wouldn't want to make your dick cry. No longer than date fifty, for sure." She patted my chest and I grabbed her hand, keeping her close.

"I'd wait forever if you wanted me to. I don't want that part to be a joke. I mean it, okay? We don't have to rush anything," I said sincerely.

She tugged her hand from mine and wrapped her arms around my neck, pulling me down to her waiting lips. "Thank you," she whispered before kissing me.

I soaked in the perfection of the moment, wondering if it would always be this good.

"I should probably get back to the bar and close up. If Ryan even looks at the books, I'll be fixing that mess for days."

She giggled as she nodded. "I can see that."

"Come on. I'll take you home," I said and reached for her hand.

When we got to my bike, she grabbed her helmet and tugged it on, fastening the chin strap as she asked, "Do you know where I live?"

"No."

It was hard to hear anything when you were on the bike other than the roar of the engine and the machine cutting through the wind, and asking her for directions while we rode would be close to impossible. So I pulled out my phone and opened the map application, then handed it to her so she could enter her address. When the directions loaded, I made sure her helmet was fastened securely and enjoyed the feel of her body pressed tightly against my back as we headed back down the Pacific Coast Highway and toward her apartment.

While Claudia and Britney technically lived in Venice Beach, they were right on the border of Marina del Rey. I'd had no idea how close she lived to me this entire time. I could have walked over to her apartment every night if I wanted to. It was probably a good thing I hadn't known before now.

I pulled the bike to a stop and waited. Claudia maneuvered her leg around my back and hopped off before I turned off the bike and followed. After removing her helmet, she shook out her long, dark hair and ran her fingers through it with a grimace.

"It's a little tangled."

"Sorry about that."

"It's not your fault," she said, then gave me a teasing look. "Well, maybe technically it is."

"Is that so?" I wrapped my arms around her and pulled her close. "Thank you for coming tonight."

"Thank you for dinner."

"I had a really good time."

"I did too."

Pressing my lips to hers, I thrilled at the feel of her melting against me as her mouth opened. The world stopped every time we kissed. All other sounds except the ones coming from her disappeared. Nothing else mattered except this moment, and I never wanted it to end.

As soon as the thought entered my mind, she broke the kiss. "You should probably go before I try to lure you inside."

My body instantly reacted, and I tried like hell to ignore it. "That's not really a good way to get me to go."

"I know, I know." She grinned. "Forget I said it."

"Not a chance. But you're right, I should go. I'll see you tomorrow."

Her eyebrows flew up. "Tomorrow?"

"Yeah. For date two."

"Oh." She rolled her eyes. "You're just trying to get to date three quicker."

I bit back my grin, playing dumb. "What happens on date three?"

"No idea," she said, laughing as she smacked my arm. "I know what happens on date fifty, but I think date three is fairly uneventful."

"Good night, Claudia." I dropped a kiss on her head before giving her one more on the mouth. God, those lips were going to be the death of me.

"Good night, Frank," she said before heading toward the

door of her building.

I watched to make sure she got in safely, but before she reached the door, she turned around and ran back to me. Her arms looped around my neck as she pulled my mouth to hers.

"I just needed one more kiss."

That kiss lasted even longer than the one before, leaving me breathless as I watched her until she disappeared through the doors of her building.

Shaking my head, I couldn't remember ever feeling happier and more content. I was one lucky son of a bitch.

No offense, Mom.

THE THIRD DATE

Claudia

FRANK CALLED AND texted me often when we weren't together. He was sweet, attentive, and caring.

Long gone were the days when I thought Frank Fisher was a shy, reserved guy who was afraid to make a move on me. In his place was a man who was in touch with his emotional side and not afraid to show it. He was confident in what he wanted, and was one hell of a man's man. The many facets of his personality were almost as hot as he was.

Coordinating our schedules so I could spend time with Frank had never even occurred to me. I could have smacked myself for not considering how difficult it might be to date someone who owned a bar until I was knee-deep in it. Not that I would have changed a thing, but I might have been more mentally prepared for it. Frank worked long hours and spent the majority of his time at Sam's, which I understood completely, but it meant I spent a lot of time there as well.

He came over to my place on Thursdays, his only evening off, but fell asleep as soon as his head hit my lap on the couch. Instead of waking him, I let him sleep while Britney and I watched our TV shows around his snores. He apologized profusely once he woke up, but I assured him there was nothing to apologize for. The man worked hard, and if he wanted to sleep on my lap every night of the week, I'd gladly let him.

If I hadn't been spending so many of my evenings at the bar, then I wouldn't have met Jess as soon as I did. I was beyond thankful that Nick's girlfriend was nice and welcomed me with open arms.

"I'm so happy to meet you," Jess had said, her eyes bright. "And thank you for making Frank smile again. I've never seen him so happy. But then again, I haven't known him very long, so maybe I'm not the best reference," she said with a laugh, and I liked her instantly. She was career-driven, motivated, and smart. And she adored Nick just as much as he adored her.

We spent a lot of time together while our guys worked, and she filled me in on her history with Nick. Amazed, I asked her no less than ten times if she was joking, or maybe making up parts of their story, and she assured me that she wasn't. I wouldn't have believed it if I'd heard it through the grapevine, would have been sure that the truth must have gotten lost somewhere in translation like a bad game of telephone. Nick and Jess's story was insane, but in the end, it only proved to strengthen my belief in the power of love and what it was capable of.

"Do you think you two will get married?" I'd asked her as we'd hung out at the bar one evening. I had never met a couple, regardless of age, who had overcome the number of roadblocks to their relationship that they had.

"Without a doubt," Jess said with a smile. "But not any-time soon."

I smiled back at her, loving her practicality and her heart.

"Not in a rush?"

"I know I want to spend the rest of my life with Nick, but I don't want to get married yet. A piece of paper doesn't change how I feel about him. And I'm not ready for kids, so the whole wedding thing can wait, as far as I'm concerned."

I laughed. "You're so not a typical girl."

"Tell me about it," she said with a grin, lifting her glass in a salute.

I tapped my glass to hers, still processing all that she had told me. After taking a sip, I said, "I still can't believe everything you two went through. That must have been really hard."

"It was at the time. I was a mess. You and Frank don't have an easy story either, you know. Maybe all the drama is some sort of prerequisite to landing a Fisher brother."

I hadn't thought about it that way before, and would have never considered comparing my story to Jess's, but maybe she was right.

"They better be worth it." My gaze slipped to Frank pouring a beer, and his eyes instantly darted up to meet mine from across the room as if he had sensed me staring.

Jess laughed as she sipped her No Bad Days cocktail. "You know as well as I do that they are."

I couldn't have agreed more.

*

DATE NUMBER TWO hadn't happened the night after date number one like Frank had planned since he couldn't get away from the bar for very long. The nights we spent together at the bar didn't count as real dates, he'd said, so our next official date had to wait.

With those rules in place, the second date had actually been over a week later, a daytime date on a Saturday morning before he went to work. We rode out to his favorite spot in Malibu and spent hours lying in the sand, talking, eating from the picnic basket he had packed, and making out. Being with him excited me so much, I felt like a teenager again.

"You live in Marina del Rey and you work in Santa Monica," I said to Frank as I lay back in his lap, sunlight soaking into my skin as he ran his fingers through my hair. "Why do you come all the way out to Malibu to go to the beach? You realize this makes no sense, don't you?" Malibu was gorgeous, but it wasn't the easiest place to get to with all the traffic.

He looked around us, and I followed his gaze to the surfers catching waves and the paddleboarders keeping their distance. Then he shrugged, brushing his fingers through my hair like he'd been doing for the last hour.

"I've just always liked it here. It's a little less crowded. The waves are nicer, and if you time it right, you can watch the dolphins."

I popped up. "Dolphins?"

"Every morning and every evening. They're incredible."

"And the waves." Curious, I squinted at him. "Do you surf and I didn't know?"

"Yeah. I can't get my board on my bike, though, so I haven't surfed here in a while."

Crap. Imagining Frank on a surfboard, all wet and muscular paddling in the water, took my fantasies to a whole other level. I leaned back into his lap and grabbed his hand, moving it back onto my head.

"Now who's the bossy one?" he asked, teasing me, but started playing with my hair again almost instantly.

"What can I say?" I sighed as my eyes fell closed. "I like the way your man hands feel in my hair."

*

TONIGHT WAS OFFICIALLY our third date, even though we'd hung out together way more than three times, and over two weeks had passed since our first date. I had no idea where we were going or what we were doing, but Frank had said to dress casual.

I still hadn't seen his place since I left the bar before it closed during the week, and he had insisted that I wasn't allowed to come over for the first time at four in the morning on the weekends. No matter how hard I begged, he refused to give in.

"Are you ready for tonight?" Britney raised her freshly threaded eyebrows at me, and I scrunched up my face in response.

"What's tonight, exactly?"

She stomped her foot and pointed at me. "Don't play coy with me, young lady. Everyone knows that date number three is the sex date. Not that the two of you can count for shit, but according to your boyfriend, tonight is it."

My cheeks burned when Britney called Frank my boyfriend. Our relationship was still new, but I couldn't hide how I reacted to that word, or how it sparked a whole slew of butterflies to take flight in my stomach.

"Who's everyone?" I asked, trying to play it off like I wasn't nervous as hell.

"Don't act like you don't know this."

"I have no idea what you're talking about." I tried to hide the smile that wanted to sneak out, but teasing Britney was too much fun.

"Fine. Play dumb. Answer me this then. You're wearing a matching bra and underwear, right? True or false."

I wanted to crawl into a hole and hide, so I threw a towel at her instead of answering.

"Answer the question," she demanded, already knowing my answer.

"Maybe?" I shrugged.

Glaring at me, Britney folded her arms. "True. Or. False."

"True," I admitted, thinking about the matching red lace set I was wearing under my ripped jeans and off-the-shoulder black top. My hair hung down my back with long loose curls only at the ends, a style that I knew drove Frank crazy.

"Totally having sex. Not to mention the sex hair."

Our apartment's intercom buzzed, and I was thankful for the interruption. The very idea of my potential first time with Frank was nerve-racking enough; I didn't need Britney's help freaking out about it. Even if I wanted it desperately, had planned for it, and fantasized about it constantly.

"Who is it?" Britney sang into the intercom.

Frank's voice boomed through the speaker. "Delivery!" He didn't even have to be in the room, and his charisma still filled the space.

"Ooh, I hope it's the sex toys and porn we ordered," she called out before hitting the button to let him in.

Mortified, I shook my head. "Really, Britney?"

She cracked up until Frank walked through the door, then she stopped. "Why are all you Fisher brothers so damn hot? It's not fair to the rest of the male population, you know."

"Take it up with my mother," he said with a wink. "I'm pretty sure it's her fault."

I died inside as I took him in, realizing that we had unintentionally matched. Again. He was wearing faded blue jeans and a black button-down shirt that fit him snug around his arms and chest.

"We match," I said as he bent down and pressed a soft kiss to my forehead.

"We always match."

I stifled a laugh because it was true. Frank and I were always showing up in the same color scheme as if we'd planned it. It was as embarrassing as it was adorable.

"Okay, go already. Take your matchy-matchy selves out of here and go do what people do on their third dates," Britney said as she shooed us out of the apartment. "She has no curfew, by the way. Keep her as long as you want!" she shouted as we walked down the stairs.

"She's totally trying to get rid of you," Frank teased as he smacked my ass playfully. "By the way, you look beautiful." He was always doing that, complimenting me and making me feel special.

"Thank you. You look quite handsome yourself."

When we got outside, I looked around for his motorcycle but couldn't spot it. "Are we walking somewhere?" I glanced down at my high heels and prayed he'd said no.

The sound of a car beeping diverted my attention, and I

was surprised to see Frank open the passenger door of a sleek gray BMW.

"You got a car?"

He gave me a nonchalant shrug. "Figured it was time."

I moved to get inside before I stopped. "Wait. Did you get rid of the bike?"

I was surprised at how sad I was at the idea. I loved riding on the back of Frank's motorcycle. There was nothing like the feel of the air whipping around you from every direction. It was exhilarating and a little scary, but I always felt safe holding on to him.

"No way. I love that bike. It's just not always practical."

Thank goodness.

"Oh. Okay." I sank into the soft leather, inhaling deeply as he folded his long body into the driver's seat. "It smells amazing in here."

"Love that new-car smell." Frank grinned and placed his hand on my knee. "Ready?" He pressed a button and the car purred to life, vibrating gently underneath me.

"Where are we going?"

"Don't freak out," he said, giving me a wary look.

"What is it?"

"My parents."

"What about them?"

"I want you to meet them?"

The fact that he'd phrased it like a question made me smile before I started freaking out. "I'd love to meet them. But where are we going? I'm wearing jeans, Frank!"

He laughed. "I'm wearing jeans too."

"Yeah, but you could make a garbage bag look good."

"So could you." He reached for my hand and kissed my knuckles. "We're going to that Mexican restaurant around the corner from Sam's."

"The one with the seventy different kinds of tequila?" I said, thinking of their ad.

"That's the one. My mom really wants to meet you."

"You could have warned me." I narrowed my eyes at him in mock anger.

"It honestly came up last minute. My parents aren't usually out this way, but Mom called right before I was heading out to pick you up. I couldn't tell her no. Plus, I really want you to meet them." His expression was so sincere, his tone so excited, that I couldn't help but be excited too.

"So date three is now meeting the parents." I gave him a somewhat disappointed look. "The ultimate cock block."

"Ha! Date three is dinner with the parents, then dessert at Frank's." He gave me a sweet smile before pulling onto the road.

"I really get to come over?"

"That's what I was planning before my mom called."

I clapped my hands like an excited child because I was more than ready to see where my boyfriend lived. Even if said place used to be shared with another woman. I could handle that because I was an adult, and adults did things like live with their girlfriends and break up with them too.

Then a horrible thought occurred to me.

"What do your parents know about me? Do they think I broke you and Shelby up?"

"No, no. They don't think that at all. No one thinks that."

"Are you sure?"

He let out a laugh. "Of course I'm sure. They don't think that because it's not true. I talked to them the night I broke up with Shelby. They both gave me advice."

"What? They did?" I hadn't known anything about that. Not that I would, necessarily, but I was still surprised.

"Yeah. They hated seeing me so torn up and miserable. They told me it was okay to want to end things with Shelby. That the world wouldn't stop turning because of it, you know?"

I nodded. It felt like that awful time had happened a thousand years ago instead of about three weeks ago. It was funny how quickly things could change, how drastically your emotions could overcome the feeling of being wronged, and how easily you could let go of the things that no longer served you. I could have held on to my feelings of anger and betrayal toward Frank, but it wouldn't have done any good. Hurting him would mean hurting myself as well, and that didn't make sense.

Glancing at Frank, I asked, "So they're happy that you're happy?"

"You have no idea." He grinned, and I admired his profile as he drove us to the restaurant.

We walked through the swinging doors holding hands, and I recognized his parents right away. Their faces practically lit up the room the moment they saw us.

His mom was naturally beautiful, with long light brown hair, and his dad was ridiculously handsome, a mix of all the boys in one. If there was any question how the three brothers had gotten so good-looking, the proof was standing right in front of me in the form of their parents.

His mom hugged me hard. "Claudia, it's so nice to finally meet you."

"It's a pleasure," his dad said before pulling me in for a hug too.

We all sat and ordered margaritas, and when they arrived, agreed how much better Ryan's were. Dinner was easy, casual, and the conversation flowed like the all-you-could-eat chips and salsa that kept appearing at our table. Frank's parents were accepting, kind and generous, treating us to the meal and sending us home with all the leftovers, which would keep Frank fed for a week.

I thanked them profusely, not only for the meal, but for raising such a great man. I'd thought I was lucky before meeting Frank's parents, but now my gratitude cup was overflowing.

"I've never seen my son so happy." His mom hugged me as we said our good-byes. "Thank you."

My eyes welled up with tears. "Thank you for being so kind."

She gripped my shoulders as she said softly, "We loved Shelby. She was a nice girl but she wasn't right for Frank, and I always knew that. This is different. You're different. And I know that too. I hope my son makes you half as happy as you make him."

"Jeez." I launched into her arms once more and hugged her tight. "He does; he really and truly does. I never knew I could be this happy."

She pulled back and touched my cheek, her eyes shining. "I'm glad. You both deserve it."

I watched as she and her husband walked out of the door,

his arm draped around her shoulders. Frank and I followed close behind, our own hands intertwined. My heart was so full, I thought it might burst.

"They're really great," I said once we were in the car.

"They loved you," he said, his words pushing away any lingering doubts.

It was far too easy fitting into this family. I'd never experienced such a thing before, and honestly, had no idea that I could.

Maybe this was how fate worked. Maybe all the pieces fell together perfectly when you were with the right person.

I wasn't sure, but a girl could hope.

FOREVER FRANK

Claudia

W E DROVE TOWARD Marina del Rey, and I shouldn't have been the least bit surprised when we pulled into one of the only high-rise buildings in the city. He drove us underground and parked in an assigned spot. The number of expensive foreign cars parked around us was a clear sign that this wasn't affordable housing.

"This is where you live?" I asked.

"Wait till you see the view," he said before opening my door and helping me out. He clicked the remote, and the car beeped as it locked.

Frank led us toward a small bank of elevators, and one appeared less than ten seconds after he had pushed the button. The doors opened and I stepped inside, noticing how perfectly clean the mirrored walls were. There wasn't a single fingerprint that I could see, making me wonder idly how often they cleaned them. As the doors closed, Frank pressed the button for the twelfth floor and the elevator rose quickly.

We stepped into a hallway lined with doors, and I followed Frank as he led the way. He took a sharp right before stopping at number 1235. He unlocked the door and held it open for me, waving me inside. Stunned, I walked into one of the nicest apartments I'd ever seen. The space was huge and open, with floor-to-ceiling windows that let in a lot of light, even at night.

I made my way straight over to the living room window and noticed an oversized balcony. "Frank, this place is amazing."

"I know. I fell in love with it the second I stepped inside."

"I can see why. Is it yours?"

"I rent it. I could have bought one, but I wasn't ready. And I wasn't sure how I'd feel living in this kind of setup long term." He stepped next to me as I absorbed the amazing view. "I've never lived in a high-rise building before, and I always saw myself living in a house with a yard. So I figured that this was temporary until the time was right."

"I don't know." I shook my head, unconvinced. "Is there a gym?"

"Downstairs. A gym, pool, hot tub, sauna, gift shop, tennis courts, racquetball, and a country mart." He listed off the amenities like a hotel concierge.

"Uh, yeah. I'd never move. You're crazy. Who wants to take care of a yard when you could have all of this taken care of for you?" I turned away and looked back out the giant window. "This view, Frank," I practically purred as I looked at the marina down below and the boats bobbing in the water. It was spectacular and so peaceful.

His lips pressed against my exposed shoulder, and I sucked in a breath at his unexpected touch. He kissed me again before moving to my neck. I reached behind me, finding his head and weaving my fingers through his hair as I pulled at him. His mouth roamed over my exposed neck and shoulder, sucking and licking until I couldn't take any more.

I turned, grabbing his face and crushing my mouth against his, tasting the salt from my skin on his tongue. His hands grabbed my ass, squeezing and kneading as he whispered my name, only fueling the fire inside me. I wanted his body on mine. I wanted him inside me. I wanted to connect with him in the most primal way possible.

"Up," he demanded, pulling at me until I jumped up and wrapped my legs around his waist.

My back crashed against a wall as he ground his hardness against me, kissing me until I was breathless. I couldn't get enough of him—my tongue pressed against his, our mouths moving in perfect sync as heat built within us.

"I want you," he whispered into my mouth, and I couldn't help but smile against his lips.

"What are you waiting for?"

He pulled back to look deep in my eyes. "You're sure?" His chest rose and fell and I stared at it, mesmerized by the man before me.

"I'm sure," I whispered back, and he pulled us away from the wall and carried me into his bedroom.

It was only once we were in his room that I remembered he used to share this space with someone else. Would I be having sex on the same bed where they used to sleep and do whatever they used to do?

He laid me on top of the down comforter and moved over me. Instead of arching into his touch, I hesitated, my body tensing.

"What's wrong?" Frank asked immediately, sensing the change.

"I just—" I wasn't sure how to say it. "The bed? Is it . . ."

"It's new. Brand new. I swear."

"You bought a new bed?" I leaned up, taking his face in my hands so I could look him in the eye.

When he nodded, I couldn't believe how damn lucky I was. Frank was considerate and thoughtful, always one step ahead of me.

"Thank you," I said before lying back down, my hands working to unbutton his shirt.

"You're welcome." His eyes feasted on me, taking me in as I pulled the shirt from him and tossed it to the floor.

"Are you okay?" I asked, and he smiled, but it didn't reach his eyes. "Don't worry. If you're bad at it, I can always take back my whole forgiving you."

"Don't worry," he said with a low chuckle. "I'm not bad at it."

And he wasn't. Lord, how he wasn't. If there was a book on how to make love to every single inch of a woman's body, I would have bet money that Frank had written it.

He kissed me from head to toe, literally, telling me over and over how beautiful and perfect I was. I had never felt more attractive naked than I did when Frank touched me, drinking me in with his gaze. A fire burned in his eyes when he looked at me, and that fire was for me. Nothing ignited me more than seeing the passion he had for me, for us.

He made love to me like he couldn't get enough, like he'd never get enough. His body worked mine thoroughly the first time, so slow and sweet. But the next time was harder and rougher, more demanding, and so was the next. The man filled me in every way possible, and I loved it. I'd had no idea how much I could love having a man inside me as much as I loved having Frank there.

"God, Frank, harder." I pulled at him, wanting him to go deeper than was physically possible. His dick was a thing of beauty, hitting all the right places like he was made for me. Maybe he was?

"You feel so fucking good," he said, his breathing labored as he moved in and out of my body, thrusting so hard and deep, I thought I might fall apart in his arms.

I moved with him, against him, our bodies crashing into each other in a sweaty, hot mess of ecstasy. I came once, and then just when I thought it wouldn't happen again, my body reacted with his, the two of us finding our release in unison. I'd heard about that kind of thing happening, but had never experienced it before.

We fell asleep in each other's arms, our limbs entwined, the sheets a tangled mess.

*

WHEN I WOKE up early the next morning, I had to gather my bearings to remember where I was. The heat of another body wrapped around mine should have been my first clue. The utter soreness of every part of me should have been the next.

I pulled myself out of Frank's arms and tiptoed quietly across the wood floor. He groaned but didn't wake as I made my way into the bathroom for a quick shower. My plan for making us both breakfast before I had to leave for work was thwarted when the glass door of the double-headed shower slid open and Frank stepped inside.

"I can't escape you." I eyed his naked body, taking note of

every hard part.

"Were you trying to escape?" His eyes were wicked in the morning, and before I could answer, his mouth was on mine, stealing my words and my breath. Hot water splashed off our bodies, ricocheting around us.

"I don't know, Fisher. Not sure how long I'll keep you around."

"How can I convince you?" He licked his lips and dropped to his knees.

"I'm just waiting till Christmas so I can see what kind of gift-giver you are," I said before his tongue found me.

"I'm an amazing gift-giver," he mumbled, then devoured me like I was his last meal.

I struggled to stay standing, struggled to form words that made sense in response. "Says the person giving the gift," I managed to get out between breaths.

He stopped worshiping my body and looked up at me. "I'm rich, Claudia. That automatically makes me a great gift-giver."

I swatted his shoulder because he was right. And then I dug my nails into it as he brought me to my release. When I could catch my breath, I panted, "Well, mine will be more romantic or more thoughtful than yours, because I'm not rich."

"We'll see about that." He winked before grabbing the soap and lathering up my body.

"Yes, we will."

It gave me pause for a minute, wondering how on earth I could ever compete with him in that way, but then I realized that Frank would never expect me to. It was ridiculous for me to even think that he would.

Frank pressed my naked body against the shower wall, and I gasped at the coldness of the tile. Taking advantage of my open mouth, he kissed me like he owned me, as if every sore and aching inch of me belonged to him.

"I'm going to fall in love with you," he said between kisses. It was a declaration, a promise of what was to come.

"I'll probably be okay with that," I whispered back, knowing I was already falling.

He held me suspended as he entered me slowly at first, inch by excruciating inch. It wasn't until he reached the depths of me that he started working me harder. The warm water still fell around us as I tightened my legs around his middle, taking him as deep as the position would let me.

Wild, we moved and bucked against each other, his biceps flexing as he held me up easily, as if I were weightless. And when I came, I yelled out his name over and over again, like there would never be another name I'd speak in my entire life. Because I knew deep in my heart that there wouldn't be.

There was only Frank.

There would only ever be Frank.

And nothing in the world felt more right.

EPILOGUE
Frank

Ten Months Later

A FTER STARING FOR the hundredth time at the diamond ring in the velvet box, I closed the top and stuffed it back inside my drawer, hiding it behind some clean socks.

Each day I went through the same routine. I took the ring out, looked at it, smiled, and quickly put it back in its hiding place. I'd always known that Claudia was the one, which was why I'd had the ring for months.

I guessed it was true what guys always said, that you'd know it was the right girl the moment you met her. Hell, I knew she was the right girl the second I first saw her.

That fact was a lot easier for me to swallow and admit now. Everything with Claudia had fallen into place so quickly and easily, but in the back of my mind, I had kept harboring residual guilt over the way our love story had started.

It took me a while to get past what I'd done to Shelby by moving on so quickly, even though my heart told me with every beat that I had done the right thing. Regardless, my conscience still liked to punish me over it every now and then.

But an email from Shelby where she actually thanked me for breaking up with her helped me a lot. She told me she could see clearly now how we had stayed together for all the wrong reasons, and for way too long. Hindsight for her had been twenty-twenty once we finally split up, she'd said. She also wanted me to know that she had moved on, had found love, and was really happy. It helped me tremendously to know that she was okay.

It helped Claudia as well, who had teared up when I told her that Shelby was dating someone. Claudia genuinely wanted Shelby to be happy, and it only made me love my girl more. Neither of us had wanted our coming together to be at someone else's expense, but it had been, and that fact had taken a toll on us both. Even though we tried not to focus on it, some days were harder than others. Shelby had given us a huge gift by sending that email.

Claudia still worked at the bank and lived with Britney. Even though I wanted her to move in, I respected her decision to wait and give our relationship time to grow. It was ironic, considering she spent almost every night at my place anyway, but I knew better than to push my feisty Colombian before she was ready.

"What are you doing?" Claudia called out from the kitchen.

"Nothing, why?"

"Then where the heck are you? Your food is getting cold!"

I hustled into the kitchen with a smile.

"It's like you don't even appreciate my culinary skills," she said before kissing my cheek and sitting next to me.

I looked down at the burned toast and rubbery scrambled eggs on my plate and laughed. My girl wasn't a chef, but I couldn't have cared less. She was the best at all the things that mattered, like keeping me on my toes and smiling and challenging me in the best ways. Claudia made me a better man, and I hoped I made her a better woman.

Our relationship was give and take, so perfectly balanced that sometimes I felt like I should pinch myself to make sure I wasn't dreaming. I didn't even care when Ryan made fun of me for turning into such a romantic sap, especially when he admitted that he was just jealous. I finally understood what he had been whining about, the one thing he claimed to always be searching for. I'd found it, and everything made sense after that.

When I took a tentative bite of my toast, it crumbled into tiny black pieces. "Delicious. Thank you," I mumbled while I chewed.

"I got distracted," she said.

"Huh?"

"That's why it's burned. I got distracted online and forgot I was making it."

Her words made me smile. My girl was always burning things. A cook, she was not.

"It's okay. I don't mind burned toast."

She laughed. "You're a terrible liar, you know that?"

Reaching out, I wrapped my arms around her and tugged her onto my lap. "I'm not lying," I said against her skin as I kissed her shoulder. "I don't lie to you."

I kissed her neck and her head tipped to the side, an invitation that I didn't have time to take her up on, unfortunately. I moved to her mouth, my tongue sweeping along her bottom lip before dipping inside.

"I'd love nothing more than to make love to you right

now, babe, but I'm already late."

When she grinned against my ear as she sucked and bit at my lobe, I instantly hardened.

"Claudia," I growled, and her whispered response into my ear only made me even harder, if it was possible. "Dammit, woman."

I stood up, carrying her giggling in my arms as I moved this conversation into the bedroom.

Tossing her on the bed, I pretended to scowl as she scooted away from me playfully.

"Naked. Now," I demanded.

She didn't hesitate, every bit of fabric that had been on her body stripped away before I took my next breath. Ripping off my own clothes as fast as possible, I threw them on the floor before hovering over the most beautiful woman I'd ever laid eyes on.

"I'm sorry I can't be gentle right now," I said before pushing into her. She cried out in pleasure, her nails raking down my back, stopping at my ass as she pulled me harder.

"Yesss," she hissed out before I hooked an arm underneath her and flipped us both over.

Claudia riding me was one of the sexiest things I'd ever seen. I found myself wanting to memorize the way her eyes opened and closed, how she moved up and down my length, the way her hair and tits bounced in unison, and the seductive way her hips rocked, like she was dancing to a song only she could hear. She was a fucking work of art, my girl, and she knew I saw her that way.

When she climaxed, I came hard and fast, simply from watching her. That was how deeply she affected me. I could find my release simply from watching her have hers.

When she slipped off of me and headed toward the bath-room, I sat up and followed her.

"I need a note."

She wrapped a towel around herself, covering up all that delicious nakedness, and scrunched her face at me. "A note for what?"

"So when Nick yells at me for being late, I can make sure he knows it was all your fault."

Claudia giggled and left the bedroom as I grabbed my clothes and quickly dressed again. As I was putting on my shoes, she reappeared with a folded piece of paper in hand.

"Here you go. One late note."

I unfolded it and grinned from ear to ear.

Please excuse Frank Fisher for being late today; he had some work to do at home.

On his woman. In the bedroom. Naked.

Please call me if there are any problems or issues.

Thank you for understanding.

—Claudia

"Perfect. Thanks, babe."

"I'll see you later," she said as she swatted my ass. "Go, you're late."

I kissed her once more. "I love you."

"Love you too."

I rode my bike to the bar, and just like I had expected, Nick busted my balls the second I walked through the doors.

"You're late, jackass."

I tossed the note at him and walked into the office to put

my bag down. When I made my way back behind the bar, I found Nick grinning.

"This is great. Can I hang it up in here? Frame it?"

Ryan snatched the paper out of Nick's hands before he could protest. "What's it say?" He scanned it quickly, his eyes wide with awe when he looked back up at me. "Damn. I want a note like this."

When I clenched my jaw, he quickly backtracked.

"Not from Claudia, you idiot. From my own woman. Jesus, caveman, calm down. No one's trying to steal your girl."

I bit out a sarcastic laugh because that was a flat-out lie. Every time Claudia was in here, some idiot who didn't know she was with me hit on her. Everyone was always trying to steal my girl. The same thing happened with Jess too, but the second Nick saw it happening, he made another declaration to the girl of his dreams, the love of his life, or whatever shit happened to spill from his lips in that moment. Guys usually backed off after that.

I could have done the same sort of thing, but that wasn't really my style. And I was pretty sure Claudia would have my balls if I tried. She'd told me on more than one occasion that she could handle herself, but if she needed me, she'd let me know.

"Look who it is. Dr. Claudia," Nick said with a laugh. He lifted his chin in the direction of the front door and I whipped my head around, searching for her.

"Did you like my note?" she asked as she took a seat at the bar.

"We all liked it." Ryan grinned, pointing to the wall where he had just pinned it up.

"Oh my gosh, get it off the wall! Frank!"

I shrugged, knowing that if I pulled it down, one of my brothers would put it right back up unless I tossed it in the trash, and that wasn't happening.

"Thank you, sweet baby Jesus, for blessing me with the most perfect girl in the entire world," Nick called out, which could only mean one thing. Jess was in the bar. "No offense, Claudia."

"None taken," she said with a laugh.

Jess moved to the empty stool next to my girl and they hugged, laughing and talking like the best friends they had become.

Claudia had fit into my family dynamic like she was born to be a part of it. Nothing had ever made me happier than seeing us all together. And I would know, because I'd lived without happiness for far too long, and I recognized the difference now.

I'd been true to my word about being the best gift-giver ever. For Christmas, I had bought round-trip tickets to Colombia for Claudia, her mom, her stepdad, and myself. Her parents knew about the tickets, but Claudia had no idea. When she'd opened the envelope, she burst into tears, claiming I was the best boyfriend ever. The trip was happening later this year, and I planned to propose when we were there, surrounded by her family.

Her mother and stepdad had gladly given me permission when I'd asked if I could marry their daughter. I think they loved me as much as my parents loved Claudia, and that was saying a lot.

I knew from the moment I saw Claudia; I was certain she

was my future. There was no question. There was never any question.

She was it for me.

She was the one. Forever.

And I couldn't wait to make it official.

I supposed that meant there was only one Fisher brother left on the market. What kind of girl was going to snag Princess Ryan's heart?

I couldn't wait to find out.

The End

ACKNOWLEDGMENTS

This story was, as usual, a labor of love. I know it may not always seem like it, but I write with a transparent heart. If you know me at all in real life, then you hear me in my books; you feel me and see me there. Whatever my heart is going through comes through in each story I choose to tell, and in the way I choose to tell it. This story was absolutely no exception.

So with that being said, I have to thank *him*. Because without *him*, this story wouldn't have wings, wouldn't have formed in the way it did. *He* affects and influences everything in me; I can see that now. I might have been in some serious denial before, but I'm not anymore. So, thank you, babe. Because of you, I'm no longer drowning. Thank you for saving me when I needed it most.

To my professional teammates and partners in crime, I am forever thankful to have you by my side: Tara Sivec, Jillian Dodd, Kyla Linde, Meghan March, Kendall Ryan, Claire Contreras, Colleen Hoover, Tarryn Fisher (#ThirdWheel), Michelle Warren, Pam Berehulke, Krista Arnold, and all the girls in TPGC group. I appreciate you all so much!

And of course #TheBoy. He gets his own line. Otherwise, he cries. Just kidding. Thank you for being the best thing in my life.

OTHER BOOKS BY J. STERLING

In Dreams
Chance Encounters
10 Years Later – A Second Chance Romance
Heartless
Dear Heart, I Hate You

THE GAME SERIES
The Perfect Game – Book One
The Game Changer – Book Two
The Sweetest Game – Book Three
The Other Game (Dean Carter) – Book Four

THE CELEBRITY SERIES
Seeing Stars – Madison & Walker
Breaking Stars – Paige & Tatum
Losing Stars – Quinn & Ryson (Coming Soon)

THE FISHER BROTHERS SERIES
No Bad Days – Nick Fisher
Guy Hater – Frank Fisher
Adios Pantalones – Ryan Fisher (Coming February 5, 2018)
Available for Pre-Order now!

ABOUT THE AUTHOR

Jenn Sterling is a Southern California native who loves writing stories from the heart. Every story she tells has pieces of her truth in it, as well as her life experience. She has her bachelor's degree in Radio/TV/Film and has worked in the entertainment industry the majority of her life.

Jenn loves hearing from her readers and can be found online at:

Blog & Website:
www.j-sterling.com

Twitter:
www.twitter.com/RealJSterling

Facebook:
www.facebook.com/TheRealJSterling

Private Facebook Reader Group:
www.facebook.com/groups/ThePerfectGameChangerGroup/

Instagram:
www.instagram.com/RealJSterling

CPSIA information can be obtained
at www.ICGtesting.com
Printed in the USA
LVHW110040150119
603948LV00001B/42/P